TIME
OUT

TIME OUT

SEAN HAYES,
TODD MILLINER,
and
CARLYN GREENWALD

SIMON & SCHUSTER BFYR

NEW YORK   LONDON   TORONTO   SYDNEY   NEW DELHI

SIMON & SCHUSTER BFYR

An imprint of Simon & Schuster Children's Publishing Division
1230 Avenue of the Americas, New York, New York 10020

SIMON & SCHUSTER BOOKS FOR YOUNG READERS
and related marks are trademarks of Simon & Schuster, LLC.
Simon & Schuster: Celebrating 100 Years of Publishing in 2024
For information about special discounts for bulk purchases, please contact
Simon & Schuster Special Sales at 1-866-506-1949 or business@simonandschuster.com.
The Simon & Schuster Speakers Bureau can bring authors to your live event.
For more information or to book an event, contact the Simon & Schuster Speakers Bureau
at 1-866-248-3049 or visit our website at www.simonspeakers.com.
Also available in a SIMON & SCHUSTER BFYR hardcover edition
Interior design by Hilary Zarycky
The text for this book was set in EB Garamond.
Manufactured in the United States of America
First SIMON & SCHUSTER BFYR paperback edition May 2024
2 4 6 8 10 9 7 5 3 1
CIP data for this book is available from the Library of Congress.
ISBN 9781534492622 (hc)
ISBN 9781534492639 (pbk)
ISBN 9781534492646 (ebook)

Dedicated to our younger selves, who wish we were as courageous as Barclay, and to anyone who's ever felt different. It turns out, we're all the same.
—*Sean and Todd*

To Brandon and Izzy
—*Carlyn*

CHAPTER ONE

TODAY'S MY SIXTEENTH BIRTHDAY.

Through the grogginess, I take a moment to really absorb the feeling of it. My first few seconds in my bedroom as a sixteen-year-old.

My last day being in my room before the world knows I'm gay.

That's right, I'm gay. I've said it to myself a hundred times, but I've never spoken those words out loud. Not even in here.

My TV is still buzzing with ESPN that I left on last night, next to the basketball medals and trophies on my dresser. Posters of LeBron James, Trae Young, and Dominique Wilkins plastered on the walls. My gaze skims over a pile of laundry I need to do, lying next to the Xbox I may have spent too long playing last night. It's a model behind what rich people like my teammate Tim Ostrowski have, but it does the job and I've gotten in the habit of zoning into it before important days. I don't linger on the Xbox now, though, instead I turn to my phone sitting on top of it, and the stupid text from none other than Ostrowski waiting for me in the team's group chat:

Ostrowski
5:59 A.M.
GOOD MORNING BOYS. PEP RALLY TODAY!!! AND YOU
KNOW WHAT THAT MEANS. TIME TO ACT LIKE FUCKING

CHAMPIONS. LETS WEAR ALL BLACK. INTIMIDATE THE FUCK OUTTA EVERYBODY AND BE READY FOR TONIGHT'S AFTERPARTY 💀

I roll my eyes, glad to see no one else has responded, then turn to shut off the TV and check my clock. Sure enough, it's flipped from 18,616 to 18,615 and my stomach sinks. I bought the countdown clock barely hours after my grandpa Scratch died and set it to fifty-one years from now, when I'll be the same age as he was. Every day since then, I've been panicking, watching the time tick away, thinking about the years I've already wasted in the closet. I force a slow breath, knowing the next time I look at it, all that panic will be gone. Even if I only have 18,615 days left, after two p.m. today, they'll be spent with me living my fullest life. Like he would have wanted. I just wish I'd realized it while he was still here.

I throw on gym shorts and a T-shirt and head down to the kitchen, wondering what birthday surprise Mom will have cooked up this year. She makes super-elaborate cakes every birthday and covers the house in decorations that change depending on what team, movie, or hobby my siblings and I have adopted over the last year.

But when I get to the kitchen, everything's just as we left it last night: plain walls, sunken couch cushions, and dishes stacked in the sink. The only exception is a card displayed on the counter and my little sister, Maggie, sitting on the neighboring living room couch rifling through a box of Oreo Pop-Tarts with her science textbook splayed open on the coffee table. Maggie never wastes a chance to study, not even to enjoy a Pop-Tart.

"That's not even a breakfast-adjacent flavor," I comment as I swipe a protein bar out of a box I left out after practice last night.

Maggie eyes the bar in my hand and glares at me. "You're eating the *exact same flavor*, jerk."

I take an annoyingly large bite and grab my card. Nice of Mom to at least leave me this. But when I open it, I'm confused. It's a hand-drawn anime-style cartoon with a spiky-haired boy holding an over-the-top cake; definitely not Mom's style. I look closer, though, where I find the words HAPPY BIRTHDAY BARCLAY!!!!! LOVE, MAGGIE on the picture of the cake.

Heat rushes to my face as I glance back at Maggie, *really* feeling like a jerk. "Thanks for the card," I say.

She sighs. "Whatever. Scratch would have made me make it for you."

I give her a nod even though just hearing his name hurts and let the unspoken *I find you unbearably annoying but still do care about you* agreement settle between us as I glance outside. Mom's missed so much work that it's fair to assume that she's just gone in early to make up for lost time. Can't really blame her for not getting a birthday display up when she's covering the funeral expenses and the second income we lost when Scratch died. But when I look outside, her car is still in the driveway. As if on cue, I hear footsteps behind me—and spy Mom still in her pajamas, lines under her eyes that no makeup can hide. But the thing I notice most is she's still. Mom's usually a blur of motion, rummaging around the cabinets, looking for her inevitably misplaced keys or shoes, but now . . . she just stands there, saying nothing.

"Are . . . you going to work today?" I ask, shifting my weight back and forth, trying not to notice she hasn't wished me a happy birthday yet.

"Not yet. The morning got away from me and . . ."

She trails off and adjusts a piece of her thick honey-brown hair—the same color she gave me—and the pit in my stomach starts to deepen. I need this day to go exactly according to plan. And that plan happened to involve Mom being at her best—or at least the best she can be after what we've been through. Today is clearly already not Mom's best day. Today isn't even as good as yesterday. I can't take this as an omen, so I press ahead.

"Well, that's okay," I say. "No one will be working this afternoon anyway since the pep rally's today."

This, at least, gets Mom to half smile. "Right. Kick off the season." But she says it like a sigh, not a cheer.

"I'm gonna"—*I'm going to come out at it*—"be doing a big speech as captain, so I'm glad you'll be there." I practically hear the countdown clock upstairs ticking as I chicken out. Again.

"Hon, I've got to take Maggie to her sketching sleepover with Emily tonight."

My heart squeezes. She's been making excuse after excuse to avoid seeing anyone since the funeral, abandoning her book club friends, ditching drinks out with her coworkers, refusing to let our out-of-state family drop in. Still, I never thought she'd actually miss a Chitwood pep rally.

Maggie glances up from her phone, frowning. "Emily said she had a ton of homework, so we canceled. It's okay. It gives me more time to work on my portfolio for the Chitwood Young Arts Award—"

Good. Perfect, actually. Thank you, Emily and Maggie's never-ending quest to be the best students and artists under age fourteen in Chitwood.

"Well then, you should come too, it's not that long," I say.

"Are you sure?" Maggie presses. "I really need to finish."

All she really needs to be there for is my speech, so yes, I'm sure. Besides, when she says "work on" her art portfolios, she usually means adding a sixth unnecessary layer onto an already incredible piece. None of the Neanderthals who judge the competitions will be able to tell.

But then we're all left in silence. Silence that should be filled with Mom assuring me that she'll get herself and Maggie to the pep rally come hell or high water.

A second more passes before she finally speaks.

"Barc, I've—" She massages her shoulder. "I'm barely back at work and I'm just not up for seeing so many people right now. Zack's mom always records the rallies, right? I'll—I'll watch it after." She gives me the most feeble smile, as if willing me to say it's fine. "I'm sure you'll be incredible."

Mom's not coming to the rally.

I can feel the blow hit me, pushing me to take a seat at the kitchen counter as a stinging prickles across my eyes and nose. But worse than Mom flaking, worse than Mom being definitely not okay, is the new issue she's created for me.

I was really planning on coming out to her before the pep rally regardless, since it feels like information a mom should know before a whole town, but with her so overwhelmed already . . . now I don't know. I know being gay isn't a bad thing, but we've never talked about girls or guys. Most of what we talk about lately is just basketball. How's she going to take something else she's not even expecting?

"Hey, Mom, can you look at my newest sketch?" Maggie starts to say, but Mom overlaps her, saying, "Speaking of basketball, how're you feeling about the season?" Mom tries to smile, like she's making up for not being there today, but Maggie deflates.

I reach over to her mega box and grab a packet of Pop-Tarts, trying to let Maggie get Mom's attention again, but Maggie's eyes lock onto me like a video game enemy, shooting a laser glare my way.

"Has your school list changed?" Mom continues like she didn't hear her. "I hear every state school will have scouts here at the first big game, it was in the paper and everything. You know it'd be something to have you at Georgia Tech with your brother."

As Maggie's hands clench into fists, I feel myself getting frustrated too. If Mom's too wrecked to go to my pep rally, why bother talking basketball at all? And especially not the stuff that's already keeping me up at night, the pressure that sits heavy in my chest. The worries about if I'll even be able to get into Georgia Tech, let alone Villanova, or Kansas, or any other big-city D1 school I dream of being able to attend. The possibility that we'll lose in the championship again this year and all those dreams will dry up. The fear that I can't do any of it without Scratch.

"Those reporters haven't stopped calling," Mom continues, eyes now back on the stairs, like she can't wait to be back in bed. "I swear they're going to cost me a listing one day, but it'll be worth it." I'm sure she's teasing, but I still sweat a little. "I know you're so good, but you can't rest on your laurels now. Make sure you're taking it all seriously." She squeezes my arm, then moves to the stairs. I check my phone; I'm going to be late if I don't leave right now. And I can't be late today. Another opportunity has slipped by and this just . . . isn't how I thought today would start.

"Well, can we talk after?" I say, trying to salvage it.

—and Maggie slams out of her chair.

"Can we *ever* talk about anything besides basketball?" Maggie exclaims, her voice high and sharp.

She rockets out of the kitchen and toward her room. Mom takes a long, deep breath and heads up after her. My moment to come out to Mom has officially passed.

I force myself to walk toward the back door but glance at the Georgia nature calendar on the wall as I do. At the little heart on the date.

This birthday, this pep rally, will be the first family event without Scratch. She hasn't even mentioned it. No one wants me to be distracted. Like Coach keeps saying, *Just swallow it all, push harder*. But this feeling and this secret are like lead, weighing me down. I can't end up like Mom. I won't. I'm going out there and taking control of my life, just like my grandpa would've wanted. She'll understand. I'll tell her about the gay thing once I'm home again. Once I have everyone else's support.

I step outside to head to the detached garage for my bike, but right away I notice something's different out here too. The baby hoop that Scratch bought me years ago is gone. I outgrew it before we could put together the time and money to install a standard size, but now in its place, there's a brand-new adult-sized basketball hoop, the rim a shining bright orange, with a red ribbon around it. A piece of printer paper is taped on the backboard that reads KEEP DOING YOUR AMAZING THING, BUT WITH #SWAG. LOVE YOU. DEVIN. I smile at it so wide it hurts my face. My older brother, Devin, must've come home from college and put it up while I was sleeping. It's the big gesture I was expecting from Mom, a sign I didn't know I needed.

I grab a worn ball out from the garage and shoot a perfect arc. It flies through the net with that beautiful swish. My tension released, I scoop it up again. Despite the time ticking away, I don't stop until I make ten in a row.

Once my shoulders have finally relaxed, I send Devin a **Thank you! see you tonight!** text and load up my bike.

Today's finally starting to feel like the good vibes I was hoping for. My phone starts to ding with happy birthday messages as I pedal out. Each one feels like a reminder—*This is right. I've got this.*

The good feeling continues to grow as I enter town ten minutes later, passing by businesses decked out in Wildcats blue and gold. Neighbors shoot me a wave as I pedal by, some even making signs already for the first game of the season tomorrow. Then people I barely know look up from their phones to smile and say "happy birthday" when I walk into school. Most of the team is lined up right by the entryway, slapping me on the back as they yell, "It's Barclay's birthday!" so even the teachers in their classrooms can hear.

When I make my way over to my locker, it's covered top to bottom in homemade cards—more than I think I've ever gotten. My fingertips put in my combination as I look the cards over. But even that small amount of concentration is lost as a pair of soft lips press against my cheek, accompanied by the scent of expensive perfume. I know without looking it's Catherine Finney, the cheer captain.

"Good luck today," she says, her voice a purr. "I'll be there cheering you on the whole time."

I feel a little guilty. We made out drunk at an off-season party last year, but it just confirmed for me that *yeah*, I'm pretty gay. I know I should've just let her down easy right after, but I didn't know what to tell her without outing myself before I was ready. At least we'll probably laugh about it after today.

My best friend, Zack Ito, slides up and replaces Catherine in her perfume-y wake. "Hey, man! Look at you. Birthday! Championship season start day!" He grins a little wider as he pushes his long, dark hair back. "Finney wants to blow you day. When I push her your way after we win tomorrow, you better fucking ask her out this time."

It's not that I'm upset that Zack and the rest of the guys will throw around comments like this, but I feel the unspoken words between us, the curious glances they give me every time I say I have to work or want to go stag to a school dance, the way I have nothing to say during locker room talk. Not quite at *He's gay* yet, but it's only a matter of time. I hate that feeling, but this is the last time I'll feel it. Two words and it'll all be out there. On my terms.

But for now, I just give my locker another try and say, "I don't even think she *wants* to blow me."

Zack glances back and Catherine gives me a tiny wave like she was waiting for me to look. There's a flirty smile on her face as she tucks a light brown curl behind her ear.

"Okay, maybe she wants to blow me," I admit. *Not for long.*

"Oh, I see you, Elliot!" a voice says behind me, shaking me out of my thoughts.

It's Ostrowski. Great.

"But remember, can't stop at just one. Especially not after we"—his voice suddenly rises—"WIN! THIS! GAME!"

He even pulls me into a bro-handshake, like he's not the reason we lost last year's championship.

I grab my books as he runs off chanting and turn to head to class with Zack.

"Now that that moron's gone, sorry I didn't get you a card like everyone else on the planet," Zack says. "I bet you'll like this better, though." He shoves something in front of my face. It takes me a second to realize it's a newspaper. I look at him, puzzled as to A) where he got an actual physical newspaper and B) why he's showing it to me. "Just read this column here." He points to the top left. When I do, my heart leaps. TOP TEN COLLEGE BASKETBALL RECRUITS IN GEORGIA. And there's me, BARCLAY ELLIOT, my name written in that sports news font I've daydreamed about, sitting right at number one.

Holy shit.

"Dude, is this real?" I ask, grinning.

"It must be if they wasted actual paper on it. With this kind of press, scouts will be falling over themselves to come see us. This season is *it*, bro," he says, punching me in the arm. He's bouncing with excitement, but the more I look at him, the more I start to notice a tightness around his smile and in his shoulders, like an invisible pressure sitting on him. It's a feeling I definitely recognize, but Zack is the chillest guy I know; he didn't even break a sweat before the championship last year.

I'm about to ask what's up, but I've been so focused on the paper I almost run smack into this girl, Tabby. Her eyes look bigger than usual in her thick glasses, but her bright red hair is the same as always. She's positively shaking as she hands me a cupcake, neck craned to look up at me. The cupcake is clearly homemade, with what I think is an animal on the top.

"I made these for you for the game," Tabby says. "That's supposed to be a Wildcat." It looks more like a horse. "Well, here's one. There's more, so . . ."

It's pretty common that one of the cheerleaders will bake for us before the game, but I'm not really even friends with Tabby. I wish I could remember where I even know her from. Science class? Math class? She's definitely not a basketball fan. But, whatever, I'll take it. I'm about to thank Tabby for the gesture, but she gets swallowed up by a group of freshmen going the opposite direction, all walking and talking down the middle of the hallway. One high school traffic hazard and she's gone. Which is good because then I can pass this off without hurting her feelings. Thinking about the rally has already killed my appetite.

"Do you want this? I had something sweet for breakfast," I say.

Zack plucks it right out of my hand and takes a bite as we walk to first period. He makes a "mmm" sound, like he's on a baking show. "Looks like shit, but tastes pretty good." All traces of worry that I saw before are gone. I wonder if they were even really there.

I snort and feel the good vibes grow. People at this school *love* me; hell, someone I barely know baked me cupcakes. And I've been gay this whole time. Nothing's changing except now I'll be leading us to victory without this goddamn weight on my chest. After I say the words, the whole team will surround me as they cheer. We'll be united and play the hell out of the first game of the season. Hell, there might even be newspaper articles that talk about me like Jason Collins, *first openly gay athlete in Chitwood, Georgia, history*. I bet there are other gay kids at this school who just need someone to pave the way for them. I can do that. Show them it'll be okay.

And I'm finally going to be free.

The rest of the morning flies by in a rush of cards, birthday wishes, and Wildcat chants. I'm about to head to the cafeteria for pizza day when a black-nail-polished hand that can only belong to one person thrusts a Cane's bag in front of my nose.

"Have I ever told you you're my best friend?" I say, turning to see Amy Baltra staring back at me, her red lips in a mischievous grin. Her self-cut bob falls into her light blue eyes, perfectly done in eyeliner.

Amy's said many times she'd gladly live at a punk concert and always look the part.

"Yeah, yeah, happy birthday, but this won't be a usual thing," she says. "My senior connection is only going to last so long."

As in: she made out with some senior in band at a party earlier this year and he proceeded to never stop asking about hanging out with the team. She hates it, but since he agrees to buy food for both of us, she keeps the complaining to a minimum. I peek into my bag, the steam from the chicken heating my fingertips.

"Besides, this is a bribe," Amy says, grabbing my arm and pulling me into the journalism classroom before I get a chance to dig in. With anyone else, I'd be annoyed to be thrown off from enjoying my usual table with the team. But Amy and I have been friends for so long, I don't think there're many paths I won't let her lead this friendship down.

"All right, what's the catch for my birthday lunch?"

Before I can respond, the classroom door opens again. A guy walks in and Amy waves. He's average height, slim, white with the kind of pale skin you can only get around here by actively avoiding going outside. His lips twitch, like he was about to smile but changed his mind.

"Hey . . ." I know this guy, but as with Tabby, I just can't place from *where*. He looks like he answers questions correctly in class. Did we work on a group project together or something?

"Christopher Dillon," he says, holding a hand out. He scrutinizes me, but his expression doesn't change past this neutral look, like I'm not worth engaging his facial muscles. His semi-rimless glasses highlight his gray eyes, surrounded by dark eyelashes. "Not Chris, not Topher. Christopher."

Oh shit, yes, *that's it*. Christopher is the band guy Amy always talks about on the newspaper. He's also the only guy I know who's out at Chitwood High, but he flies pretty under the radar. He's definitely changed since the last time I saw him, though. Gotten taller, new glasses, changed his fashion maybe? He's got one of those hipster-y dressy-casual outfits—a vertical-stripe peach-tone button-up, slim jeans that stop before the ankle. I don't know, it's not my vibe, but it works on him, almost like he's . . . *cuter*. It comes into my head and like a reflex, I look away, locking onto his dress shoes.

"Yeah, yeah, you're an old man," Amy says. "We get it. This is *Barclay*. Stephan Dixon used to bark at him in elementary school, so I think his name is more tragic than yours."

I frown. "Thank you for bringing that up, Amy."

Christopher drops into the desk next to me, darting his gaze to my food, then his notebook. He pulls out a pen and clicks it against a mole on his sharp cheekbone to get it open. "All right, let's get this over with."

I look right over to Amy, like I'm a kid again not understanding long division or what *himbo* means. "Get what over with?"

Amy smirks. "Well, you know how I was always fighting the last newspaper advisor about writing something that actually matters for the paper? The new advisor, Ms. Cho, is totally on board. She and I came up with a way in. I get to write my column on voting rights if I interview you for a shiny worship piece. Lead the meatheads and admin in with you, then slip in some hot button issues. But no offense, I'd rather vom than interview you, so Christopher is doing it. He owes me."

She punctuates my roast with a wink at Christopher, who rolls his eyes and rakes a hand through the dark locks framing his face. It goes right back into his eyes before he even pulls his hand away. "I owe you nothing and yet still I'm writing this article. A good, old-fashioned hand-to-dick piece, the pinnacle of journalism. So let's make it as painless as possible, considering it's just about high school basketball."

I don't think I'm the most important person to ever walk these halls, but man, Christopher has a chip on his shoulder. From the corner of my eye, I see Amy holding back laughter as she dips a chicken tender in Cane's sauce, enjoying this lunchtime theater she's set up for herself.

"Why don't you want to do this?" I ask, annoyed.

Christopher clicks his pen in and back out on the desk. His index fingernails are painted blue. "Just a little outside my interest sphere," he says, deadpan. "Before you ask, you haven't been on record, but let's start now. What do you think of the team this season?"

"I—" I fidget with my trash. And of course, instead of distracting from me, it just gets Christopher to watch me do it. "This year is gonna be different. You'll see. This game is going to be one for the books, and that's only the beginning of the path to the championship."

Then—silence.

"Wow, I can't believe your life is a word-for-word sports movie," Christopher says, raising his brows. "Well, how's it going to be different? I mean what do you think went wrong in last year's championship?"

I can still smell the exact punch of ammonia from the cleaner on the court that day. It was down to the buzzer, *two points* between us and the title, the one we hadn't won since Scratch was a senior at West Chitwood fifty years ago. The crowd was screaming so loud it felt more like a concert than a game, chanting my name—*Barclay, Barclay, Barclay!* I whipped around to find my opening, squaring up for the shot. But the opposing team's defense collapsed around me, shouting taunts about the *sophomore prodigy losing his steam*. The shot wasn't there, so I'd passed Ostrowski the ball back outside the arc, then raced down the lane so he could feed it back to me. But he didn't even pause, didn't even look. He lobbed up a shit shot no one in their right mind would have taken, and as it died in the air, the buzzer sounded. I hadn't had time to make the rebound, hadn't had time to fix it. My soul sank to my feet watching the ball roll off the court. The shrill alarm of the buzzer sounded in my ear as I looked helplessly to my equally shocked teammates, the wilting painted faces of every Chitwood business owner in the stands, then finally to the fallen look on Scratch's face from the front row of the bleachers. That slow, dizzying realization that it'd all come crashing down in one moment. A moment I can't stop thinking I could've done better.

A voice in my head keeps telling me there was a way we could've won. That my grandpa could've seen another championship before he died. That maybe some effect in the universe would've kept him from dying all together.

But it'll be different this year. When I come out today, this team is going to be tighter than ever—no secrets, no distractions, no ball hogging. We'll rally around each other, because like Scratch used to say, *Championships are won by teams, not players.* I'm gonna set the example.

But I can't tell Christopher any of that. Not yet.

Before I can think of anything else to say, the bell rings. Christopher looks to the clock hanging on the wall and closes his notebook.

"I guess we'll have to pick this up later. Oh joy," he says, his speed seemingly turned up three times as fast. "When we meet again, Finn."

Definitely the weirdest school paper interview I've ever done.

Whatever. I have so many other things to worry about than one singular person in this school not liking me. I'll give him plenty to write about at the pep rally.

"My name isn't even Finn," I mutter as I collect my trash.

Amy just laughs.

As much as the rest of the day has flown, getting through this last class feels impossible. Spanish with Mrs. Shue is usually a solid okay—she's one of the cooler teachers—but my mind is drifting hard today.

"The reflexive goes before the verb when that verb is conjugated. So in this sentence, 'Please pass the mustard,' you would say, 'Me puedes pasar la mostaza.' Does everyone understand that? Sí? Todos entienden?"

One last period. One last period until the pep rally.

I run my fingertips along the wood of the desk, antsy. After all this buildup, I'm beyond ready to do this. God, I can't wait to get back in my uniform. In a way, the Wildcat uniform changes the way my body feels, making my blood pump better and injecting me with energy. It keeps my head clear when it needs to be, focused, like I can do anything. Most of all, though, it makes me feel like I'm part of something, along with everyone else in class already wearing their Wildcats apparel and whispering about the game.

"Guys," Mrs. Shue says when no one responds, her voice laced with frustration from probably the seven classes before us combined.

"Sí, Sí, entiendo," everyone but me says.

"Bueno, moving on," Mrs. Shue says. I draw circles on my desk with my fingers. Little basketballs, imagining their rubber on my fingertips instead. "Barclay?"

Shit. I look up, heating rushing to my ears. "Yes—sí?"

"I'm sure you're as excited for the season to start as I am," she says, a smile forming across her face. "I'm thinking about letting you go early. . . ."

Scratch is looking over me today. Getting out early from Spanish before she can ask for the homework I definitely didn't do? Hell *yes*. "That would be awesome, Mrs. Shue."

She smirks. "Say it in Spanish and I'll let you go."

Even *I* know that one. "Este es tan bueno, Señora Shue."

She smiles again and says, "Consígamos una victoria, Barclay."

The room erupts in cheers of "Go, Wildcats!" that feel like I've already won. As I pack up, Señora Shue leads the class in a Spanish rendition of "Happy Birthday." I might only have 18,615 days left, but the 18,615th day has been pretty damn awesome so far.

And it's only going to get better. I can feel it deep in my bones as I hustle off to the lockers to get ready. When I peek out through the locker room doors fifteen minutes later and see the crowd filling the stands with excited energy, the feeling grows.

"I think the whole town is here," I say to Zack as he adjusts his uniform.

He grins. "They better be."

I go back to scanning the crowd. Mom isn't here. One promise she managed to keep. Still, I find myself looking over the crowd a couple more times, a lump forming in my throat as I fail to see her again and again. But I shake it off as quickly as I can. Focus on who is here—Maggie, Devin, Zack's parents, the team's families, our sponsors, people from town who serve us ice cream and fix our bike tires and check out our groceries. Random town personalities and politicians. People I've known my whole life and some whose faces I barely know, all holding signs with *my* name on them.

I wave at the people who spot me as I peek out, and I find Amy, who's sitting with that girl Tabby who baked me cupcakes and that annoying guy Christopher. They're both holding up these posters done in elaborate tiny calligraphy that just say *yay*. But even Amy, who thinks pep rallies are equivalent to nationalist propaganda, can't hold back a smile at the infectious energy around us. Prerecorded wildcat roars fade into the school band playing an awesome version of our fight song, and I feel like a warrior ready for battle, blood pumping, itching for action. I start jumping up and down to release some of the energy, and the team follows suit, all getting hyped around me. I can feel it. We're really in sync, comfortable in each other's spaces for the first time since we lost last year. And I know, *I'm ready*.

I can hardly wait as Principal Horvath takes the stage. He's got a Wildcats jersey on awkwardly over a suit and tie. I glance at Zack and we bite back grins.

"Dibs for my Halloween costume this year," I whisper to him, and he curses under his breath that I beat him to it.

Coach stands at the end of the line, farthest from me, yet I can sense the tension in how he stands. I know he loves these pep rallies, but he's ready for tomorrow's game to get started too, to put last year behind us.

"Hellooooo Wildcats!" Principal Horvath says as he waves his arms to quiet the crowd. Everyone leans in. The man usually doesn't have this much enthusiasm for anything. "This is one helluva team! Undefeated last year and went all the way to the state championship! And, if I know this team, they are hungrier than ever. This is the year we win our first state title in decades! Let's welcome the Wildcaaaats!"

The crowd goes even wilder as the guys and I run onto the court. I find myself joining in, screaming my lungs out. So many friendly faces are cheering and grinning and jumping to their feet around me. For me and this team. God, I can't believe I'm here, leading this team out as captain. I can't believe we're gonna win this year.

I can't believe I'm finally doing this.

"Special thanks to Gus Verrier from Verrier Electronics for the new uniforms," Principal Horvath says, almost as an afterthought. "Thanks, Gus."

Gus, a sort of tiny, former–AV Club–looking guy who fixes my iPhone whenever I drop it, which is a lot, waves to Horvath.

We all take our seats just behind Horvath's podium, but I can practically feel everyone's legs twitching as we try to sit still, itching to scrimmage.

"This kind of season doesn't just happen without the best coach in the state of Georgia," Principal Horvath continues, his voice rising like he's in the WWE. "Folks, give a giant Wildcats roar for our coach, Brian Ferris!"

We focus and join in to give Coach the introduction he deserves. It's like watching a legend strut onto a stage. Coach takes a moment to smile and even put his arms up a little, relishing in the attention the most I've ever seen him.

"Thank you, thank you," he says. "I just want to say it's an incredible honor to lead these fine young men seated behind me. But the Wildcats wouldn't be the Wildcats without the support of all of you and the entire beautiful community of Chitwood behind it. And, as you know, we're kicking off the season with one hell of a test against the Panthers tomorrow."

The crowd boos.

"Now, now. We're going to welcome them onto our court with respect and dignity—that's what the Wildcats do." He holds the mic closer, like he's performing. "And then we'll kick their asses!"

The roar that follows is deafening, and the heat in my body just spreads.

"In my twenty-three and a half years, this is the best team I've had the privilege of coaching. But we all know we wouldn't be here if it wasn't for the exceptional play of one special young man."

My stomach flips.

Now or never.

I can hear the ticking of my clock. *Now. Now. Now.*

Someone shouts, "Go Barclay!" and the crowd picks up on my name and starts chanting. But Coach cuts them short with another hand motion. He waits patiently as everyone calms. Zack claps me on the back as everyone jumps up around me in excitement. *They're all here for me. They've got my back.*

"Last year, as a sophomore, he broke the Georgia state record for three-pointers. And, thanks to his leadership, talent, and exceptional, God-given purpose in this life, he leads us into what I believe is going to be a very special season. My fellow Wildcats, it is truly my honor to introduce to you, our team captain, Georgia's reigning Gatorade Boys Player of the Year, *Barclay Elliot.*"

With my name, the crowd goes fucking nuts. Like I'm talking the whole bleachers swaying as everyone stands in unison.

"Barclay! Barclay! Barclay!"

This is it. The next time I walk back to this seat, I'll be out. I run up toward the podium, but it feels more like taking the first step on a tightrope. I won't look down.

Time is the enemy. I know now there is no time guaranteed other than the present. The cheers drown out any thoughts or doubts in my head until all that's left is the thundering of my heartbeat.

"Um. Hi," I say. The mic screeches with feedback. I launch back a step, resisting the urge to clutch my ears.

A voice from the crowd fills my moment of hesitation. "Happy Birthday, Barcs!"

Cheers erupt once more and I grin pointing at the voice in the crowd, but it's hardly five seconds before I'm back in the silence.

The awareness of time gives us the courage to face our fears. Scratch said that all the time, but I never really appreciated it until now.

"I don't have too much to say, uh, other than you guys are awesome. And I'm so proud of this team."

And if we face those fears, we can defeat them.

I turn to the team. To Zack's two thumbs up and grin, to Ostrowski rocking on his feet, antsy. To Coach watching me, nodding along as if I'm saying something profound.

"You guys are my family. And I'm proud to be your captain."

They all smile back. Some of that confidence from this morning returns in a swell of energy.

"Hell, this entire school is like a second home to me!"

The crowd cheers again. My people, my family. They're all here for me and nothing could stop that, nothing can stop us. It's everything I could have ever dreamed of.

". . . And you should be able to share everything with your family."

Today is the day. I only have 18,615 of them left. What am I waiting for? Let's fucking do this.

"So I want you to know . . ."

Two measly words and it'll be done.

"I'm gay."

And then—there's silence.

CHAPTER TWO

THE SILENCE ISN'T JUST FOR A SECOND. IT HOLDS LIKE something sticky thrown at a wall. My chest constricts as I wait for it to fall. For the thunderous applause to start. They're shocked, I get that. But shouldn't someone be saying . . . something? Finally, the silence shifts, but to whispers, not applause. People lower their signs with my name on it, and look away from the court. The whispers start to ping-pong through the stands, and the growing static feels like a hot needle driven into the same spot over and over again.

What is happening?

I look away from the crowds, over to my team, sure my boys are about to surround me. But the new recruits who looked up to me and players who hyped me after game-winning shots all look to each other with furrowed brows and tight jaws. Ostrowski, no surprise, looks ready to jump out of his seat and murder me. I look for Zack to exchange a *Can you believe this?* look, but for once his face doesn't match mine. He looks . . . like he has no idea who I am. And I can't look away from him.

Why is no one—

And then one single "YEAH" echoes through the gym. Amy, I realize. She's standing up to cheer, her hands around her mouth to amplify the sound.

Then Tabby—who I never even got to thank for the cupcake—stands up too. "Go Barclay!"

But no one else joins them. I might throw up. I seek out Devin's face to hold myself together. But he's got his eyes on Maggie, who's staring in slack-jawed shock.

Principal Horvath skids his way back onto the stage, ever-so-gently shoving me away from the microphone. "Anyway, thank you everyone for coming to this year's pep rally! Let's go Wildcats!"

As soon as Principal Horvath leaves the stage, though, the whispers just grow louder, gobbing together into a mixture of sound loud enough that I can't think, but garbled enough that I can't make out any words. Cameras flash in my face, only adding to the chaos. I've never had nightmares as intense as this. I think back to the newspaper Zack shoved into my hands this morning. Is this . . . going to be in the news? In a bad way?

"Warm up! It's time to scrimmage," Coach snarls at us, no, not us, at *me*.

The whole team looks to me and doesn't move.

And it's just . . . over? Shit, I—was that it? It's somehow like the moment never happened but won't end, the silence echoing in my head, two cheers, turned faces, and that's—that's it? This is happening too fast. *What did I just do?*

Maybe they thought I was joking. Maybe it was a bigger shock than I thought and they just need a minute. Maybe I should play it off like it was a joke. . . . No, I just need to make a great shot and—

"NOW!" Coach bellows.

Everyone starts warm-ups, and thankfully, I don't get any more time to spiral. The drills pass me by in a blur and by the time the scrimmage starts, I can't even *feel* my body. The sacred minutes where I

23

usually feel most comfortable in my own skin, in the most control of limbs, calculating the tiniest movements needed for jump shots or weaving around guys a foot taller than me, are gone. And not just for me, it seems. Half the shots we take end in basketballs flying off the backboard. Lochman and Zack bump into each other with poor footwork. Ostrowski jumps his way into my space so much you'd think we'd switched to hockey. When we finish, the crowd's cheers are lukewarm and I'm hardly less tense than before.

Coach calls us all to a huddle in the locker room. An abrupt one, where he's rubbing his hands the whole time.

"Okay, guys, pep rallies don't matter. Put it all—all of it—out of your heads. Tomorrow is the first game of a season that's going to change this town," he says, his voice clipped. I look to Zack and Lochman, but both have their eyes squarely on Coach. The new guys on the team are all fidgeting like mad. "That's what matters. And that means the *only* thing in our heads right now is getting that ball into the hoop. Now shower off and meet tonight at seven thirty for our pasta dinner. The Wildcats are back!"

Coach dismisses us. I wait for him to call me over, sure he just wants to talk about it and check in in private. He's not a showy guy. Coach Ferris and Scratch were practically best friends. My grandpa was his first coach too, and he's always felt more like family than just my basketball coach.

But he walks away like I'm a stranger. When I look around, I realize I've been watching him walk away so long everyone on the team is already gone. Even Zack. For the first time all day, maybe even all year, I'm alone.

With a couple inhales of air, my brain starts to shuck off the panic and my heartbeat slows. I expect it to go back to, well, normal. But as I start a slow pedal out of the parking lot, nothing *feels* normal. I know every inch of this town; nothing ever changes here, but it feels like I've put a different filter over my life. Chitwood's a hodgepodge of different generations, Historic Main Street bleeds into mom-and-pop craft stores, then Shakey's Pizza. A church marquee stands with one of the letters in "Jesus" tilting a little. It'd only take one drunk teenager to knock it loose. Old buildings that once had other purposes now house new restaurants that attract a line around the block for a couple weeks before fading into the background with everything else. There's something haunting now to me, though, about how old, solid things that everyone thought would be around forever are just gone at random, no signs they were ever even there.

The one thing that is consistent, though, is the Wildcats. Wildcats stickers are slapped onto store windows, team signs stabbed into lawns as I bike into the neighborhood. Even the chain stores quickly jumped on board with the decorations, like it's an initiation ritual. People will always talk about hope with me—hopes for the new basketball recruits, hopes for a winning record each season, hopes we'll bring home a huge trophy come March. They've been holding on to this hope for so long, and like some of the crumbling storefronts, I wonder how long it can survive. Last year brought a lot of energy back into town, but it also feels like it'll be a bigger failure if we lose again. If I lose again. And somehow it feels like I already did.

I pull out my headphones and put on some Halsey-heavy playlist Amy made me, looping back to the school, not ready to go home yet. I need something to slow down my thoughts. And for a couple blocks, it works. My brain focuses on Halsey's lyrics and lets my feet pedal on autopilot.

But then as I near the school again, I ride by the memorial right outside.

It's a small thing. A couple candles, teddy bears, flowers. Still, it hits me like a kick to the back of the knee. Car accidents aren't how grandpas are supposed to go. You're supposed to expect it, be able to say goodbye, tell them all the things that matter. I thought for sure there'd be time for that. Scratch was the bravest man I knew. He served a tour in Vietnam, beat *cancer twice*, even stepped up to be a father after my piece of shit dad left us when I was a kid. My mom, siblings, and I even changed our last name to match his. And then one Chevy Malibu barreling through a stop sign right next to Chitwood High ends it all? I can't make it make sense.

I *didn't* get to say goodbye. There *wasn't* time to tell him the important things.

The urge to turn away from everything I didn't do hits me, but I stay put.

The last time I saw him, we were talking about tryouts. *Pay attention to all your teammates. You only win together, so find a way to bring everyone together, tear down the walls between you*. But isn't that what I just did? Isn't this what he would have wanted me to do?

I always thought when he said stuff like that that he knew what I was hiding. But there was always something going on and coming out just didn't feel as *important* as basketball. I thought I'd have time to deal with it once the Wildcats won a championship.

But after he died, I just kept thinking of it as a wall, boxing me in. If my healthy grandpa's life isn't guaranteed, then nothing is. I'd never get to see that smile on his face, that little laugh as he said he loved me that I'd imagined a hundred times. I'd never know if he really knew or if I was just bullshitting myself. How would I know that the next street I step into won't have another Malibu ready to mow me down? I wouldn't. Coach always tells us not to take it down to the wire and that's exactly what I was doing. It was too late to tell Scratch, but it wasn't too late to tell someone. Everyone.

I know I did the right thing, I tell myself, pedaling off, leaving the memorial and the empty gym behind me again. But as I pass more and more people whispering instead of raising their hands to wave or cheer, it feels like maybe they don't think I did. Not at all.

CHAPTER THREE

WHEN I GET HOME, FOR THE FIRST TIME I'M ACTUALLY thankful Mom's still in her room. Clearly the news hasn't reached her yet. But Devin is waiting for me in the living room, looking wary.

"Barc. Are you okay? That—" He shakes his head. "That was really public." I pause from the hug I was about to go in for. I thought he was going to say, *That was so messed up.* Or *Everyone is a moron, they'll be over this in a second.* Not talk about how *public* it was.

"What do you mean? It was school. A place where people *love* me. I know these people, Dev. They're not assholes, they're practically family. In fact, I thought I *should* do it publicly to prove there's nothing to be ashamed of. Maybe pave the way for other gay kids who don't have a platform, you know? That they don't have to lie or hold it in anymore. . . ."

"But Barcs—"

I shoot him a nasty look. "Or do you think I have something to be ashamed of?"

Devin's face falls a moment, his hand rubbing against his barely there cheek stubble. But when he looks back at me, his expression is resolved. "You know better than to think I believe that. But this is Georgia *basketball* we're talking about. People around here are like bandwagon sport fans. When you're winning, they cheer, they scream, they worship you. But the moment you start losing, the moment they think you let them down, it's all boos and they're throwing away their gear. . . ."

It's not like I don't remember what it was like when we lost. Of course I do. Since I was seen as the leader of the team, most of the disappointed looks ended up falling on me. "No one likes losing, but they made signs again, bought the gear again, cheered with me again. I'm not some random pro team, they *know* me. They just . . . they were surprised, that's all."

"Barclay, come on, you know this is different." Devin scoots closer to me and while part of me wants to move away, I don't. "*I* love you no matter what. When you're ready to tell Mom, which probably needs to be soon, by the way, she'll love you no matter what too. But those people who were in the stands don't know you the way we do. I—" He grimaces. "I will always support you, but just . . . be prepared that things might not end up the way you're imagining."

Devin is my anchor, and I know he's holding on to me, but it's like I can feel the links in the chain stretching, moments from snapping all together, like everything else.

"Things have already gone pretty wrong. Mom's never here and even when she is, she still can't mention Scratch without crying. She sobs all night like after Dad left. You're gone and everyone expects me to be fine and lead the team to a huge championship—I can't do that if I'm distracted by even one more thing," I say. "I was walking around every day with this huge fucking secret weighing on me and I had to let it go. It was the only way to feel better."

There's this long, almost painful pause as Devin swallows and stares at me. "Y'know, he's barely been gone a month. . . ."

His words leave a weird, creeping feeling on my skin. "I'm

fine, Devin. This is to *honor* him! He'd want me to be an example."

I walk out without another word and go get changed for the team dinner. I don't tell him about my countdown clock or that feeling of being too late. He doesn't get it; he's never had to keep a fundamental part of himself a secret like this. But I have to believe one day he will see he's wrong. When we win the championship, this will be the last thing on everyone's mind. He'll see.

Ostrowski's house is so nice that it literally came up when Amy and I got high in the off-season last year and searched Georgia homes at ANY PRICE and sorted the listings HIGHEST TO LOWEST so she could plan which locals she'd guillotine during the Inevitable American Class Uprising. Now I'm back in it, under a chandelier that is so huge that it could kill me instantly if it fell, adjusting my thrift store tie. It's dark blue, but has this small stain Mom couldn't get off it from last year. I didn't even ask her to try again this year, but I hope no one notices tonight. Though I guess that's the last thing they'll be thinking about after this afternoon. I take a deep breath and am about to head over to the fancy pasta bar set up on a kitchen island as big as my whole kitchen when I feel a hand on my arm pulling me aside.

It's Zack. He's barely looking at me, and practically radiating that anxious energy from this morning that sits all wrong on him. Zack scrunches his face to get it back to relaxed. I look to my fading sneakers, focusing on the squeak over Zack. "Barc, you—you have to know I support you."

That should make the knot in my chest release. That should be enough to pull me to turn to him. But if that was so true, why didn't he show up for me? Why did only Amy and Tabby cheer to break up that horrible silence? Why does it feel like there's a "but" coming?

I can feel it hover in the air, but he doesn't say it. Instead Zack cracks a smile like everything's blown over now. "I always knew, you know."

"Oh, really," I say, waiting for the punchline. As if I'd want to hear a joke right now.

"Dude, you used to get a boner every single time we hugged."

"Fuck you."

I take a turn toward the kitchen, but Zack stops me from storming off with a hand to my chest, his other rubbing his temple like this conversation is hurting *him*. "No, hey, I'm sorry."

"I'm glad this is funny for you."

"I just—I guess I don't understand why you did it this way. Why didn't you just tell the team privately or like in postseason? We could've taken the time to process this—"

"What is there to process? I'm the same guy everyone was cheering for five hours ago. I'm your teammate, your friend."

"Dude, of course you are! I know that, but do you think Ostrowski and his idiots are gonna think that?"

"They'll get over it," I say, sounding more sure than I feel right now.

"But how soon? We can't afford a slipup this season." His hands are clasped so tight in fists they're practically white.

"What's got you wound so tight?" I ask, unable to hold it back any longer.

"It's . . . Look, the grocery store let my mom go," he says. "With my dad being laid off last month, we're—"

Screwed. He doesn't need to say it.

"If I don't get noticed by a big-time scout and get a scholarship, I can pretty much kiss college and getting out of this shitty town good-bye," Zack continues.

A tiny bit of shame creeps up on me, inching heat up my neck and tingling in my fingertips. Zack's got shit to deal with too. I'm not the only one going through it.

"Zack." I push my hair out of my face. "I—I know you hate all the 'sorry' bullshit. But that really sucks. I can't do much about your mom, but basketball we've got. We have twenty-three games to show you off before playoffs. We're getting you a scholarship. No matter what it takes. I promise, me coming out isn't going to change that."

Zack straightens out as I speak, but the glassiness in his eyes is still present.

"Look, let's be honest," I say quickly while he tries to get himself together. "With the way we play, we don't have to worry about getting a scout to notice. These scouts will be *fighting* to get both of us on their teams." I smile. "Maybe we'll even get recruited by the same school. How badass would that be? I can hear it now." In a hushed voice, I start the cheer I've been saying to him since we were in middle school, "Zack Attack, Zack Attack!"

Zack smiles and finishes it off—"The Panthers better watch their backs"—but his voice is soft, his smile not quite meeting his eyes. "Thanks." He shakes his hands out. "I'm sorry about—"

"Don't. Shit's hard. I know."

"No offense, man, but with basketball, it doesn't seem like it for you. I just hope . . . I hope you're right about everyone else."

We stand there for a moment, then Zack pats me on the arm and jogs over to join Lochman in the pasta line. I watch him go, focusing on the drag of his feet and the way he knocks his ears to each shoulder to crack his neck. The stress is radiating off him still, but I know no pep talk works as well as that first win. Once they start coming, he'll know I'm right. But part of me can't help but still be disappointed that he doesn't get why I did this. That this is going to help us.

I'm about to follow him in when I hear my name said in a low, urgent voice coming from the cracked door to my left. I recognize Coach's gruff mumble, but it takes a minute to place the snooty drawl answering it—Ostrowski's father. Local travel agency owner, school board president, and grade A tool like his son.

Why would Mr. Ostrowski be saying *my* name? Usually the only name he's saying is Tim, whining to keep his son on the team despite how much he sucks. I find myself stopping, ears perked.

". . . disgrace," Mr. Ostrowski says, "and it's the perfect excuse optics-wise to get Elliot off the team."

I thought it couldn't get any worse than that silence and the glares from my teammates at the pep rally. I've heard homophobia on TV and, frankly, as close to me as dinners with our really extended family on my dad's side. But there's something curdling about hearing the word "disgrace" and knowing it's about *me* being gay. I peek in and see Coach sighing.

"Look, I know it's attention-seeking and we didn't need it now, but the team needs Elliot to win. He could paint the school rainbow and we'd still need his skill."

I don't even realize I was hoping Coach would defend me until I'm deflating even more at "attention-seeking."

But then Mr. Ostrowski leans in close. Threatening close. "Let me remind you, Brian, of what's at stake here. *My* company is the reason the team got to go to the preseason tournament in Orlando. Now, that might've been a win-win, but *I'm* the reason no one on the board makes a peep about all the travel and new equipment you ask for, despite the school having to lose a whole spring theater lineup to pay for it. You think Barclay Elliot is the reason this team has a shot at glory? Chitwood kids haven't gotten this team shit since his old man played; *I'm* the reason you're even close. And I can take that all away like that." He even snaps for effect.

Holy. Shit.

I always figured there was some favoritism that was keeping Ostrowski on the team, especially after he fucked up the championship game. But what Mr. Ostrowksi is talking about is more than that. I mean, what's he doing to the school board? Bribing, threatening like he's doing to Coach now? And is he really using the basketball team as a way to direct school funds back to his travel agency? A wave of dizziness hits me as I remember trying to console Amy after the spring play got canceled midway through rehearsals last year, texting her through quiet periods at the tournament. Not only was I not there for her, but my team was the reason she was upset in the first place?

But I can't think about it long. Mr. Ostrowski and Coach head to the door, so I speed away, beelining for the pasta bar, and the safety of Zack filling up a plate. I do my best to focus on the food. There appear to be more sauces in the spread than I've ever even heard of. I'm tempted to follow Zack and try pesto for probably the first time in my life, but trying new food while my stomach's still in a wash cycle probably isn't the best idea.

A couple of the other guys—Lochman, Anthony, and a new sophomore named Derek—all have empty seats next to them, but they avoid my gaze. So instead I make my way to the two empty chairs next to Pat, the only freshman who made the team. I remember being so nervous before my first game on the varsity team, and a good captain knows and prepares for that. And I'm still captain.

But after I drop my brick-heavy plate onto a pristine white linen tablecloth, Ostrowski's dad struts into the room. I'm not even exaggerating how this man walks. There are ostriches who'd laugh at him. I stab a couple noodles as he clears his throat, draping his hands over the back of his son's chair at the head of the table. Of course.

"Welcome, Chitwood Wildcats, to yet another pregame pasta dinner," he says in his perfectly Georgian elite accent. "Another big thank-you to my lovely wife, Mary, for this wonderful spread. In a town like ours, so rooted in our meaningful tradition, particularly in the sport of basketball, we're so humbled to contribute to that legacy."

I accidentally make eye contact with Coach, who's sitting next to Ostrowski, as I resist rolling my eyes. They "contribute" all right, but Coach doesn't blink or smirk.

". . . As we all know, this year is going to be history-making, and the town and I cannot wait for the recognition you will bring to us and your own lives going forward. Let's go Wildcats!"

Everyone at the table cheers, and I force myself to join in. Coach stands up and I sit back and settle in, wondering what he's going to say. I always look forward to Coach's preseason speech, but now I'm practically holding my breath.

"We've made it, boys," Coach says, puffing his chest out. "After getting closer than we've gotten in far too long, the Wildcats are going to take their first championship in *fifty years*." A few of the guys stand up and clap, making the lines around Coach's eyes crinkle. "I know we have the talent, the determination, and the *will* to go all the way this season. This team is full of star players, players who'll rise up to NCAA championships and maybe even the NBA."

Coach doesn't look at me, but my whole body buzzes with energy, the commotion of the room falling away as I chew on that. Me, getting such amazing scholarship offers that I can afford to go to any college I want. Me, dribbling the ball down a televised court. Me, signing with a professional team in a super gay-friendly city like San Francisco or New York, making enough money to allow my kids to never worry about the price of sports equipment. Me, *being* someone. Away from all this Chitwood and Ostrowski bullshit.

Then the sparkle leaves Coach's eyes, and I know he's about to slide into a lecture. "But to do that, we need to talk about unity." I sit up straighter and glance at Zack. His eyes slide to me briefly before turning back to Coach. "We can have all the talent under the sun, but winning is about having a great *team*. These young men around you are your brothers and for the next several months, our priorities have to lie with each other. We need to be willing to be cogs in the machine as much as stars on the court. We need to trust that we have each other's backs and stop putting ourselves first. Do y'all have each other's backs?"

I look around. If you'd asked me this morning, I would have shouted a *Hell yeah*. I've got everyone's back in here, but . . . do they have mine? It doesn't seem like it. Instead of that *Hell yeah*, gazes just slide my way from all across the table. Even from Zack. Coach grimaces and doubles down.

"The next few months have to be about one thing: basketball. Your team needs each and every one of you at top performance. That means absolutely no screwing around. No ruining your bodies or minds. No distractions *of any kind*. Your *girl*friend trouble or video games can wait."

Am I imagining the emphasis on "girl"? Is he being serious? The gazes feel hotter on my neck, and I start pulling at my tie.

". . . You have one shot at this, and I know no one wants to be the guy who lets the team down," he continues, now staring unmistakably at me.

"And I know y'all hear this lecture every season, but it's paramount this year. There won't be any other chances like this. No other lineup with players as good as this year. Everything's riding on this, and I sure as hell hope you boys are ready to *man up* and tackle this challenge."

I take a deep breath. *I'm* ready to tackle this challenge. I'm here. I put everything out there so there wouldn't be any distractions or secrets between us. Yeah, it was for me, but it was for us, too. For the second time I think, no pep talk is better than the first win. Once we get that, it'll convince everyone nothing has changed. *You shouldn't have to convince them,* I think, but as Coach wraps up, I push that out of my mind.

The moment Ostrowski announces that the team is headed out to "go get ice cream," I'm not gonna lie, even with how in my feelings I've been, I get hyped the way I used to as a kid when we'd go to Chuck E. Cheese. I jump into one of the senior players' cars, squished between Zack and the window as we pack too many bodies into the back. The speakers reverberate with a hip-hop song I don't recognize, something where the bass line causes the hairs on my arms to stand up it's so good.

"Do you know what we're doing this year?" I ask Zack. He shakes his head.

While our little mission is technically a secret, something we don't advertise to Coach, pretty much everyone knows exactly what goes down. It's a tradition for the seniors to plan a prank on the Panthers right before our first game, before they can prank us. Last year, we rigged buckets of glitter above the gym to rain down in Wildcats colors when they ran out on the court for their pep rally, and the pictures across Instagram were absolutely epic. There's nothing like the adrenaline wave shared with my teammates as we try not to get caught and pull off something legendary. It may also be my only shot to get everyone back united with me as captain. Time to show them I'm still their friend before we have to get serious about the season.

The lights to Winder High are completely off as we all park out in front of their gym. Chase leads the pack like our very own Fred from *Scooby-Doo*. He stops short of the door, giving it a couple tugs before his gaze rises above it. When his flashlight lands on a window that's cracked open maybe eight feet above us, he nods at Zack and Lochman like that was perfectly within the plan all along.

Lochman lifts Zack up and through the crack in the window so he lands with a *thud* and we all wait, painfully tense until the door opens on the other end with Zack grinning. I take another deep breath as we all file into the school, three flashlight beams and an emergency exit sign our only light. I'm careful to make sure my shoes are making as little sound as possible, but a heavier set of footsteps sounds from a hallway outside the gym. *Security.* Shit. Luckily, Lochman shines a beam on a sign reading GYM, which must be our destination. I pick up the pace and Zack follows suit.

One step inside, and my chest loosens as I inhale that awful, familiar scent of sweat, adrenaline, and stale body spray.

"Freshman, watch the door," Chase says as he ventures deeper into the locker room.

Pat goes scurrying to it.

"I'll go help!" Derek says, clearly still eager to impress too. He runs over to Pat, who seems relieved to have the company.

Kyle lifts Boris up to grab on to one of the Panthers' hoops. Zack and Lochman remove their shoes and start sliding their way across the court. Anthony, Russell, and Ostrowski appear to be trying to get the equipment shed open. I want to join in on the shenanigans, but I can't shake the awkwardness, so instead I decide to hang by Pat and Derek, who look too nervous to be weird around me. Maybe that's the inroads I need.

"We can't get in trouble for this, right?" Derek asks.

"Nah, they always look the other way," I say. Still, I listen for the security guard. I can't decide if he'll end up being a real issue or just, like, a Diet Threat.

"But there was a security camera out there," Derek says.

I tug on my tie, but when I look around, there's so little light coming in here and what's the chance they have a camera that's so nice that it could get a clear picture of our faces? No, it's fine. Everyone knows we do shit like this to each other anyway. It's tradition, expected, a good laugh. Every part of the basketball team is supported in this area, including the sillier stuff like this. We're untouchable.

At least I thought we were.

"It's fine, man," I say, shaking off my doubts. They exhale, clearly relieved, and it feels like a sign, things are going to turn around.

Chase finally reemerges a few seconds later, a huge grin on his face as he holds the sunken skin of the Panther mascot costume in his arms. It's magical, the way that everyone collectively exhales or says, "Holy shit, dude!" as we all take in this costume. It's the thing I've always loved about being on this team. I don't even know what we're doing with it, but I can *feel* this memory getting engraved in my head to tell my kids and grandkids. Just like the stories that Scratch told me, Devin, and Maggie. Chase tosses me the costume, a little harder than necessary, and leads us back into the hallway.

Sure enough, there's that security camera. And I'm now the one holding the stolen costume.

Ostrowski comes up next to me and oh, boy, is that desire to roll my eyes strong.

But then Ostrowski does something so stupid, rolling my eyes couldn't possibly be enough. He points to the camera, saying, "Hey guys, check this out!" and *drops his goddamn pants*. He bends over and moons it. Then he turns to me. "Don't get too excited, Elliot."

The guys around me crack up, half of them genuinely laughing and the other half awkwardly chuckling like they know what'll happen if they don't suck up.

Then the gym door slams open. "HEY!"

Shit. There's the security guard, a burly dude shining his flashlight directly into the hall, right on us. Chase takes off first and a second later the rest of us rush out like we're all freshmen again. I don't even bother looking back to see if Ostrowski can run without his pants. I hoist the costume over my shoulder so it won't slow me down, and I book it.

"GET BACK HERE!" the security guard bellows.

But we keep running until we make it back to the door outside, the fall air smacking us in the face. I jump back into the first car I see, costume and all, and watch with bated breath until the last guy slams the door shut. Chase gets into the driver's seat, turns the key, then slams on the accelerator just as the guard busts through the door. I'm launched into Pat and Derek, who're both red-faced but laughing their asses off now that we're on the move. We all whoop and cheer, letting that sweet victory feeling seep into our veins for the first time this season.

Twenty minutes later, we regroup on our football field. Chase grabs the mascot costume from me without a word and holds it above his head like he's a hunter with a fresh kill, everyone chanting "WILDCATS WILDCATS WILDCATS" as we all take our places surrounding him.

"So here's the plan, everyone," Chase says as he lays down the Panther costume on the grass. "It's time to show the Panthers that we know what they are. The other seniors and I talked, and we're gonna put on a show with this guy." He smirks. "We're gonna take our Wildcat costume and set it up doggy style, really make it look like the Panthers are getting *railed*."

My stomach starts to sour. A few guys immediately respond in laughs and rounds of "fuck yeah," but I'm disgusted. These rivalries are about *basketball*. What's fucking fun about implying that the Panther is getting sexually assaulted? Or is it supposed to *just* be a gay joke? Maybe the shit Ostrowski pulled and all the looks are starting to compound in my brain. I can't grimace through this one. Has Chase always been this gross?

That's when I realize Chase is looking straight at me when he says it, a nasty grin on his face. The dude who days ago was telling me what a legend I am. Who asked for pointers on his jump shot even though I'm a junior and he's a senior.

And I know without a doubt that what I do next matters. If I let it happen, they might pretend I didn't come out. They might tolerate me enough to help them win.

But I came out to stop swallowing down harmful shit like this. And I'm not going to walk it back now.

"Chase," I say. My hand moves to the back of my neck, but I force it back to my side. I'm captain, I remind myself. "I know you guys might not be psyched to have a gay teammate, which I don't get, but *this* isn't funny. And there's no reason to risk anyone being forced on the bench if we get caught. Can't we just tie it to the goalposts instead?"

Ostrowski is of course the one to step forward. "Seriously? You're gonna be a little bitch about this, too?" He takes another step toward me. "Just like the Panthers. Maybe you belong with them, Elliot. They'll be *begging* to suck our dicks." His lips turn up into this ugly smirk as he laughs.

I clench my fist and take my own step forward. Every bit of this day seems to hit me at once. One swing and I could see that smirk knocked right off his face and—

Coach steps out of the darkness. I jump back to friendly distance from Ostrowski, and he physically turns so he's facing Coach and not me.

Coach looks down at the Panther costume. "You know, you boys really shouldn't be doing stuff like this. It's illegal, not in the spirit of good sportsmanship, and takes your head away from the game and what we can do to win." His words are sort of scolding, but he can't stop smiling as he speaks. He crosses his arms. "No displays with the costumes. The stakes are much too high for us to have this Panther costume in our possession."

There's a brief lull, where it seems like Coach is letting the air out of basketballs as the team deflates. And I can't help it—it's a relief that even though he hasn't had my back, Coach doesn't think the underwear thing is funny. *Someone* is sane around here.

Then Coach smiles again. "Let's save screwing the Panthers for the game and return that mascot suit." He pauses. "But let's give it a Wildcats jersey as a souvenir."

Everyone cheers, but my stomach sours more that he stops there. The team runs inside to grab a practice jersey and I turn to go running with them, hoping no one notices the drag in my step.

"Hey, Elliot, c'mere a minute," Coach says.

Cold washes over me as I turn and walk to Coach. His expression is unreadable. And I wonder why he's just now pulling me aside.

"We are not going to discuss this afternoon. Not today, hopefully not ever. Because you have big opportunities ahead of you and I can't stand to see you squander them. Whatever possessed you to air your personal affairs isn't as big as this game. Doesn't mean as much to your future as this."

Doesn't mean as much to your future. Except . . . it does. This is about who I am. This is about building a life full of people I love, not having to hide or lie. I want, I don't know, for being gay to mean more than being anxious about coming out, having fleeting crushes that can never go anywhere, and jacking off to whatever pops up on the first page of gay porn sites in my room late at night. I want to start living my whole life now, instead of watching the days tick down, missing chances. Being all of me is the only way we *can* make it to the championship, the only way I can lead. They just have to let me.

I want to say all of that, but before I can even open my mouth, Coach is walking away. And instead of following the rest of the guys into the locker room to get the jersey, I just walk home.

CHAPTER FOUR

W E'RE FIFTEEN MINUTES AWAY FROM THE FIRST GAME against the Panthers, and I don't feel any more comfortable with how the guys are looking at me than I did before the scrimmage the day before. Somewhere deep in my mind, I knew there wasn't anything a pasta dinner, Coach's speeches, or a prank could do to change anything. Still, as I bounce a fresh, newly inflated basketball that can be dribbled to the sky (I wonder if Mr. Ostrowski manipulated the board to get that, too), I feel as deflated as the ball at home, so old the surface is coming off in ribbons. Maybe even as sad as I imagine Mom feels (she didn't get out of bed at all this morning, and is still the only one who doesn't know I'm gay).

Everyone on the team is clumped in circles, stretching or staring off at the bleachers like we're not going to be playing this game together. Scratch used to prep me on the possibility of being captain one day, but he never talked about what to do if *I* were the problem. I do everything I know how to keep my breathing steady, save the anger to pump into adrenaline for the game. There are scouts and journalists out there. People who can make my future. People who can make Zack's future, I think as I notice him still tense even after stretching.

I quick pass the ball over to Zack, just to get his attention. He barely catches it in time, but smiles as he does a dribbling maneuver. Exactly what I need from him.

"Got any other revelations before the game, Elliot?" Ostrowski asks. "Gonna tell us you're dating Ito to 'bond us' even more?"

I hold my breath to keep from saying anything. Zack palms the ball, frozen a moment. Then he turns to Ostrowski. "Fuck off, man."

He says it like he's already defeated. "Try not to dwell on it," I say to Zack, even though some part of me wishes he were saying this to me. "He'll stop making the jokes when he's on the bench."

Zack squeezes his eyes shut. "There's just a lot going on right now. I'm having a hard time focusing."

Because of me. He won't say it, but I know it. "Even if nothing changes with Ostrowski, trust me. I'm gonna get us to that championship."

Zack nods, half-hearted. It's not enough, but I take what I can get.

I take a deep breath and zero in on what's important right now—getting in position behind all six feet four of Lochman as he gets ready for the tip-off against a Panther who's surprisingly taller than him. He turns and I open my hands to do our pregame handshake. He hesitates—so long that I almost don't think he's gonna do it. But just as the ref walks up the court with the ball, he reaches over and does, hardly a whisper of a touch between us. I shake it off, focusing on the Panthers' forwards. The center seems to be favoring his left as he bounces side to side. I can use that.

The Panthers win the tip-off, but I anticipate the ball's direction. A few seconds later, I've stolen it. I charge down the court, weaving my way to a layup at the basket. It slides through easily. There's a burst of cheers, but nothing like I'm used to. Nothing like an opening game should be. Still, my game's good and that's what counts. Once we get our win, this'll all be a blip. Everyone knows what they're here for.

The Panthers bring the ball up, and I run over to meet their point guard. I signal to Ostrowski, but he meanders like we're on a stroll through the gym, completely missing my plea for a double-team. The point guard blows by me, taking a shot—but misses. Thank God.

But when it bounces off the backboard, Ostrowski doesn't jump for the rebound, and a *fucking Panther* grabs it instead. He runs it back to the top of the key, but instead of following him, Ostrowski runs alongside me instead. He's sweaty and red-faced, even though we just started, but he's also smirking.

"Always knew you were a fucking fairy," he says through a stupid grin.

Anger shoots out of me like a volcano. No more slow burn, no more excuses. For a moment, the haze is so heavy I can't even see the court.

"That's not what you said yesterday, asshole," I snap.

Zack materializes, running between Ostrowski and me. "Watch it, Ostrowski, the clock's running."

I try to refocus, but I realize there's no anger in his voice. He's warning Ostrowski like he's joking around at practice. Not like . . . Not like he's defending me.

"May be an asshole," Ostrowski continues. "But at least I don't want dick up mine."

It's not even a good insult. He's *never* been able to come up with good insults. But I am raging all the same. I want him gone. I want him hurt. I want him on the floor and that stupid fucking smile off his face. I want Zack to help, but he clearly won't, so I reach around Zack and shove him.

He shoves me back. And I run at him, ready to—

"Are you two kidding me?" Coach says.

One moment he's on the sidelines, and the next he's charging into the game. The game that, I realize, has stopped. Panther and Wildcat players alike are all just staring at me. Zack is doing nothing.

"TECHNICAL!" the ref calls.

"Bench," Coach roars. "Both of you."

I can't believe this. Ostrowski is clearly throwing the game, baiting me, and *I'm* out? I didn't even get a full quarter to at least show my teammates that I can still play basketball.

The anger's the only solid thing I can hold on to as Ostrowski and I make our way to the bench. The other feelings, the bitter and heavy ones, I can't deal with right now. At least Coach'll have to rip into Ostrowski, too, for tormenting his own teammate on the court during our first game of the season.

We sit almost at opposite ends of the bench. It would've been polar opposites, but Pat and a couple sophomores have all bunched onto one side to avoid the drama. Coach stomps his way over to us, a vein in his neck visibly throbbing.

And he goes right to . . . *me.* "You better cool it with whatever crisis you're having by the time this half ends, Elliot. You're embarrassing the whole team."

Embarrassing?

God, was that what those unreadable expressions on the team's faces were? On Zack's?

I open my mouth to say something to Coach. I have to make him understand.

"If another word comes out of your mouth, I'll bench you for the second half," Coach says, and then he walks back to the sideline, ignoring Ostrowski completely.

I close my mouth, wishing there was some way to make myself

smaller. Ostrowski looks over, grinning like he's won the lottery. And for the first time in as long as I can remember, I'm on the bench an entire half. It passes by in a complete blur. I can't even focus on strategies or watching the Panthers for weakness or even really breathing. I don't dare look into the crowd. Like if I don't look, those scouts and reporters will have never come at all. Won't have seen me get into a stupid fight with my own teammate. Won't get the story all wrong.

And things don't get better when halftime hits. The Panthers lead us 35–20. My teammates sit farther from me than is even reasonable as we huddle for Coach's halftime speech in the locker room.

"Now guys, let's keep our heads in the game," Coach says, clapping his hands like we're distracted dogs. "We're champions, remember? This is our year. We were *one* mistake from a championship last year. I know my juniors and seniors remember. *One shot* from a championship. And you know what happened? Everyone, including my so-called star players, got so caught up in their own egos, their own bullshit, that they ruined an easy play." People glare at *me*, buying the way Coach is rewriting history all of a sudden. "An *easy play*, guys! I thought the summer would give everyone time to humble and get your heads on straight, so let this be my last reminder to you new folks." The implication is clear, he's ready to sculpt the next group if I don't perform. Nothing else about me matters. "We're a *team*. So start acting like it!" The hypocrisy is so rich I almost laugh.

Coach at least calls my number in the lineup for the second half, though, and I try to regroup. I take a deep breath, ready to swallow down the bile taste in the back of my throat.

But I guess the rest of the team isn't.

We're immediately out of sync. Nobody's looking at each other at the right time. We're tripping over each other's plays. I make shot after shot, but the Panthers just run it right back down the court and erase it.

I don't lead us back to victory. There's no sports movie comeback redemption.

In the end, we just lose. And this time, I know exactly who they'll blame.

I've gone through practices so hard that I threw up, or couldn't walk properly for days. Games that threw shrouds over my confidence and false alarm injuries that I thought could end my career. But I've never felt *this* exhausted after a game. It's sunk into the fabric of my body, making me feel like cartilage and blood has turned to lead and molasses.

"Great job, Elliot," Chase says with a sneer.

"MVP my ass," Boris says.

"Hope you're happy," says Derek, even though he was practically peeing himself last night until I calmed him down.

I force myself to look to the stands. People are heading out, leaving signs with my name on them torn and abandoned on the seats, but the absence of the scouts has been there for nearly an hour. They left before the game even ended. Once the deficit hit the double digits again in the second half, there wasn't anything left to see.

A refrain keeps running through my mind as I turn back to the team. *It didn't have to be this way.*

"Oh, boo-fucking-hoo," I growl. "I had your backs out there, I was still our lead scorer tonight. But you guys couldn't handle having mine."

"Elliot!"

I stiffen at the sound of Coach's voice. It's not the barking anger of

49

before, but there's still a sternness. Lecturing dad voice when I haven't done shit to deserve it.

This time when I follow him, I'm not scared. I'm pissed.

He shuts the door to his office and drops himself into his chair. But I stay standing.

"Look," he says. "I don't care if you're gay." He winces as he says it, though, like he's getting a shock from a lie detector test. "But you went about this the totally wrong way. The only way we all succeed is if we work as a *team*, and what you did threw a spotlight on you. For God's sake, you're already the star of this team. You didn't *need* more attention. It was selfish and a distraction for everyone that took them off their game. This isn't the time to stray from our goal. It's—" He pinches the bridge of his crooked nose. "It's got nothing to do with basketball. You see that, don't you? It's not what basketball players do, what real men do."

There it is.

But he isn't finished.

"Men don't need to *talk* about these things. Why couldn't you have kept it to yourself?" He pauses, as if realizing how bad it sounds, which is how I know he means it. "At least until after the championship. You see what this kind of stuff does to the boys, especially the ones who need a leader like you. Ostrowski got so overwhelmed he had to let off steam mid-game."

Let off steam?

So all the times he's shoved other players or said horrible comments, were those just *letting off steam* too? Were his tantrums that have gotten him benched in at least a quarter of the games last season now suddenly okay?

Ostrowski has actually done shit that hurt the whole team. Hell,

50

even Chase and Boris have jeopardized a game to act tough. But I—I what? Say something honest about myself at a pep rally, let them into my life, and now I've caused some huge upset to the team? It's not like I even asked for the goddamn spotlight. They pushed it on me, making me captain when I'm not even a senior yet. Not because they believe in me. Because they believe in my jump shot.

I stand up straighter. "I've—I've given so much to this team. To this town. I've put the whole team on my back, turned my friends down countless times, skipped family functions, spent less time with my *now dead grandpa* so I could lead us to a championship that now everyone feels entitled to. That we would have had last year by the way if Ostrowski hadn't 'blown off steam' being a ball hog. And what? What did I really do here yesterday? Oh, I admitted I was gay so I could stop holding a secret in that was going to let the pressure get to me and mess this season up. Something that doesn't affect the game for anyone but me. But I should've *held it in*? To be a man? Scratch always said a real man owned up to who he was and supported his teammates no matter what. Or do you not think he was a real man either?"

I think back to Devin and what he said last night. How people here are all bandwagoners. The moment I venture from their perfect idea of me, they drop me. Even my team. Even Coach. Was I only ever a way to win games and get scholarships and sell shit at the hardware store to all of them? I'm the exact same person everyone *loved* yesterday.

But it wasn't love. None of that was real. That's so clear now. And I'm not going to let them reduce me down to just the parts they're comfortable with. I can't take back what I said, but neither can any of them. So there's only one thing left to do.

"I quit," I say.

Coach doesn't beg me to stay. He doesn't say anything at all. So I walk out.

All my effort. Everything my grandpa and I worked for. I watch it tumble down the drain as I walk out into the gym where the rest of the team waits. Out into the hall. Out of the building. Out of basketball. For good.

CHAPTER FIVE

BEING OUT, I HAVE TO ADMIT, DOESN'T FEEL LIFE-CHANGING. Being off the team? Way weirder. My arches, calves, and core ache from hustling at the game. I wake up on Sunday with new plays and clips of the game playing in my head. But it's all useless. My phone, usually constantly dinging with messages by now, is silent after I blocked everyone on the team's numbers and deactivated all my socials. Well, except for approximately a hundred messages from Amy that I haven't been able to even face yet. I just know she's going to be a little too happy that I quit and even though she's probably the only support I have right now, I'm not ready for that.

Even worse, when I came home, there was a box with a bow right outside my door. From Mom.

When I finally open it, my throat closes up.

It's a pair of the newest Air Jordans, pristine and so far out of our price range I'd feel guilty even if I *hadn't* just quit. Which she still doesn't know. Devin walked me home after the game, psyching me up to tell her everything. Sure enough, we'd walked past her bedroom door and heard her sobs through the walls. Devin entered while I slammed my bedroom door shut and passed out.

I tuck the shoes in my closet, like maybe if I ignore them long enough, they'll go away. Maybe the same thing can happen for Mom and me, maybe she'll stay in her room long enough that—

"Barclay!" Mom screeches.

She's in her suit when I make my way down. It's her best suit, but something's wrong with her makeup. She shuts the door, but stands in front of it. I look to Maggie, then Devin, but both look blank. I scrunch my shoulders, wishing this could just be about me not taking the trash out or something.

"Do you want to know who's outside our house right now?" she demands.

I haven't ordered anything on Amazon in weeks, so no. I really don't.

"Reporters!" she says when I don't say anything.

And suddenly everything comes back into focus. I cross my arms to try to stop them from shaking. "Shit."

Maggie rushes to the windows, and Devin jumps to his feet. He swears too low for Mom to hear and steps outside.

"And you know what they asked me?" She blinks really hard for a few seconds. "They asked about your sexuality, and how I felt about you *quitting the team*!"

All I wanted was to come out once, yet here we are *again*. Me having to justify myself over and over. She hasn't even asked me how I am. Or if it's true. So I don't say anything.

She takes a deep breath, sighing hard. "Barclay, why would you not tell me first? How could you *blindside* me like this? I love you. I love you no matter who you love. But how could you . . ." I wait, my muscles painfully tense, a wave of guilt washing over me. I've known this was coming since I chickened out of telling her that morning.

". . . quit the team like this?"

I'm all but knocked back. Like a cartoon character not expecting a hanging piano beaning them.

She's mad that *I quit the team.*

She just found out her son is gay and told everyone but her and is more concerned about the team.

The guilt disappears as I rocket to my feet. "And?"

"How could you be so selfish? Do you ever think about the sacrifices I've made to keep you on that team? To give you a future? Or even, for one second, how *I'd* feel about finding out from *reporters*?" She's taken steps toward me and is close enough now that I can see her mascara is running. "What would Scratch say?"

"Scratch would've been here to talk about it for more than five minutes!" I blurt out.

She's stunned by this. Like I've slapped her. But I'm not done.

"When was I supposed to tell you? All the nights you're crying in your room? Or when you are out here just asking me about my basketball numbers?" Tears well in her eyes, and a lump grows in my throat but I'm not going to cry. "Yeah, reporters are asking you all this stuff. About *me*. You haven't even asked me if I'm okay. Or *why* I quit the team."

Devin comes back in then, eyes wide and helpless as he sees how close Mom and I are, as we both bite back tears. "Hey, guys, come on. Mom, please, he didn't tell anyone before the rally. And last night I told him not to—"

It's not just Mom who whips around to see Devin. Maggie does too. Maggie's eyes get watery as Mom's fill with fury.

"You what?" Mom demands. "You *knew*?"

"So did I—from that stupid rally he made me go to! But no one talked to *me*. Like always!" Maggie squeals before darting out of the room with her usual drama.

Mom runs after her and gives me a look that tells me not to follow.

I look to Devin. Once more, it's just the two of us. Dad gone, Scratch gone, Mom gone, Maggie gone.

Devin sits back down on the couch and pats the spot next to him. "Barc—"

"Don't be a dick," I snap. "I get it. You told me so."

Devin frowns, rubbing his hands along his thighs. "I would never say that to you. I have your back. You know, not everyone is against you." He glances toward Maggie's bedroom. I tense to hear what they're saying, but they're talking too quietly. "It'll just take a little time." He gives me a tiny smile. "At least you're free to live authentically now, right?"

I snort. It sounds like he's quoting a humanities course or something. "What does that even mean?" So far, it's cost me basketball, most of my friends, and now maybe most of my family too. What's authentic about it besides how much it sucks?

"Well, you get to decide that."

I don't think my options are very good.

When it comes time to return to school the next day, I try to stay focused. Without the team, the only reason I'm at school is to go to class and maybe hang out with Amy if I can catch her between newspaper, drama club, and the underground guitar lessons she gives people in the ceramics room during her free period. I've just got to keep my head down, ignore the team, get through the day, and not overload myself with any more BS before I can finally head home again. But the second I walk through the door to get to my locker, Zack approaches. His jaw is set so hard that I can see the tendons in his collarbone throbbing. "I've been trying to contact you all night."

A little bit of guilt creeps in. With all that Zack and I have been through together, I probably shouldn't have blocked him along with the rest of the team. With what he just told me about his mom, he can't afford to quit in solidarity I guess, though I still think he could have said *something*. But Devin says I decide what my authentic life looks like—well, I'm ready for Zack to jump into the new fold.

"Sorry, man, I couldn't talk to anyone after the game. It wasn't personal."

But Zack isn't done. "So, what, you're just gonna quit the team and not even talk to me about it?"

Quit the team. His words, like Mom's, knock against my brain as my thumb hovers over the unblock button on his contact.

"You sure I'm the one who quit? Because it feels like the team quit *me*. What were all your messages about? Basketball? Because I'll bet they weren't asking if I was okay after you all left me up there *and* out on the court."

"I told you yesterday, I support you, but you were totally selfish, bro. You didn't think it would affect things, but—"

"Why aren't *you* thinking about what you and team are doing to me? Why should I have to make everyone comfortable with something that has nothing to do with them? I've been uncomfortable holding this in and lying about myself for *years*. I was ready to play better than ever with that off my chest and once again, *Ostrowski* threw it all off. But no one called *him* out!"

Why is everyone acting like I tried to do a promposal at a game? This wasn't just some spectacle. I *needed* to do this. No one gets to tell me *I* came out wrong. *They* reacted wrong.

I shake my head. "What I did wasn't selfish; it was brave. A hell of a lot braver than you all just sitting there saying nothing."

Zack's chest heaves; he's suddenly furious. I almost take a step back. "Brave? You call this *brave*? No, dude, you thought you were too popular to be touched. That's not brave. You were showing off. *Just* like Ostrowski at the championship last year. And then when it didn't go perfectly, you quit on me, your best friend, when I told you how much I had riding on this season."

"How the hell was I supposed to know that being a 'team' was just lip service? I didn't think I was fucking popular, I thought I had actual friends. I thought they'd all have my back. I thought you would because yeah, I do know how much you have riding on this season, so I went out there and tried to have yours the whole time." I say, "Besides, look at you! It's perfectly fine when you unload your parent troubles and all that pressure onto me, but *my* secret is crossing the line?" It feels below the belt, but so is everything he's said to me. The warning bell rings and I turn back to walk the last few feet to my locker. It's not near Zack's, so now would be a great time for him to get the fuck away.

But before Zack can even cobble together another weak response, we both stop dead. My locker's a rainbow, but it's not for pride. It's dozens of different layers of spray-painted dicks in all colors and a hell of a lot of slurs that start with *f*. It's . . . I can't believe what I'm seeing. It's not like I haven't seen this scene hundreds of times. In movies, when I'd doomscroll through hate crime articles, I know this shit happens. But then right in the middle of the layers of paint, I realize someone has drawn a re-creation of Chase's mascot prank outfit idea.

It's my fucking team.

"Do you really think I should've stayed on a team that'd do *this* to me?" I say, gesturing to it, my voice deeper, strained.

Zack's dark eyes dart to seemingly every individual word, fury gone. "Barcs, I—I can help you clean it off. Let me get—"

For a second, there's a flash of my friend. The one who spent his allowance to buy me the newest Hot Wheels set to cheer me up when my dad left. Who opened doors for me when I sprained my ankle in middle school and had to walk with crutches for months. Who sat with me every minute of my grandpa's funeral.

But he's also the one who five minutes ago was taking their side. And I can't feel that right now. The only thing that feels okay, feels tolerable as my world collapses, is the steady boiling heat of my anger.

"Why are you acting all scandalized when you agree with them? You're just as bad. Just go," I say, but it doesn't feel like enough, so I hit lower. "If you only care about the scholarship, you won't find one with me anymore. So why hang around?"

Zack's face falls. It doesn't make me feel better, but I can't stop replaying the past couple days, all the moments I looked to him and felt even more alone than before. How when he needed support I was there, ready to help. It's easier this way than hearing him pretend he cares *but*. Even if everything feels so, so much worse as Zack walks away, leaving me alone with my slur-covered locker.

The locker sets the tone for the rest of the day. If people aren't gaping at it like it's a car accident on the highway, they're whispering about me as I pass. Jake glares at me as he blocks my usual seat in English class. Teachers who used to let me coast start calling on me for every question, telling me to pay attention when I space out. I don't even go to the cafeteria because I know my invitation for the team lunch table is revoked. And of course, I find out Amy somehow managed to get dress coded for a third time, so she's serving an unjust one-day suspension on the worst possible day. I try to block it all out until I'm finally back in my bedroom.

It's so weird to be in there with the sun streaming in, to look at the time on my phone and it's before four. To not be in practice. Mom's actually at work, and I haven't seen her since our fight about the reporters, though I haven't exactly been trying. Maggie's at home too, playing CW shows really loudly while she assumedly works on some new masterpiece for her portfolio in her room. Strange that she's not posted in her usual spot at the kitchen table, but maybe she's still being angsty over not being the center of attention. Still the volume doesn't make it any easier to focus on the Spanish homework I'm trying to do (Señora Shue says I'll need 100 percent completion to get a "grade that'll impress colleges," which no one has ever said before). What should feel weird but doesn't is that Devin is still here. He decided to stay home for the week to help smooth the drama in the house. He groans as he takes a makeup test over Zoom.

"Going that well, huh?" I say.

"What's not going well is that Mom says you're ignoring her now," Devin says.

I glance over at his test. "Don't you have something else to focus on?"

"I . . ."—he dramatically clicks his mouse, ending the test—"don't now, bitch!"

I drop deeper into the sofa, rolling my eyes. "I don't want to deal with her. She's the mom; she's supposed to come talk to me."

"At least she wasn't crying herself to sleep last night."

"Not my problem."

He stares at me, long. Long enough for me to realize he kind of *does* think this is my problem. "Fuck off, man. I know—"

He touches my arm to stop me. "You're old enough to fix things with Mom on your own, I'm not gonna push on that. But I—I dunno, Scratch dying was hard on all of us. I'm worried about you, too. You need a break."

With all the extra work I need to do in school now, I'm not so sure about that. "Yeah, I wish."

He throws an arm around my shoulder. "I'm serious. This town is cancer, anyway. How about you come visit me at Georgia Tech in a few weeks? It's Visitors Weekend. I'll be done with midterms and there's always parties to go to. Mom'll have a chance to cool down and focus on Maggie, and I can introduce you to some dudes."

No offer has sounded better since I made varsity as a freshman. But as I hear the screeching TV sounds coming from Maggie's room, I have no idea how I'm going to make it through the next few days, let alone a few weeks until then. I'm seconds from going into Maggie's room to ask her to turn it down when the doorbell rings.

There's a rustle as Maggie leaves her room to answer it.

"Amy's here!" Maggie calls to me, and Devin takes that as his cue to go back to his room and avoid the rest of his work.

When I get to the door, Amy's holding a huge box and her arms are shaking, but there's a grin on her face. "Happy late birthday! Blame our underfunded postal service."

I take the box from her, enjoying my first shot of any positive emotion in what feels like forever. "You know, you can text instead of ringing the doorbell."

She heads up to my room. "Are you saying you would've actually answered? Besides, miss the creepy alien tone? No way."

I tense as we take the steps, suddenly very aware that we haven't talked about the pep rally since it happened. The last of her hundred texts said she'd give me space if that's what I needed.

But apparently space is over and now I don't know what to do. *What if she thinks I was wrong too?*

She beelines for Maggie's room first, yelling, "Keep it down, squirt! I'm about to change your life!" before heading to my room. She doesn't even flinch when Maggie shouts, "Get the hell out of here, Amy!"

Amy gently sets the box on the floor and sits cross-legged in front of it. I take a deep breath, ignoring the strain in my hamstrings as I bend down and unwrap it.

It's a record player.

"Oh," I say, breathing in sharply. It's expensive, way too expensive like the shoes, and red, my favorite color. And I can't believe I wanted space from one of the only people who cheered when everyone was silent. That I was even worried at all. "This is so cool. You didn't have to—"

"Shut up," she says as she hands me a second present, an unwrapped record. *Out of Time* by R.E.M.

"What's this?" I ask, honestly too used to Amy shaming me about music to care about the judgment I know will come in response.

Amy throws her hands up. Thank God we're on the floor. When she gets really impassioned, she tends to knock stuff over. "It's your starter record. It's R.E.M. It's like, the best album of all time. Michael Stipe is one of the greatest singer-songwriters to ever live."

As Amy takes the record out of the jacket and puts it onto the record player, I have to ask, "Isn't it easier to just play on Spotify?"

"It's not about what's easiest. It's about what's *authentic*. I'm not gonna let you be one of those basic white bread boys who only listens to Top Forty on Spotify while sending dudes bad dick pics on Snapchat."

I like the way Amy saying "dudes" doesn't feel weird. It actually feels . . . kind of awesome. At least *someone* knows how to switch "girls" to "boys" but keep our friendship the same as it was. As I think about that, the music draws me in. I reach for the jacket and read the song name. "Losing My Religion." The tempo's upbeat, soft, but the singer, this Michael Stipe guy, has this sad, rich voice. It *does* fill the air differently than playing out of a speaker.

"I like the sound *a lot*," I say.

Amy smiles. "Well, they're a huge part of my life. They'll become a part of your life too." She motions to my clock. "What's left of it, anyway. It's way more morbid in person, by the way."

Amy asked what it meant when we were FaceTiming after the funeral, and when I told her, she said it was "super emo" and sent me a Yungblud playlist on the apparently now very inauthentic Spotify.

"Maybe the clock is off by several thousand days and I'll die tonight," I say.

"It's not every day the best basketball player in the state quits the team and that's the second most interesting thing that's happened that week." She leans over and punches my arm. It reminds me of picnics when we were little kids, her punching me like that when I took too many of her chips. "You didn't even tell me."

She doesn't seem mad, or even particularly serious, but it's almost a little too light. I know there's some truth there. "I didn't tell anyone. Not even Devin."

"Barclay, we've known each other since we were six years old."

I give her a play punch back. "What, are you upset? Because you're into me?"

Her face scrunches, genuinely offended. "Ew. I was never into you. You're bland as hell. I'm into Michael Stipe." She motions to the

63

record player, as if I've forgotten the god on Earth we're listening to. A beat of silence passes, and the playfulness slides off her for once. "You know you could've told me. You know that."

"I know. I just . . . I've spent most of my life trying to convince people I'm somebody else instead of using that time to just be myself. I thought if I just told you, I wouldn't go any further. I'd just keep doing it."

"Well, I'm into it. I think it's cool you're gay. Now we can live the problematic cliché life of gay guy, best girlfriend. Do you think it still works if I give you the dating advice and have the superior sense of style?"

Unlike Zack, Amy joking around like this actually makes me feel better. This time it's a confirmation that nothing has changed between us and nothing will. And suddenly everything I've been wanting to tell someone just spills out. "I honestly thought it'd be tougher to do. But, once I got up there . . . it was freeing. I guess it was stupid to think everyone else would get that."

Amy scowls. "*Fuck those guys*. It's about time you purged the assholes from your life. Even someone previously thought to be semi-decent like Zack. Bye." Zack moved into town at the beginning of middle school, and the two of us bonded quickly over basketball before we hit our growth spurts. But Amy always tolerated him rather than liked him, I think. In all my years bringing them together for hangs and birthdays, I think they've only bonded over how white Chitwood is and liking Fall Out Boy. It stings to hear how easily Amy can shrug off their connection, even if I burned Zack twice as hard today. "Though," she says as she plops onto my bed, "I'm not surprised that the team reacted like that. Most of them are a bunch of Neanderthals. Which is offensive to the Neanderthal population."

I sigh and look down. "I was. I was so thrown. They've always had my back."

She seeks out my eye contact. "Yeah, but be honest with yourself. You know the way they treat people who aren't members of your little team. Ostrowski and Chase comment every time Eddie Davis gets two slices of pizza at lunch. Boris asked Iris Dekermenjian to homecoming, then laughed in her face when she actually showed up. The seniors steal all the oat milk at lunch when we only got that put in for people with dietary issues. And you've never really known what it's like not to be part of it."

Her comment goes in like a needle, deflating me again. "You really think that?"

Amy straightens up, cocking her head at me. "Barc, it doesn't mean you were wrong to do it. I believe that you buy into all that rah-rah team stuff, but did you really think that was going to cure those heteronormative toxic masculine fucks of their homophobia?" She laughs humorlessly. "Babe, those guys were never going to throw a Pride parade for anyone. Even *you* aren't that popular in white rural Georgia."

"I didn't think I'd cure homophobia." My cheeks heat. "I just . . . can't believe we still let assholes get away with this shit. Why the hell hasn't anyone stood up to them before?" *Why haven't I?* Then I think about Christopher. "I'm not the first gay kid in this town, but I've never heard whispers or drama like that about anyone else."

Amy shrugs, a mischievous smile on her face like she knows what I'm thinking.

"Speaking of *Christopher*, now that your busy schedule has opened up, maybe you can join us on the newspaper." And for the first time since she got here, Amy goes silent on purpose. Her face twitches like she's in pain and she looks *right* at me. "There's not really a good time to drop this on you, but here we go. You know how I am when I'm pissed off, so I did some digging. That bush covering the stop sign at your grandpa's accident site? People *reported* that and the school board ignored it. I just know there's more to it and I think we can expose it."

I feel the sound of the record distancing as the words sink in. Amy obviously hasn't said this before, but somehow the information doesn't feel new. People *reported* the obscured stop sign that caused my grandpa to die.

"I bet if someone on the board gave a rat's ass about traffic safety so close to a school, something would've been done. But I started going to their meetings, and they only ever talk about the basketball budget because Lord Ostrowski is in charge," Amy continues. "Maybe if someone like you, someone who was close to Scratch and to basketball, said something, it would change." She tips her chin in my direction. "You could do some real good."

"I think any clout I had is essentially gone," I say with a sigh, but heat settles in my stomach like storm clouds as I remember what I overheard the night of the pasta dinner. I'm the reason the team got to go the preseason tournament in Orlando. I'm the reason no one on the board makes a peep about all this despite the school losing a whole spring theater lineup. If I tell Amy about this, there'll basically be no stopping her. And I don't really know what will happen to me if I let myself sink too deep into *just* how preventable my grandpa's death was, but I know I can't afford to find out. Not with everything I'm already juggling. I need to stay as far under the radar as I can.

But why should I stop *her*? I still think basketball is important, but could the cost of new uniforms that aren't that different from the old ones have kept my grandfather alive? The answer matters.

So I tell her everything I know about Mr. Ostrowski somehow convincing the school board to funnel the musical money into the basketball team's trip to Orlando. About the way I think he's using the basketball team travel to enrich his travel agency. The way he got up in Coach's face about trying to get me off the team.

Amy grabs what I tell her like a dog with a bone. "That makes so much sense. God, Barc, that—that connects to everything. Christopher and I were just—holy shit. That fuckbird really is as bad as I thought. We have to find out what he's doing to the school board to keep them doing his bidding! God, I can't wait until we tear him down—"

I hold my hands out. "No 'we.' Pretend I didn't say that to you! In fact, don't tell anyone yet. That's all I have. Go do some digging yourself if you and Ms. Cho want to use it for newspaper or whatever." I force myself to meet Amy's glower. "Aim, please. I have so much bad publicity as it is. I need some time to stop being news and figure out what to do next so I can still leave this shitty town with you."

I wait, watching every micro-expression and movement Amy gives to see what she'll do next. Slowly, God, so slowly, the rage melts out of her dark eyes.

She waits a few moments, seemingly lost to the R.E.M. Then when she speaks again, she looks at me. "I can't believe I'm saying this since this is basically my dream, but are you really, seriously sure that you want to quit the team? I'll support you either way, obviously. But I'm also happy to raise some hell with you if you want to go back."

I love that she's angry in her acceptance, ready to punch people for me. I need that. I look down at my feet, still wishing I could run across the court. No exercise I can do outside of practice will give me that same happy exhaustion. I don't know what I'll fill my head with if not basketball, let alone my future. But . . . I can't forget and shove down who I am. This can't be for nothing. I don't see another way.

"I don't know that it's what I want," I admit. "But I know I can't go back to the team."

Amy grins, shameless in her bias. "Great!" She takes my phone from my bedside table. "Newspaper meets every Wednesday at lunch, and Christopher and I meet practically every other day to try to actually make it useful. I won't make you give me anything else, but newspaper is a great extracurricular for college apps and I think you'll really vibe with what we're doing."

She's already in my phone putting it all into my calendar.

"How do you know my passcode?" I ask.

She rolls her eyes. "Oh, ha-ha-ha, you mean your former basketball number twice? Don't insult me."

Laughter bubbles in my chest, and I let the moment last longer than it needs to.

CHAPTER SIX

THE GOOD THING ABOUT NOT BEING ON THE TEAM THE past two weeks has been that I've had time to start picking up shifts again at Beau's diner and save up a little for college now that my scholarship dreams are over.

The bad part is it's the perfect place to see how my actions at the pep rally have rotted the townspeople's brains too.

During Amy's *very intense* musical theater phase in middle school, her parents took her to New York City. And of course she came back home buzzing about Broadway and how beautiful the piss smell was and everything artsy people say about New York. But she also vividly described some diner she waited three hours to get into where the waitstaff would all perform songs for the customers as a way to practice for auditions. The regulars would have favorite staff members and stan them the way Amy stans all her emo musicians.

Working at Beau's used to feel kind of like that, like I was part of a performance team I didn't know I signed up for. The job started off pretty basic over the summer—I wanted to save up for basketball supplies, and Amy worked there and said it was boring ever since her e-girl coworker friend graduated. But I couldn't get through a single lunch rush table without someone calling me over and wanting the inside scoop on the Wildcats and how we were preparing for the home opener, wanting me to sign an article in the paper or take a photo.

Every friendly face just made the resolve grow inside me. People love and support the Wildcats; they would do the same for me.

Yeah, right.

Now just like school, customers have been glaring at me, making comments about letting everyone down, about being selfish, about my actions being "unfortunate," and the tips have been essentially nonexistent. The Wildcats have been obliterated in half their games since I quit, carrying a 2–3 record when last year we were 5–0, and the comments make my feet feel like lead weights I have to drag through every shift.

Today is no different. It's Thursday, the usual dinner rush at Beau's, and I try to stay focused on the stress of balancing seven milkshakes on one platter. A group of regulars, some construction workers, keep loudly wondering why I won't come back to the team while I refuse proper eye contact.

One of the guys looks up at me as I drop the bill off. "So, what's the deal? Does being queer keep ya from physically being able to play?"

They all snicker as they pull out crumpled bills. I stuff my hands into my pockets, holding my tongue.

When they leave, I hold my breath as I take their bill.

Sure enough, no tip.

"What the *fuck*?" I mutter under my breath.

"Language," Amy says as she glides past me, imitating the way Richard says it to her every shift, and adds, "even though they *are* dicks." At least Amy's been ranting about it every free chance she gets. It was one thing when the student body was being shitty about me leaving the team, but the town being like this is even more infuriating. She doesn't understand how these fully grown adults can really care *that* much about high school basketball and thinks they need a new fucking hobby. I finally agree with her.

She's wearing red lipstick to go with her raccoon-adjacent eye-liner as she rushes off to prepare milkshakes for a pack of middle schoolers. I catch her mid–death glare as all three of the kids rotate in their chairs, making the old things squeal. My anger fades a bit as I can't help but chuckle; Amy's pissed-off reaction to Richard telling her to smile more was said raccoon makeup, and her tolerance for buf-foonery has been at a negative five to start and declining fast.

I rest my arms on the counter and try not to look as exhausted as I feel.

"Excuse me!" an old lady screeches, making me jump.

Amy covers up a laugh as I head to the old lady and her husband's table. They've got finished plates, full waters. Not sure what the prob-lem is. Or I do, which is worse. "Yes?" I say, trying to suppress my annoyance.

"Could you be bothered to/serve us?"

Only five more hours on shift. I have a break in three minutes. I'll be with Devin at Georgia Tech tomorrow. "I'm sorry, *ma'am*," I say, so careful to keep my words even, but I can feel my hands balling into fists. "What would you—?"

And suddenly Amy swoops in, dropping two mugs of coffee down. "Sorry about that, you two," she says, her voice extra high. "The machine was conking out on us, but it's fine now."

Once the coffee is down, she hooks onto a chunk of my shirt, steering us back to the bar.

"Thanks," I mutter, embarrassed to have forgotten something so basic. Again.

"Just keep it together, man," she says. "Maybe you'd be better off with that creepy night shift where all the truckers and serial killers come in."

Honestly, at least the serial killers wouldn't care about my jump shot.

It's a few minutes before my break, but clearly I need it. "I'll be in the back room."

Right before I can head that way, though, someone straight-up *bursts* into the diner and rushes over to me at the bar. It's a middle-aged dad type, sunburned skin, beer belly, and stained T-shirt.

"Pickup order?" I ask.

"You should be ashamed," he sneers at me. He has a really strong Southern accent, but it's not Georgian. "Think you're so high and mighty, that nothing'll ever affect you? My kid'll never go to college because of you and your *lifestyle*. Fuck you, Barclay Ell—"

And before this man can finish cursing my name, Pat of all people runs in, wide-eyed in humiliation. "Jesus, Dad, please don't—"

I pin my gaze on him, remembering how he cowered on the bench as Ostrowski went off, how he didn't even try to approach me. "Don't even bother," I snap.

I shove a to-go bag into his dad's arms, relieved it's prepaid, and storm off to the break room.

Amy finds me head in my arms a minute or two later. I look up, rubbing my eyes. "Please spare me the pity."

She snorts and hands me a milkshake. Mint chocolate chip. "Wouldn't dare." She takes a seat and rolls her shoulders and neck, cracks sounding through the tiny room. "Do you want a distraction or a shoulder to cry on?"

I can't tell if she's being sincere, but I answer anyway. "Distraction." I sip my shake.

"So I finally figured it out," Amy says with an air of victory as she sits next to me. "I've been going crazy thinking about a game plan since we talked. You know I could angle the systemic issues of Chitwood like, five ways. Between the deplorable sex ed, glorifying *Christopher Columbus*, and the incredibly biased budget you told me about—it's just, ugh. But everything we print in the newspaper has to get vetted by the same administration we'd be exposing. We have Ms. Cho on our side now, but we have to be creative. I've felt voiceless since the spring play was canceled and I bet a lot of other people do too."

"Wait," I say, interrupting. "You didn't try to print what I overheard, did you?"

Amy sighs and rolls her eyes. "No, I didn't. But I've been looking into it and that's where I got my inspiration." She leans forward, close enough that I can smell her floral shampoo and the soda syrup stuck to her hands. "Voter suppression isn't just a state-level issue. Obviously. It trickles down to local stuff too. From what I've seen so far, the corruption in Chitwood is astronomical. Yet everyone is so convinced that the only change we can make is huge, state- or nationwide, when there are so many issues we need to fix here. People just tell themselves it's not worth the effort to vote if there's no president or governor on the ticket. When's the last time your mom voted for the Chitwood city council or school board, right? And yet they're the people who we have the easiest access to lobbying to get them to change things."

"Hey! Waitress lady! We need napkins!" one of the middle schoolers says through the crack in the door, his prepubescent-but-trying-to-sound-deep voice slicing through Amy's conversation.

"Which brings me back to the school board. They're pouring so much money into basketball." Amy nabs a pile of napkins and drops them onto the breakfast bar without breaking her narrowed eye contact with me. She doesn't even glance to make sure the napkins actually landed *on* the table before she returns to the back. "But I bet Ostrowski isn't the only one profiting off it. A lot of them have businesses in town that get a boost from the basketball buzz, and nearly every other activity gets shortchanged as a result. And it's not just the arts. Test scores are falling too! I found last year's numbers and they are abysmal. And the regular people of Chitwood don't even *realize* that because they're so busy cheering on the team, so they'll funnel all their resources into keeping Ostrowski's dad elected because he's a "team dad." And then what do we become? I mean, what kind of society is just sports and business? Even you have okay music taste and know who Marx is. Imagine someone *you* think is boring, times a thousand."

"Okay, okay, I follow you," I say, even though I'm still kind of struggling to keep up, "but then what can you do about it? What does that have to do with Ms. Cho?"

"That's exactly the problem, it's so ridiculous that teenage voices are so devalued," Amy says, polishing the same cup over again. "And then even the seniors who can vote just don't care. But they should. There's a school board election coming up in February." She takes a deep breath. "I'm working on a project that can run alongside and go further than what Christopher and I are doing with Ms. Cho on the newspaper. An underground club to get people involved in voting and local elections. We help get them registered or get them to ask their parents to vote if they can't yet. I know the administration won't approve, but they can't stop us hanging out or police what we talk about, so we'll just meet in the hallway or something."

Wow. As usual, I get a flash of all the incredible things Amy and her amazing brain are going to do after Chitwood. "This all sounds great, Aim." I pause, stirring my milkshake as I consider saying anything at all. *But do you really think that's what's going to change everything?* is what I'm thinking but instead I ask, "But are you worried about meeting in public anywhere on school grounds? We both have college to think about."

Amy shrugs. "We meet until they make us move. If it's not the halls, we move here. If not here, I'll meet in the goddamn woods. Power comes in numbers, not fancy classrooms."

"How will you get people to join, then?"

"I already have a few people besides us, but I think the best way to get the word out is to partner with an actual candidate and have a rally. And I know it's a sore spot, but you actually gave me the idea," Amy says, and I wince. "So I reached out to someone who aligns with most of our ideas and it kinda all came together super quickly so . . . it's going to be next weekend, meaning we've got to start planning like yesterday. I need you on the ball."

"Well . . ." I glance at my phone for the time, almost wanting to get back out there. I know it's normal for Amy to assume I'll join in on her latest venture. But nothing is normal for me right now. I just— this is already sounding like a lot of troublemaking. Good trouble, but not the kind I can make right now—

The door squeaks and at first I think it's Richard saving the day for once, but it's only then that it occurs to me that Amy brought in three shakes. A cookies 'n cream sweats by her knee.

"Is Vote Squad so underground that we have to meet in closets *outside* of school too?" Christopher says as he walks in.

I turn to him, heat hitting the back of my neck. Yeah, we've been sitting together at lunch since I hide out in the newspaper room, but I haven't really been socializing with anyone besides Amy. We haven't really talked since that first interview. Not since I came out.

"Barc here is trying to avoid full-grown adults physically assaulting him for his gayness apparently destroying the basketball team's one shot at glory," Amy replies, deadpan.

Christopher frowns as he takes a seat and pulls his milkshake to him. It's the kind of frown where I tense up, waiting for some gay-to-gay empowerment speech I'm *not* in the mood to hear.

But it doesn't come.

"Well, no better time to focus everyone's attention on people who don't suck, then." He turns to Amy, like I've left the room entirely. "You told Barclay about the rally yet?"

"Just started to." She turns back to me. "Have you been to a political rally before? I need to know if you're ready for the vibe."

Christopher fiddles with the straw on his shake, eyes more on his phone than me. Like he's spacing out on the tutorial section in a video game. Yeah, so much for me being out improving our relationship.

"No," I say quickly, hoping Amy will take the hint that I'm definitely not ready.

"Well, it's"—she waves her hand like a witch casting a spell—"you just kind of get to hype people giving speeches about mobilizing and policy and actually giving a shit about the same things you do, and you get local businesses involved so people will actually come out and then stay and listen. None of the current candidates against Ostrowski's dad have offered clear views on budget distribution, so we're hoping by partnering with this candidate, Brianna, at this event, we can show her and even the rest of them that that's what the students want to hear." She slaps Christopher's shoulder hard enough to startle him. "Chris explains it better than me."

Christopher shoots Amy a dirty look at the nickname, but goes into it. "The school board race and the other local ballots are this huge opportunity to really push progressive policies that would make an impact on this sad town. Ideally, we'd be gunning for someone to pressure the board to install protections for queer classmates and improve the overall community-school relations by balancing the budget to reflect priorities that aren't just basketball. Incidentally, your coming out has made it so the board has to be aware that there is in fact more than one gay kid at school." He rolls his eyes as he says this. "That there is, in fact, a *range* of different kinds of queer kids who deserve to feel safe at school. And since you held a leadership position within basketball, Ames and I thought you might want to"—he finally looks right at me—"you know, speak."

Did Amy and Christopher set this whole thing up? Just to get me to speak at their rally thing? Even if it is a cause I agree with, it doesn't feel all that different than people just caring about my three-pointer. What would make them think I'd want to put myself out there like that again?

"We'll also make buttons and maybe T-shirts because we are all minions of consumerism," Amy adds on quickly, like she knows what I'm thinking. "As long as we get the word out."

"Will you do it?" Christopher presses.

The memories of everything from the pep rally all the way to Pat's dad still sting fresh. No one wants to hear me, anyway. Not anymore. "I don't think that's a good idea."

Christopher scowls. "I *just* explained why it's a good idea. Do you know what it'd mean to other closeted students to see you *still* put yourself out there and see your value despite what shit you just went through? Come on. You had the nerve to come out at a goddamn pep rally in rural Georgia, so do it again."

My anger flares, but a little piece of me perks up. Is Christopher *right*? Would Scratch have just caved and never shown his face again? I wanted to be an example like he was, but the only thing anyone could possibly have learned from that rally was that they should stay hidden. I don't want that.

"I . . . I mean, if you write the speech," I reply, finally, even though I immediately want to take it back.

"I knew you'd want that, so it's already in the works," Amy says, exchanging a conspiring look with Christopher. "Wanna know the best part about this particular rally besides you speaking?"

"What?"

"It's gonna be at the same time as Ostrowski's dad's campaign event. You know, the one where he shouts from a bullhorn and rains Walmart gift cards into the crowd."

I'm always down for sticking it to an Ostrowski, but if I'm being *completely* honest, I can't see anyone our age picking either political rally over just about anything else. "Any other pull for people from school besides messing with Ostrowski's dad?"

She sighs. "I'm seeing about getting a local band to play." She swings an arm around me. "And you'll be there. Good or bad, people still seem interested in you."

God, I hope we can swing the interested people into the liking-me territory.

The room spins with the onslaught of information. I look away from Christopher and Amy, to the clock on my phone. I've been in here too long. I stand up, pulling Amy up with me. "Sounds good, but I think we gotta head back out."

But Amy's way ahead of me. She gives Christopher a pointed look and straight-up sprints out, leaving us alone with three half-drunk milkshakes.

"By the way," Christopher says, exhaling. "I'm sorry about being so annoyed about our newspaper interview. You were clearly going through a lot and"—he tucks a hair behind his ear—"I of all people should know."

The sentiment is nice and all, but . . . "You shouldn't have to know I'm gay to not treat me like shit."

He winces for once. "Yes, you're right." He chews on his lip a moment. "Still would like to do that article about you. I'll take it seriously this time. And not just because it's way more interesting now."

I scoff. "Why? Would Ms. Cho even be able to print it?"

"Yes, she thinks so, and now it serves even more purpose if we're gunning for LGBTQ+ student protections too." He smiles as he says it, strangely charming in his confidence now that he's not looking at me with annoyance.

"Yeah, well, let's see if I do anything interesting and then we can talk."

What I'm really thinking is, *Let's see if I'm worthy of being noticed outside of basketball at all*. I really want to make a difference, but I thought that was what I was doing last time too.

CHAPTER SEVEN

T'S HARDER TO CONVINCE MYSELF THAT I'M NOT AVOIDING Mom now that she's not hiding in her room as much. Especially as I literally tiptoe to the front door. It's not that I'm not relieved to see Mom more up and about and actually spending full days at work. But despite her pleas to have a real conversation, I always find a way to get out of it because I'm afraid it won't be any different or she'll just end up pitching me on going back to the team. And I don't think I can handle that right now.

So I keep tiptoeing, duffel bag in hand, fingers inches from the doorknob on my way out to catch my train to Devin's for the weekend. "Barclay?" Mom says as she stands in the kitchen, her Friday suit loosened after a half day of work.

I guess Devin told her what train I was taking. Traitor.

"I gotta go, Mom," I reply. "I'll be late for the train."

But Mom grabs my arm by the sleeve. "Baby, please. Really quick. I know you've been avoiding me and don't deny it, you're still on your tiptoes."

Called out, I feel my ears go red as I yank out of her grasp. "Everything's just been a lot. And I don't *want* to talk about it."

"Well I'm still your mom, and I do," she insists. "I reacted badly to finding out about you. I know. And I'm so sorry."

The pain from that day still stings, waiting just below my skin, but I don't want to feel it. "Mom, I have to go," I say again.

She grabs my shoulders this time, turning me around despite the several inches I have on her. "I love you, Barclay. I love everything about you. There is nothing in this world you can do to change that, including"—she sighs—"quitting the team."

"Thanks." The words should feel so good. I want them to. But everything comes off hollow the second she says "team."

"You have a bright future ahead of you no matter what you do," she continues. "When you're back from visiting Devin, we can talk about it and make a new plan."

Long talks with Mom used to be such a normal part of my life after my dad left. I should feel good at the thought of having them back. But all she wants to talk about is my future. A new plan for college. Questions I don't have answers to and not the ones I want her to ask. But I need to appease her to get out of here.

"Love you too, Mom."

But the way I yank myself out the door right as she leans in for a kiss doesn't say that very well. I'll have to deal with her when I get back.

For now, though, I rush my way over to the train station. I barely make it on in time, but once I'm on, I prepare for a few hours of peace.

Well, *an* hour of peace, maybe. I promised Amy that we'd have a call (like she put it on my phone calendar) to discuss me speaking "in detail."

In my last hour on the train before getting to Georgia Tech, Amy calls me a minute early, of course, startling me out of the game I was playing to pass the time. I stick my earbuds in, hoping they're not so broken that the sleeping guy next to me will wake to Amy probably yelling at me.

"Hey," I say.

"Hey, you still have time to talk while you're trapped on a train?" she asks.

"Yeah."

"Great. The least you can do for leaving me *the weekend before* the most important rally of our movement." There's shuffling in the background behind her.

I don't even dare joke that it's the first event of our movement and that I only found out about it yesterday. I shift in my seat. It's super cramped and I'm going to need to do a lot of walking with Devin to shake the ache in my legs. "I'm here."

"Okay, so speakers are mostly lined up. I still have you as our closer—or I can move you to opener, whatever you feel comfortable with." I wince, not comfortable with either. I've been thinking about it ever since yesterday's shift and really regretting agreeing to it. It's way too soon. "But we need to do a lot of promo next week. Someone needs to hand out the flyers, I'm gonna set up a guerrilla booth outside school before class every day next week, then ask the not-shitty businesses in town to maybe let us set up there a couple times after school."

"I can do the flyers," I offer, putting on my best cheery voice.

As expected, Amy doesn't give me a verbal pat on the back for volunteering for the easiest job. In fact, I'm met with silence. "Well, look, if you don't speak at the rally, I won't hold it against you."

"Aim, I don't know—"

A voice pipes in from the background. A voice, I realize with a jump, that belongs to Christopher. "Amy, *come on*!"

"But people pay attention to you," Amy continues, in a way that says she's *definitely* going to hold it against me. "Good or bad.

Wouldn't you like that attention that's being glommed on you anyway to go to something positive? Your experiences right now are a perfect signal that things need to change and we need reps and authority figures who will support *all* people."

I pretend Christopher isn't clearly in the background listening.

"It's just, more attention is the last thing I need, at least right now. I mean, just look at what shifts have been like. Pat's dad coming in to yell at me, people not tipping, people being dicks. What if all I show people is that it gets worse?"

Amy snorts. "You mean that old couple you were totally ready to chew into when you forgot their coffee three times?" She sighs. "Look, Barcs, I've been paying attention. What you've been getting is so horrendous, but you've also been stuck, obsessing. All I want is to transport us to some not-shitty town so you can go kiss boys and play basketball at the same time and it's not even a big deal. But we're here, in Chitwood, for the next *two years*. Getting involved with something that makes this town about more than basketball will *feel better* than yelling at dicks in diners. If you don't want to talk about the pep rally, we can just start with the stop sign. I *know* how much it means to you to make that right."

It's so frustrating that Amy's the one saying this. She wants out of this town as much as I do now. Why waste effort to change something that'll clearly never change? I need to focus all my attention on getting out, which at this point seems to mean getting my grades up and working. And using my grandpa just isn't fighting fair. "I'd just be a distraction," I say. "I don't want to blow all your hard work. Please, just let me hang flyers."

Amy ends the discussion with a long sigh. "Okay, then you better at least dress up. Do you own jeans or just those ugly basketball shorts?"

"Yes, of course I—"

"I bet they're shit jeans," Christopher adds. "Here."

A moment later, a notification from Christopher pops up. It's a link to a Japanese imports website, for a pair of pants that are so ripped up there're random fabric patches sewn underneath the holes. Uh, *no.*

"Look, let's talk next week. But speaking or not, you're coming. And you're helping get the word out. Don't disappoint me," she says, which I take as her begrudging okay. I just wish it felt okay.

The Atlanta station I get off at is everything the Chitwood one isn't— brighter color paint, bustling people of all shapes, colors, and walking speeds getting on and off trains. Even Devin is different here, in his colored shorts and boat shoes. I don't think he's joined a frat, but he's definitely picked up the style. He hugs me hard when he sees me, lifting me into the air despite the fact that I've been a couple inches taller than him for years now.

"Man, Barc, I am *so* excited to have you here," he says, full-face smiling as he drops me. "You're gonna love the place." We start walking out of the station. "How's Mom?"

I shrug. "She tried to apologize today, but only right as I was about to go."

"Well, at least she apologized," Devin says brightly, like it's a problem solved. I decide not to correct him.

Thankfully, we don't talk about Mom after that. We head to the Georgia Tech campus and sure enough, when Devin says I'm gonna love campus, he's right. I find myself looking in so many directions as he launches into stories about his roommate and the dining hall theme nights and which classes he's enjoying so much he might major in the subject. He walks us past redbrick building after redbrick building with towering, pointy gray roofs, dodging people on bikes and skateboards without missing a beat. Then he heads right for one of them.

"Sorry," he says. "I have to ask my professor a question about an essay and it's her office hours. Then we'll let you drop your stuff off."

I don't mind. The hallways are packed, groups of students gathered together around vending machines, grabbing flyers off bulletin boards as huge as classroom walls back in Chitwood. One guy hanging by a drink machine smiles when he sees Devin. He's wearing suspenders and a pageboy cap, something I've never seen someone wear outside of TV.

"Dev, man, didn't think I'd see you before chem on Monday," he says, giving Devin a bro shake.

Devin grins. "Yeah, Henderson can't keep me away long."

He winks when he says it, which only makes the guy shake his head. Devin's friend looks over to me and nods. Confidence I haven't felt in a while resurfaces as I shake his hand, realizing he has no idea who I am or what I did.

"I'm Barclay, Dev's brother," I say. "I'm visiting campus for the weekend."

"Good to meet you, Barclay," he responds.

As we head up the stairs, I can't help but lean into Devin to say, "He seems . . . artsier than your friends back home."

Devin shrugs. "No one really separates like that in college. Killian and I are in a GE together, so we kinda trauma bonded."

I think about that while Devin goes into his professor's office. Not whatever trauma bonding is, but having friends who are into all sorts of things. Hipsters and political people like Amy, but also theater majors, STEM majors, jocks, frat guys. Not having to be just one thing.

Then I spot a sign on a bulletin board for a Queer Prom that weekend. I can't imagine that, just being in a room full of people I don't have to be worried are going to harass me or stop talking to me. Without even a QSA at school, I find myself holding in questions I bet have easy answers. What movies with gay people in them are actually worth watching? When do you even figure out if you're a top or bottom? Is my experience with homophobia extra bad or average? It makes me think, for a moment, about Christopher and his campaign to get more protections at school. Would that include a QSA for kids with questions like mine? I tense up, thinking of what I turned down at Amy's rally. What if I'm wrong about making a difference? What if it's my fault Chitwood doesn't get a QSA?

I watch a couple of girls with dyed hair walk down the hall holding hands. No, I have to focus on here and now. I'm at college, my future if I stay out of trouble. I always used to imagine Zack and me getting onto the same college team, but I never thought about what else college might offer besides basketball. The moment hits me unexpectedly, painfully, as I remind myself that Zack and I aren't going to the same college and aren't even friends.

Devin finally emerges and we walk until he swipes us into his dorm building.

"You seem kind of shocked," he says, a playfulness on his face.

I rub the back of my neck as he presses the button for the elevator. "No, I'm just—I like the people here. It feels right."

Devin nods his head, and I know I don't need to specify more than that.

"We're not in small-town Chitwood anymore."

It settles on me that this weekend I can just be me again, no basketball stardom, no embarrassing-as-hell public coming out gone wrong. In a couple years, this will be my fresh start. But for right now, I have this weekend break to preview it and I can't wait to soak it in.

By the time Devin's walking us to a house party, it's sometime after ten (apparently no college parties actually start before ten), and I'm practically shaking with anticipation. Everything has been awesome so far. Devin showed me around his dorm, took me to the underground part of the library, then the crazy state-of-the-art gym, and even up to the roof of one of the science buildings, where we ate chili dogs and fried peach pies from a local food truck. We haven't had this much fun together since we were kids. A whole day and no mentioning any of the awful shit that's happened this year.

"Now, I'm not gonna mother you, but please keep your head on straight," Devin says as he nods toward a guy standing at the door of a house and hands over a ten in exchange for two Solo cups.

It's the kind of place that was probably nice before a group of college guys moved in and caused the wood to fray, the lawn to die, and a window to be taped up with green duct tape. But people are already chatting on that dying lawn with Solo cups in hand, and the energy is so strong I swear I can taste it. And the guys—Jesus, it's like I've been living with my gay lens energy cut in half and suddenly it's at full power. I notice it all. The muscles under tight T-shirts, the sharp jawlines, the size of the hands that engulf the Solo cups.

And some of these guys might be gay. For the first time, I can actually try to find out without having to worry about who hears or what they'll say.

Devin fills our cups at the keg, taking a long gulp of his before passing one to me. I follow suit. I've never been a huge drinker, even at parties the team used to throw in offseason. After the one time

Lochman and Zack got about half a bottle of vodka inside me that led to the awful Catherine Finney make-out session, it all just felt too dangerous. Why let loose and risk that I'd end up smashing my face into a guy's face next time? Watching the guys flirt and score with the cheerleaders or the student council while I just made excuses was downright depressing, honestly.

But now, well, the giddy joy spreads easily.

Devin stops in front of a group of about five guys. They're all tall, with nearly identical short haircuts.

"Guys, this is my little brother, Barclay," he says. "Barclay, these are some guys from my intramural football team."

"How long are you in town for?" one of the guys asks me. "I'm Evan, by the way."

"Just the weekend," I reply. I wish it were longer, though. I almost feel like my old self. I wonder if Devin would let me stay a few extra days, and I look for him, but—

—he has somehow made his way across the house, talking to a blond girl in a floral dress and pink Converse. I roll my eyes; some things never change.

"He'll talk to her all night and she'll leave him the moment he laughs too hard and beer sprays out his nose," I say to no one in particular.

But it gets the intramural football guys to laugh. Evan laughs particularly hard, his body turning to me. "Oh shit, what other dirt do you have on your brother?"

Evan has these pretty green eyes. We're close enough that I notice. And it's okay that I'm noticing. I grin and keep talking. I launch into a description of his six-week *Star Wars* obsession in which he tried to teach himself piano using Grandma's old upright just to learn the theme song. After I finish up the part where Devin totally failed to impress fellow nerd Kelly Anderson with his playing, Evan asks if I want to play beer pong.

Sure enough, the girl wanders off after a loud snorting laugh from Devin. And he makes his way back over to us just in time. "Jeff and Dev versus me and you?"

I don't even glance at Devin before I say yes, the beer I've already drunk pushing aside any fear that I've never played pong with college guys before. We make our way over to one of many sticky tables and separate out. Evan dips a Ping-Pong ball in the water cup and squares up to throw.

"Y'know, I never knew any local Georgians until here. Definitely thought you all would have stronger accents," Evan says.

He takes a shot. It misses.

"Where're you from?" I ask.

"New Hampshire."

Jeff throws his ball and lands it right into the cup. As if to answer the question, he yells, "Idaho pride!" Then he adds, "Harry and his little brother, John, who're out here somewhere, are from Cali."

Evan reaches for the cup, but I take it and chug. I toss the ball, and, *fuck* yes, it lands in the cup. Evan and I high-five as Devin drinks.

"Is it just me, or was the last game unusually killer?" Jeff comments as Devin psyches himself up to throw. "My girlfriend had to help me up into the shower yesterday."

"Well, isn't it surprising that you're up and about today?" Devin says as he throws. He misses. "You sure it wasn't just an excuse for shower sex?"

Evan sighs. "Dev, shower sex isn't actually good. Next, please."

Evan makes the next shot, emboldening me. "Yeah, Dev wouldn't know about that. He has never even made his way into the shower."

It gets the guys to crack up. No one asks my opinions about girls, or assumes anything at all. As the game heats up, more people crowd around and start to watch.

And when I get the shot that wins Evan and me the game, Evan hugs me and says, "Fucking *killer shot*!" and it feels really, really good.

And it's not just Evan cheering. Devin cheers, Jeff gives me a few claps, and the other football guys howl my name. *Barclay, Barclay, Barclay!*

Even John-from-California, a Black guy about my age with an undercut, lip ring, and blue Docs, cheers from the sidelines. Riding the high of everyone's cheers, I take a chance and stride over to him while the next game starts.

"Getting a refill?" I ask, smiling.

He smiles back. "I can if you're going."

We move over toward the keg, so fast I don't even think Devin sees us go.

"So have you ever been to campus before?" he asks me as we get in a massive line for the keg. His voice is low, making something in my chest shiver.

"Only once to move Devin in. He collects so many comic books and my mom insisted that they all go with him. He needed all the manpower he could get."

John's rich brown eyes slide to my arms. I think. "Devin's lucky." He shakes his head, swiping his tongue across his bottom lip and making the ring shine. "My brother only had me and my ex-boyfriend to help him and it took us nearly two days."

A tingle creeps up my spine at "ex-boyfriend." Being right about it feels like I just took another winning shot.

I try to stop myself from letting everything rush out at once, but I still blurt out, "I just came out." Then I say quickly, "Shit, please ignore that."

John smiles. "Hey, that's awesome, welcome to the club. How did it go?"

I'm swimming pretty deep in the alcohol. I *want* to take him to a bedroom in this stranger's house, tell him all the grueling details, and ask if it's always like this. What he'd do in my situation, since he's clearly got his shit together enough to have had at least one boyfriend. But I don't want to seem like some whiny newbie.

He takes a step toward me as we move forward in line and our hips brush for just a second.

Or . . . maybe I just want to take him to a bedroom. I swallow my big sob story and pretend for a moment that it went exactly how I imagined.

"It was fine. Over with. I'm ready to just start existing, you know?" I say. "I'm trying to expand my horizons. My friend got me my first record last week."

We take another step forward. His hand brushes mine. The nerves zap from my fingertip all the way back to my chest. "Existing is pretty cool." He smiles at me. "So you seriously started a record collection last week?"

I rub the back of my neck. "Yeah. I mean, she makes me playlists on Spotify, but I'm saving up some of my tip money so I can buy my favorites on vinyl. It's actually another experience. Do you have a favorite record?"

John chuckles. "I actually don't listen to vinyl, but I like watching your eyes light up when you talk about it."

It's like I've swallowed a balloon and could float away at any moment. Is this what it's like to be flirted with? I could get used to this. My gaze falls over his whole body, Docs to his wide shoulders to his square jaw to his eyes. "Your eyes are nice too."

He laughs, raising his eyebrows. "That where you were looking?"

We're facing each other now. His fingers run over my tricep.

"Full disclosure, your brother told mine that you were gay," he whispers. His voice goes lower, if that's even possible. "Neither of them told me how cute you are, though."

I'm unsteady. I think. Or maybe there's just something in how we're standing, the words between us, the way we're looking at each other. It's all so fast. I always thought it'd take so much longer. But the next thing I know, our lips are pressing together. I exhale, in a way that feels like *finally* even though I haven't been waiting for anything.

This is nothing like kissing Catherine Finney. This is a press of lips where I'm suddenly aware there are *nerves* there. Nerves that are burning, tingling, aching. Shit, *this* is a kiss. My first kiss with someone I'm actually attracted to. At a college party.

I clutch him as the kiss deepens, suddenly desperate for the feeling of him, of the heat of his chest. The grip of his hand on my mid-back. To let out all these feelings I've held in so long. He presses his lips into mine over and over again, as if he's getting different micro-angles to my skin. When his tongue swipes between my lips, the kiss deepens.

So this is what it feels like to be wanted. To want back. To be held and not let go.

But there's suddenly three people in this kiss. Someone, a pretty well-built someone by the sheer weight, knocks into us. John and I pull apart. My lips are a little numb, my hair mussed, and I look to the culprit. Sure enough, some football-built white guy. His eyes are looking away from me, but his hand is pushing against my arm—

"What's your fucking deal? You have a problem with two guys kissing?" I exclaim. I shove his hand off me, enough to send him back a few steps. Shock melts into anger on his face.

John touches my opposite arm, hesitant. "Hey, it's okay. He just—"

I hold my gaze, steely, on this asshole, as I stand my ground right in his face. "Huh?" I press.

The guy rubs his arm, like I really pushed him that hard. "I don't give a shit who you're kissing; just don't do it on top of the fucking keg."

And that's when I see it, my organs shriveling away.

He's wearing a shirt with a bear and rainbow on it.

I'm such an idiot.

And when I look around, there are eyes on me being an idiot. So many eyes. Again. My mind floods as I cringe. John. John, who—

—is now a few feet from me now, frowning. "You *may* be a little more green than I thought." He gives a weak kind of wave. "Good luck with everything."

And John walks away, leaving me alone. Devin isn't anywhere I can see, and my whole body is on the brink of shaking as I can feel people's eyes still on me. That hushed whispering. Just like at the pep rally.

I can't deal with that.

With the keg right there, a beer seems like the only option. I fill up and drink it down, even as it burns my throat. The carbonation fizzles back up my throat. I try my best to stifle a burp, and it leaves a sour taste in the back of my throat. My stomach's starting to churn, and the beer smell all around me is doing nothing to settle it.

But just as I'm about to go for another, there's Devin swooping in with his stupid hair and boat shoes.

"Come on," he says, grabbing onto my arm hard. "You need to sober up."

I drop my cup as he forces me up the stairs. I watch the specks of gold liquid soak into an already gnarly grayish carpet, and then the sound gets quieter as we ascend. He picks a bedroom, peers inside, and pulls us both into it. It's barely someone's room, nothing more than a mattress, a plastic dresser, a single pillow and blue blanket, and a trash can. Devin helps me to the mattress and sighs long and hard. Like Mom does.

"What was that all about?" He seems to be asking genuinely, but there's an edge in his voice.

"I was—how was I supposed to know—he ran into me!" I say.

"Yeah, and? You made a wild assumption and *shoved* some stranger! At a school you don't go to, while drinking underage! Do you not see how much worse that could've gone?"

The room is unsteady again, blurring around the edges, barely in my vision. "I don't—"

"You're smarter than this."

I take a deep breath as the world spins faster out of control. "I feel like I keep messing everything up. Like I'm handling everything wrong no matter how hard I try."

There's silence. When I finally look up at Devin, he doesn't look angry anymore. He sits down beside me. "Don't be so hard on yourself. What you're going through is normal. You're sixteen, figuring out who you are. That'll mean making mistakes. I know this isn't a concept you're too used to, Barcs, but not everyone will like who you are. But that doesn't mean no one does or no one will. You can't just jump to the worst conclusions with everyone because some people let you down."

The sour feeling isn't completely gone, but the spinning slows. Still, heat rises up my neck—I made a whole ass of myself out there. I hate to ask, but—

"Can we go back to your dorm?"

Devin laughs. "Yes. Lemme help you up."

I'm feeling okay, I swear, but Devin pulls me up way harder than I was expecting. My organs all go sloshing with it. The beer shoots up my throat with a vengeance, and thank God for the trash can.

Devin is still chuckling as I puke. "Yep, *definitely* time to go."

CHAPTER EIGHT

NLIKE DEVIN, MOM'S SUDDENLY TOO BUSY WITH YET another showing to pick me up from the train station Sunday morning. I guess she's trying to make up for all the ones she missed but still. It's before noon, so thankfully, it's pretty empty when I pull in, people either sleeping in or in church, which leaves just the sound of the white pine trees blowing in the breeze and the slap of my shoes against concrete as I walk home. The rest of the weekend was uneventful compared to the party. Devin went full mom mode and didn't take me drinking again, instead opting for an improv show and exploring downtown. Still, that campus felt more like home in two days than Chitwood has felt since the pep rally. Coming back, I can just feel the drama in the air.

It's only confirmed when I spot the newspaper on our porch, which Scratch made Mom still subscribe to. WILDCATS LOSE FOR FOURTH TIME THIS SEASON, CHAMPIONSHIP SLIPPING AWAY right there in the sports section. A tension headache starts to form as I pick it up. I shouldn't look, but like comment sections on YouTube, I can't look away. Sure enough, they mention me. They don't *directly* say *Fuck you Barclay Elliot for abandoning your team and bringing shame to your whole town,* but they might as well. I thought the one bright spot of quitting would be not agonizing over reporters and scouts anymore, but I can't dismiss the bad feelings still. The team's record is now 2–4.

Last year, we won over 80 percent of our games and were guaranteed a spot. Now, unless the team suddenly wins the rest of their games, they'll be duking it out for a berth, maybe even a wildcard. The team with a 19–4 record last year needing a wildcard spot. It's truly unbelievable. I step through my front door, reading because that's not all. There's a Georgia player ranking right next to the article.

Of course, I'm nowhere in sight. Gone like a witch cast a spell on me and wiped me off the map.

Except I'm not gone. This town still remembers me very well, just in all the wrong ways. I'm just waiting for more graffiti on my locker. Work will be the same thing but with actual adults. The only gay guy for miles will be Christopher, who can't stand me. Am I really going to have to wait two years before I can be myself again and not be skewered for it?

I drop onto the couch with Maggie, who's got some network teen drama on. The sight is almost uncomfortable; I can't remember the last time Maggie was out here on a Sunday afternoon and not shut in her room studying for a test she was already guaranteed an A on. Even weirder she's still in duck pajamas and her unicorn hoodie, actually so focused on this show that she's not even looking at her open history textbook, or the blank notecards spilling out.

"I'll make you French toast if you put on *The Witcher*," I say to Maggie. Amy got me hooked on the show, and she was angrily texting me about getting caught up to her the whole ride home.

"No way," she replies, not looking away from the screen even for a second. "The main actor on that is too buff, it's gross."

I glance up at the screen, where two characters seem to be equating high school football to war or something. "This is gross too." And a little too real.

97

Maggie rolls her eyes. "I heard Amy say that the last time she was over."

I snatch the remote. "Just change it. We can watch one episode, then I'll make breakfast. Or better yet, go off with your friends."

She launches onto me, throwing her hand over the remote, and I'm taken aback. Maggie's annoying but she usually doesn't get this intense, especially not if I'm offering French toast. "That doesn't even make sense! Besides, have you not noticed that—"

The doorbell rings. We both turn to the sound and she pushes me toward it, clearly thinking I could fight off any murderers waiting outside. I stretch as I make my way to the door.

I don't know who I was expecting, but it wasn't Christopher. Yet here he is on my porch in a button-down covered in flamingos, his dark hair perfectly styled to hang in his eyes.

Wait, what day is it? Did I—no, the rally is next week, besides. Amy would've murdered me by now.

"Uh, hi," I say.

"Amy said you were back. I'm here to interview you for that article." I roll my eyes. "Look, I know you're all, 'let's see if I do anything interesting,' but you know you already did, and Amy wants to have it done by late January to go along with our last push before the voter registration deadline, so let's get going."

"Tell Amy there are way better ways to drum up registration. Everyone wants to talk about me, not read about me."

But Christopher barely blinks, completely unaffected by what I said. "That's exactly why I should write it. So they're talking about the real you. At least now it's not going to be some lame puff piece. I've been working on real questions and everything." I don't know if he's making fun of me or what. "Besides, she said you were off partying this weekend, so you must feel a *little* better."

Yeah, a little better *at* Georgia Tech. Not here. And I don't want to undo that right now. "How about next week?"

Christopher shifts his weight from one foot to another, but doesn't move to go or acknowledge what I said. "We can go for a walk," he suggests. His hand floats to the back of his neck. "If things are awkward at home, I understand."

Honestly, the idea of going for a walk has my skin crawling. The last thing I need is for the rumors to swirl about Christopher being my boyfriend. Was I actually just kissing someone in front of literal strangers only forty-eight hours ago?

"We can just do it here," I say, opening the door for him.

As he walks in, Maggie looks over at us.

"Hey, I'm Christopher." He introduces himself to her.

"Maggie," she says, but not with her usual class-president company vibes.

She slumps as I lead Christopher through. He eyes the TV as we go. Once we're in the safety of the backyard, I breathe again. But then I'm face-to-face with the basketball hoop Devin got me for my birthday. Lately, whenever I get the urge to shoot around, I've just been going on runs at the crack of dawn or working out in my room to avoid it. But here it is. I'm staring at it. So is Christopher.

No, Christopher's moving *toward* it. He leans against it, getting himself comfortable. He pulls out his notebook and looks over to me with gray eyes.

"What's your favorite TV show with a gay character?" he asks.

"*Shameless*?"

"Knew you had basic taste." I give him a look and he laughs. "Kidding, kidding. That was just a warm-up round." He pauses. "So what drew you to basketball initially?"

I think Christopher expects me to grab a ball and start shooting. Instead, I take a seat on one of the worn wooden rocking chairs out here. Scratch's.

"My grandpa played. He'd take me to shoot hoops and I got really good at it."

He glances down at me, briefly, then back to his notes. "Was there any particular draw to joining a team, or was it the actual game of basketball that you liked more?"

"I guess the game?" I've never even thought about it that way. The team and the game just came hand in hand.

Christopher sighs. "Is this all you're gonna give me? I can't print an article with . . ." He actually counts. "Nineteen words."

"Well then, ask another question."

"What were you aware of first, that you were gay or good at basketball?"

I force myself to take a deep breath, but the tightness only spreads. I do know the answer to this one, but I don't know if I want to say it. Gay, at age eight. Basketball came when I was ten or eleven. But it doesn't feel complete enough and I don't want to unpack the feelings that come with it. "I don't wanna answer that."

Christopher throws a hand up. "Can you not waste my time here?" There's something in his voice. It's not rising, like he's angry. It's almost sad. I don't know what to call it.

"You're the one who wants this. I don't. I don't know what you even expect from me," I retort. "A bunch of feelings?"

Christopher straightens himself back to his full height. "Yes, exactly, but I'll skip straight to the heart of it. Why did you choose to come out the way you did if you knew our town is ninety-five percent ignorant assholes?"

Something about it rubs me the wrong way—like it's *so obvious* that everyone here's a bigot. That I must be an idiot, too full of myself, or too oblivious to ever consider that things could go well. That I brought this all upon myself. Screw that. These people acted like my friends. Like they cared. I'm not stupid for trying to be optimistic that I'd still be treated like a goddamn person even if people weren't thrilled. It puts me on the defensive.

"You know, it doesn't seem like anyone gave you this hard a time about being gay."

In fact, he's been wearing shirts with the word "gay" on them since he first came to Chitwood. Not a single peep. I remember even thinking one of the designs, a graphic of Skeletor with a rainbow over him that says "I have all the power," was one I'd actually wear when I was out.

I'm so ready to drop into an argument with him, but that's not what he does. No, he holds eye contact with me and remains cool as ice. "It may not have *seemed* that hard for me, but I'm also not exactly the school hero. Way fewer people care about my personal life. I also didn't get up in front of the school and ask them to." He crosses his arms, his colored nails tapping against his bicep furiously. "It's not like you extended a lot of friendship my way when I arrived, by the way. Would you have even noticed if it had been bad for me?"

Cold slides its way in as I stop and consider it. I guess I don't know for sure what it was like for Christopher coming here. He's a sophomore and was already out when he came to school, so what *do* I know about it? My gaze falls to his nails. Something I'd never dare do. Something Ostrowski would probably zero right in on. It's like Amy told me, I never noticed so much about what guys like him said to other people. How shitty do I have to be to assume no one ever said shit to him just because I didn't see it? Hell, what if it was *worse* than what I'm going through?

"Was it hard?" I ask, my voice barely more than a whisper.

Christopher deadpans, "No, it was pretty easy."

A beat passes, but suddenly I start to laugh and Christopher's frown melts into a smile too. And huh, this smile—it's actually a nice one. He has perfect teeth and the corners of his eyes wrinkle. He never smiles at me, so I guess I never noticed.

Okay, that is *not* useful to be thinking about. We're working together on something Amy is relying on us for. Work. What work thing can I ask? I remember Amy texting me this morning.

"Amy says you have a specific suggestion for our school board candidate's platform. What is it?"

"What, are you interviewing me now?"

I smile, despite how annoying he's been. "Just give me your best answer."

"Well, when I first got here, my friend up north asked me if we had a secret gay club. He comes from the most granola liberal high school, and he says they not only have a QSA, but this group that meets after school and spreads through word of mouth. A queer faculty member leads the group and no one has to give labels when they go, so it's this apparently great support group for out kids and closeted ones. I just know statistically there are more closeted students at our school, but let's face it, after seeing what happened with you, of course they wouldn't come out. At least not yet." He looks to me. "If you thought you're going through shit, imagine what a trans kid would go through if they went public. I don't see us getting a QSA, at least not yet, but even if all we add is more discretionary budget for extracurriculars so it could get called something else, it could make all the difference for something like that to safely bloom."

An anonymous student group that was safe for closeted kids.

"That's cool," I say.

"That might've been a game changer for me."

Christopher shrugs. "Me too." He tenses his jaw a moment, like there's something else he wants to say. "With the gay thing, anyway. People are always a little shitty about me being half-Jewish down here, but that's another story."

I never thought Christopher would get even a little vulnerable with me, so I'm so surprised I almost don't respond for a minute. "That's so messed up, man."

"More than one marginalization isn't great, especially when your fucking name is Christopher."

"Do people really comment on that?"

He sighs. "Yeah, so, ironically, goyim just pick up on the sacrilege they perceive in a Jewish parent naming their child after Christ. In reality, my dad always says he was adamant that I get a 'Jewish' name like Jacob or Adam and my mom get the middle name, but then my mom nearly died in childbirth. In the aftermath where my dad was all weepy and guilty, she asked to have me named after my maternal grandpa. It followed Jewish naming principles, but my dad's family was verklempt for a solid year. It's ridiculous and hilarious to me, not so much to a lot of people."

Wow, what else don't I know about this guy? "I'm sorry. What a story."

He glances down at his notebook, making a clicking sound with his mouth. "And about yours. It'll be impactful, I promise." He looks up at me. "I genuinely want you to be able to tell your side. Even the people who aren't outright bigots seem to think it was some publicity stunt for you to try to go pro or something. Amy mentioned it had something to do with your grandpa. Maybe you can talk about that here."

My side. It still feels so weird talking to Christopher about something I've never told anyone else. All people can focus on is how I've somehow changed the basketball team forever, but I'm still me. Like Christopher said, everyone has the wrong script going. Maybe people just need to be reminded that I'm the same guy they've known since I was a baby, who loved his school and town. Scratch's grandson.

"Okay," I say.

Christopher nods. "But to do that, I'll have to really get to know you. As a person, since I'm not your propaganda machine anymore." He sighs. "And I guess to do that we should start by me being more honest with you. I thought you were just another dick on the basketball team who thought he was too good for everyone. But it's meant so much to Amy that you joined Vote Squad, and I really don't want to be another asshole misjudging you anymore. I'm sorry."

Wow. Christopher comes over alone, tells me personal stuff, and now he's apologizing *again*? I never thought one of those things would happen, let alone all three.

Heat rises to the back of my neck. "And I'm sorry for blowing you off when you were apologizing to me at the diner."

"All is forgiven." He raises his brows. "But interview-wise. Since this is a profile, I need to see how you are just existing on top of asking you questions. I'll observe the speech Amy is hoping you'll change your mind about and we can talk about it after. Besides, I think I've gotten enough 'feelings' from you for one day."

"I still have no idea why anyone would listen," I say.

Christopher sighs again. "Show you give a shit about other people. It's like I said, if you were going to hide, you might as well have stayed in the closet. You can do a lot of good without being on the court. I hope I see you there. Be the Heath Ledger in *10 Things I Hate About You* I know you can be."

Right when I think I'm starting to get him, Christopher says something that loses me entirely. I have no idea what that reference means. But before I even have a second to reply, he walks toward the gate to go.

He's halfway through when he turns back for a second. I wait for him to explain, but instead he says, "Oh, and by the way, your sister's TV taste is shitty and you seem woefully unprepared to exist within modern gay culture." I stiffen. "You should watch *Glee* with her. Every episode. It's a start for both of you. You'll thank me eventually."

I don't even know what that show is and I'm too scared to ask now.

"I—" I say.

But Christopher is gone before anything else can happen. My gaze falls to the basketball hoop. I take a deep breath before the mess of feelings can turn to anything physical.

God, this whole weekend has turned me upside down.

CHAPTER NINE

T'S GOING TO BE DIFFERENT THIS TIME. I CHOSE TO BE A PART of this group. I want to really make a difference and annoying as he was, Christopher's right—it's time to stop complaining. I'm gonna blow Amy's and Christopher's minds at how much good I can do at something other than basketball. As I ride my bike to the town square for the rally, it's my mantra. Mrs. Mackay at the deli looks away from me as I wave? *I'm going to make a difference.* Mr. Durkin the hardware store owner glaring at me as I ride past? *I'm going to make a difference.* Shawn from my math class throwing me the finger when I spy him loitering outside the movie theater? *I'm going to make a difference.*

Not that it really keeps my hands from shaking the closer I get. After blowing it at the pep rally, this kind of speech just feels so much huger. Even with Amy's planned words—as promised, I focus on how the grounds budget disappearing led to the bush obscuring the stop sign that could've saved my grandpa—I'm still nervous about how it will play out. She has me going last, but do I really have the charisma to pressure the new school board candidate into putting budget concerns like that into her campaign platform? Will she not if everyone boos me? I've been practicing a ton since my talk with Christopher, but I still can't imagine anyone will listen to me. And that's ignoring the possibility that this event goes totally sideways since the school didn't sanction it and it involves a ton of teenagers making bold political statements.

The vibes just keep getting worse the closer I get to the stage. When I lock up my bike by the town square, a line of cars goes driving by. Nice cars, all bearing OSTROWSKI FOR SCHOOL BOARD signs. And they seem to be trying to compete for who can play the loudest electronic music–intermixed-with-honking combination. One is trying and failing to follow the beat of the music with their horn, and I'd take a wild guess and say that's Ostrowski himself. Nothing says Tim Ostrowski like going in really confident and completely blowing it with a smirk on your face.

God, sometimes I'm really glad to not be associated with him anymore.

I roll my shoulders and stand up straight. I'm not just disconnected from Ostrowski; I'm doing something to stand up to him. Barclay Elliot is back.

When I find Amy, she is red-faced, circling around Christopher as he writes on a clipboard.

"So Brianna is pulling up now, we have the flyers printed—" Amy's saying. Neither of them look up as I approach.

"Half are black-and-white," Christopher says. "The print store ran out."

"How does that even happen?"

"Late-stage capitalism failing."

Amy glares at him as I hold back a chuckle.

"Someone else got there before. I'll get there earlier next time, boss."

Amy waves this away. "You got the intro and outro music cued up?"

"Yeah. Finished recording it last night and it's a go."

"Great. We have all the designated spots to drop the flyers picked out, bodies to—"

"Hey," I say, before either of them get too deep in it. "I'm ready to help however I can."

Amy glances at me, but there's no clear recognition in her eyes. "Oh shit, sound check is in ten. But at least Brianna's people managed to actually get the good equipment from the rental company. . . ."

Christopher, on the other hand, looks up. "Your unwavering, long-term commitment to Amy's mental health and Chitwoodian voting rights is appreciated even though you're a millisecond late."

I check my phone, but realize he's being sarcastic as hell. At least he's got a smile on. I look around and spot the electrical equipment Amy must be talking about piled in the corner of the stage, not set up. "Well, I can lift heavy things," I offer.

Only then does Amy look at me. "Hey, Barclay, yes, go do that."

I'm practically bouncing as I run over to the equipment. Amy's already taped down x's for where everything goes, so thankfully, I can complete the task without sweating over hearing yet again about the time I set up the annual art show facing the wrong way freshman year. It's good that the task is easy because I'm low-key distracted going over the speech again in my head.

Once I'm done, I head out to the corner and walk up and down the street, passing out the leaflets to everyone who'll take them (even though people mostly tell me to go screw myself). By the time I'm out of breath and headed back to the group, a small crowd has gathered. I recognize some of the people I handed out flyers to are actually here, standing around for the rally. People from Chitwood High too. People, I realize with a twinge inside, who continue to mostly ignore me at school. But they're here. Not at Ostrowski's, so that has to mean something.

It's around then that I first see Brianna. She's a Black woman in her forties with a pristine mint-green pantsuit on and one of those infectious laughs. I catch her unwinding Amy as she finally stands still for a minute. Christopher is grinning harder than I've ever seen him. I make my way over and he steps aside so I can join the circle.

"I haven't seen you before," she says, looking to me.

I hold out my hand to shake. "Barclay Elliot. Thank you so much for sponsoring our rally."

Her eyes light up. "Ah yes, Amy mentioned you. I'm Brianna Collins. And happy to support a chance to see what the kids I'm hoping to work with want in their school."

My hand goes to the back of my neck. "Honor to be here, ma'am."

Her sunny disposition drops as she looks me in the eye. "And I heard about what you've been going through. I'm sure it wasn't easy to come here, so thank you. We're going to make schools like this safer places for all of us to be ourselves."

I glance over at Christopher, who's beaming. He's speaking about the school budget supporting clubs outside basketball, including LGBTQ+ ones, sometime before me and I was nervous for him, but I just have this feeling he's gonna kill it.

But Brianna's not looking at Christopher right now; she's looking at me.

At least with basketball, when people complimented me, I usually was doing the work I was being praised for. But right now, looking at Amy as she's back to frantically checking things, I know all I've done is set up a microphone and passed out flyers. I don't deserve this praise. I resist looking at Christopher, knowing how much he's putting into getting these LGBTQ+ protections when I haven't done anything for my community until I came out. And even that hasn't really helped.

"I haven't been doing much," I admit finally, looking to Amy. She finally looks back and gives me a soft nod. *Apology accepted.* "I really don't deserve the compliment."

But Brianna shrugs. "Well, you're here now. The great thing about showing up with the right attitude is there's plenty to do if you want to start now."

Brianna wasn't kidding about plenty to do. I help adjust equipment, I put fences between the audience and the stage, I tell the food stands, mostly out-of-towners, where to set up. It's a particularly cold day, so by the time I'm helping some of the non-sports clubs Amy contacted (who are in desperate need of funding from the school board too) with setting up their stands, I can't keep my eyes off the artisan hot cider and steaming pulled pork sandwiches one vendor is advertising. In fact, I'm setting up their menu at their table when Tabby of all people runs up to me, carrying a batch of cupcakes. These are frosted in rainbow icing stretching across at least a dozen of them.

"When I heard you were going to be here today, I just knew what to do," she explains. "'Make him cupcakes,' I told myself. 'Barclay could use the boost.'"

I find myself just staring at her as her words slowly process in my brain. These cupcakes aren't for the rally. They're for . . . me. On one hand, this is the kindest thing anyone has done for me in weeks, but on the other hand, I would rather be swallowed up into the ground right here than sit behind a bunch of rainbow cupcakes like I'm begging for acceptance—

I finally unfreeze and take one of the blue ones. She has several shades, so at least it doesn't ruin the aesthetic.

"Thanks, Tabby," I say. "Um. You should offer the rest to Amy and her team. They're the ones doing the real work here."

At least it's not a lie. I mean it's 100 percent likely that Amy hasn't eaten since last night. Her own blood sugar always falls to the bottom of the list when she gets into things. In fact, I'm still strictly forbidden from mentioning the time she passed out sophomore year right behind the facade door while tech'ing *Musical Comedy Murders of 1940* and caused Kaitlyn Cooke to break her nose when she tripped over her.

Tabby beams. "Great idea!" But she doesn't leave. She's still just grinning at me and it feels like she wants to say something but she doesn't. *Why isn't she leaving?*

She takes out a pen and writes something on a napkin. Then, after another awkward second, runs off, instantly replaced with Christopher as he covers his mouth to muffle laughter. I go brighter red than I was from the heat alone.

"Leave that out of the article," I say quickly.

Christopher clicks his tongue. "Mmm, see, I don't think I can. We need more great, sweet moments like that in the life of Barclay Elliot, Angry Gay Troy Bolton."

I *have* actually seen *High School Musical*, but my stupid head and stupid mouth still can't let the image of me and a batch of rainbow cupcakes linger. "I just . . . come on, man, don't bring Tabby into the heat. It's not worth it. It's not like Tabbys of the world are going to win people to my side."

I go ice-cold the moment the words leave my mouth. Christopher bristles, his jaw tightening instantly. Those gray eyes close off completely.

"Maybe you shouldn't diss the only people who're actually supporting you," he says as he walks back to Amy and Tabby.

As I watch Christopher put a hand on Tabby's shoulder, beaming as he takes a cupcake and says it's a perfect Chanukah present, I feel like shit.

I look down at the napkin and see it says *Good luck today, Barclay!*

Feeling like shit confirmed. One step forward, immediately taken back.

The rally grows before my eyes. Within an hour, we go from a dozen people waiting around the stage as they eat their food to, like, a concert-in-the-park crowd in the middle of December. The sound of everyone's voices rumbles as the final sound check finishes. I spot Zack, Pat, and a couple other basketball guys in the crowd. The sight gets my lungs tightening; what would they be doing here? It's not like they care about the school board. But I also haven't talked to Zack since our fight after the game, so I couldn't know why he's here, anyway. He might hate me now, but is he really going to mess this up for Amy?

It's too late to look into it now, though. I stick to the wings with Christopher, who still hasn't quite made proper eye contact with me despite the fact that I apologized to a very confused Tabby, who seemed to think I was apologizing for not complimenting her cupcakes enough. Either way, she seems thrilled, but somehow I feel worse at that.

When Amy takes the stage to open the rally, running up and bouncing like all those rocker guys she loves, it's like seeing her at her most confident, happiest, most Amy self.

"It's so amazing to see all your lovely faces in the audience!" Amy says as she takes the microphone off the stand with the fluidity of a performer. No feedback or anything. "We've seen the mind-boggling change that's possible with a lot of work and engagement, and I know Georgia isn't done leading the way for every gerrymandered and suppressed state in this country. But change starts here, voting for issues that'll affect our town, our school at the local level. Chitwood, we're part of a brighter future!"

I've always known Amy has a larger-than-life charm, and that it sinks deep into any crowd when she brings it out. This is something else. I cheer as loud as I can as she keeps her speech rolling.

"Thousands of recently eighteen-year-old voters helped bridge the gap in the 2020 senate races in Georgia, an upset *thirty years* in the making. But the power of young voters isn't limited to large-scale change. We have the power to make a difference in what kind of school and town we have. One that supports *all* its students and their interests—arts, academics, and sports. One that is safe for students from all backgrounds. And the first step toward any of that is making sure that a school budget that reflects those priorities is passed by the board. We need a fair budget champion to emerge come February."

The crowd erupts in a few pockets of cheers, but I can see some commotion in the middle. Suddenly, Ostrowski and the other seniors on the basketball team come into view, shouldering their way to the front row. Including Chase, with a *fucking megaphone*.

"Go home, loser!" Chase shouts. How original.

I can't see Amy's face from this angle, but I hear the slightest tremble in her voice as she tells them to get out of here. I look to Christopher, who has his thumbnail in his mouth, bouncing back and forth on his feet. *Please just go.*

Of course, they don't. They throw in the usual suspects. *Special snowflake, SJW*. I cringe at every word, especially as Amy keeps going, trying to speak increments louder.

"This shit isn't gonna get Travis Morris to date you!" Boris shouts.

Amy has her fists clenched, and I know she's seconds from jumping off the podium to throw punches. I secretly want her to, but this is too important.

"Amy Baltra, fucking dyke!" Ostrowski shouts, which doesn't even make sense following Chase's insult.

Fuck this. No one gets to talk to someone I care about like this, and I'm not letting her get arrested for throwing hands.

I charge up to the stage, adrenaline burning through me. I drag a mic with me and look right in Ostrowski's stupid face.

"You must be pretty scared of folks actually getting registered, huh, Ostrowski? If that happens, I don't think your dad's travel agency will survive without all the school's money going toward team travel."

Electricity runs down my spine at what I've just said in front of all these people, but everything's worth it to see the guys on the team go wide-eyed and turn to Ostrowski. Every one of them looks like someone found their drug stashes, confidence melting to shock. I wish I could take a picture.

And Ostrowski. Oh, Ostrowski. I always knew he had a thick neck, but the tomato red combined with the throbbing vein on full display, it's beautiful. Security finally makes their way over, and he looks like a mad dog put on a leash as they drag him and the others away.

"Well, this would be as good a time as any to introduce none other than Gatorade Boy of the Year and former captain of the Wildcats basketball team, Barclay Elliot!" Amy says, and takes a step back. Curious, I guess, to see what I'll do next.

"Uh, hi, everyone," I say, refocusing as my heart slams. "I'm Barclay and I . . . guess I'll just launch into it. Now more than ever, it's so important that we pay attention. Voting means having the power to make huge changes in Chitwood and the town at large." My throat starts to itch, but I stick to the script. "Most of you probably knew my grandpa, Scratch. He was killed by a distracted driver earlier this year. He was a basketball star when he went to Chitwood High, toured Vietnam, and was a cancer survivor who had years left to offer." I swallow, knowing this next part will be hard. "But a stop sign on school property was covered by overgrown bushes. Several people complained to the school board, but the board had allocated money away from school grounds upkeep, so it never got fixed. Where did it go? Into the basketball team.

"I loved basketball just as much as so many of you do, but I loved Scratch more. Basketball is important to Chitwood, but it isn't the only thing that matters here. We can fix the problem by voting people who don't believe that out this year. We can vote for people who listen to the students, *all* the students, and provide us with what we need. We can make sure no spring musical ever gets canceled or no culture clubs get cut because of supposed lack of funding." I exhale, thinking about Christopher, and Brianna, and Tabby. And I go off-script. "We can make sure LGBTQ+ students and other marginalized groups have written protection from school policy that would allow them to meet and connect safely on school grounds and help them feel accepted when and if they choose to come out. Government matters on every level to keep us physically and mentally safe." I look to Amy, who's glassy-eyed. I'm glad I'm saying this, but my throat's just getting tighter and I really have to hand it off. "And now, back to Amy and the others for way more details!"

I tense, waiting for another drawn-out silence.

But then the crowd cheers. Not a ton, but definitely some whoops, a few claps, and the unmistakable shouting of "We love Scratch!" from more than one voice. When I look down, Zack surprises me by being among those cheering. I leave the stage with an unexpected twinge of comfort spreading in my chest.

Amy introduces Christopher to speak more on the clubs issue. As he starts to talk, I see the way Brianna in particular has her eyes glued to him.

Then, as Christopher continues what I'm sure will be a badass speech, Amy comes barreling over to me and jumps into my arms. I have to spin around to stay upright as she hugs me.

"I'm so fucking glad you got involved," she says to me.

I drop her back to her feet, a little dizzy and still reeling from the adrenaline. It's almost like the rush of a great basketball game. "I thought I'd be embarrassed, but I'm just energized." I shake my head. "Shit, I'm in this now. All these people showed up because they need school funding too. People do care about so much more than just basketball." There are way more people than I ever thought who care about their community. Who, judging by the fact that people aren't pelting Christopher with tomatoes or making a mass exodus, might care about queer people, or be convinced to. "It's time I help fight for them, not just me." I sniffle, the last remnant of the emotion from being onstage. "This is something I can do for Scratch, too."

I flash back to Zack in the crowd and Zack at the lockers. What he said about being brave. What if he was right? That coming out like that wasn't the bravest thing I could've done in his honor?

I run a hand through my hair. I can't think about Zack now.

I focus on the rest of the rally, watching the collection of speeches as closely as I can. I seek out Amy again as soon as the event ends. She's talking with Christopher, unfiltered joy all over her sweaty face.

"So what's next?" I ask.

Amy pulls Christopher into a side hug. "Glad you asked. We're planning a door-to-door campaign to get more people registered and involved."

"I'm in," I say. No more hesitation necessary.

Christopher smiles after I say that. A little more muted than this morning, but it still feels like a win. "You do seem to love a public moment."

I roll my eyes as Amy laughs. Once the laughter dies out, though, her eyes fall back to the crowd. To the ghosts of Ostrowski and the seniors.

"Ostrowski definitely won't let that go," she says. "This is about to get heated. But the registration cutoff is in a month and a half, so that has to be our immediate focus. Now that I'm pretty sure Brianna's on board with our suggestions, I think we should plan one more big rally right before the deadline in support of her specifically and push the budget issues before the election."

Heated? I'm counting on it. Ostrowski might have money, might have enough influence to make people forgive how much he sucks, but I'm done letting him pass and cover shit up.

I think about Ostrowski mooning that security guard during the prank. The shit with the mascot. The way Coach dismissed it all, clearly finding the joke funny.

We don't live in that world anymore and it's time they're called out for it.

"Let's go bigger this time. Let's drop so much shit on the Ostrowskis that there's no way they can crash our rally again, let alone win an election," I say. "I'll make sure this next rally blows them away. Hell, let me plan it."

The sneaky grin Christopher and Amy exchange already makes it all worth it.

CHAPTER TEN

WHILE I APPRECIATE THE SEPARATION FROM EVERY-thing happening at school, winter break isn't exactly the over-the-top joyous occasion it was when Scratch was still here. There's no walking home from the last day of school to see him hanging multicolor Christmas lights on the roof, no late nights sharing stove-popped popcorn and watching *Die Hard* until he falls asleep before Hans Gruber plummets off the roof. Devin's home, but he's chipping away at an application for a summer internship. Maggie's laid out on the couch instead of off at the annual cookie-baking party she and her friends put on every year. She's got her English notebook open, but she's weirdly sketching in the margins, even though she nearly had a panic attack that I "ruined it" when I ripped out a few blank pages for a homework assignment months ago. Guess she's figured out her perfect student track record isn't gonna be wrecked if she doesn't spend another winter break studying. And while Mom has managed to get off work before seven p.m. on Christmas Eve, she's hardly looked at any of us as she preps for Christmas dinner.

"Did you take the SATs yet?" Devin asks me, seemingly out of nowhere, as I click through Netflix from the couch.

"No, that's a spring thing," I reply. I think. Amy told me and I wrote it down somewhere now that my scores actually matter, but I clearly haven't internalized it yet.

"If you want my old practice book, let me know," he says, then he laughs. "It's barely marked up, so perfect to use."

I click on some show that I wouldn't be embarrassed for Devin to see me watching; Christopher's *Glee* assignment will have to wait. "Thanks."

"You should start soon," Mom pipes in, for the first time since I got down here.

"I have months." Besides, I'll be busy meeting with Amy nearly every day to talk about the second rally. I've been brainstorming ways for it to not just be speeches all break. No time for test prep.

"Barclay, that's *not* the attitude to have." She turns away from her prep in the kitchen and straightens up. Devin raises his brows at me—*good luck, man.* Shit. "And now that you're finally free for a few weeks, we should have a serious talk about college."

I knew this was coming, but I still feel like I'm being cornered as she sits across from Devin and me and pulls up her phone. Notes app time.

Devin, meanwhile, throws an arm around me. "Don't worry, Mom. Barc's gonna be just fine with me at Georgia Tech."

Close to home. Close to Devin. Something that should be so comforting now, but even though I loved it there, I don't know if I'll ever fully escape my older brother witnessing me making out with a dude and then having to break up a fight I almost caused. Even if it's away from Chitwood, I don't know if it'll be far enough away.

But I can't say any of that. So I just say, "I guess."

Mom's gaze whips right over to me. "What's wrong with Georgia Tech? You'd have Devin, you'd be close to home, and it's a great reach school."

God, that hits me so much harder than anything. *Reach school.* Georgia Tech was a safety school when I had basketball.

"You don't think I'd definitely get in?"

Devin, suddenly deciding to be a total shit, creeps out of the room. She takes a deep breath, glancing at her cutting boards covered in vegetables. "If you start applying yourself now, of course I think you can get in. There's Georgia Tech, but also University of Georgia, Georgia Southern, Kennesaw, North Georgia. So many options all over the state you'd thrive at."

I can already imagine the future Mom has for me. I join whatever Div II or III basketball team they have. I study for some practical degree and get a job where I can come back here and do it. I come home every few weeks, or she can be at my college in a few hours' driving, even though we barely see each other when we live in the same house.

What I see, though, is staying the same way I am now. Always worrying about who's around me, and without anything new to challenge myself or grow with.

"What if I want to go somewhere out of state?" I ask.

Mom's mouth twitches, the most painful delay before she speaks. "Why would you want to go out of state?"

Heat already rises to my face even as I think of saying it. No one told me even after being out, I'd still be embarrassed as hell to say "gay" in front of my mom for no reason. "I . . . I wanna be in a big city. A . . ." I rub my arm. "A city where there would be . . . more for me to do. To be myself."

She puts her fist to her mouth, dead silent. I sink deeper into the couch. She's imagining me having gay sex, I just know it.

But the next second I look at her, I swear she has tears in the corner of her eyes. "Barclay, without basketball scholarships, I don't know if you'll be able to—Atlanta is still—"

Her words hit me like a gut punch. Coming out publicly was supposed to secure my future. Make anything possible. But now it's become the thing that limited it. I don't want to stay in Georgia, and she thinks all my tickets out of here just went away. She doesn't believe in me.

Maybe I wouldn't be in this position if you hadn't been riding on my basketball career, I think. It's so vile that I cringe with it just in my head. But God I still feel it. The words ignite in my veins. *Maybe if she had just let me tell her that morning, I wouldn't have gone through with it the way I did.*

But what will getting angry even do? This is my life now.

"Okay," I say.

She's still frowning as she nods along with me; I can practically feel the crack between us widen.

The next few hours of Christmas Eve go by in a blur. Mom focuses back on cooking, and I try to numb myself with video games. I have no idea what Devin and Maggie do. Within a few hours of exclusively focusing on the screen, my mind's gone the perfect amount of fuzzy. It takes me a second to even realize my phone's pinged with a text.

Zack
Hey, Barcs! Merry Christmas! Listen I really want to talk. I'm headed over to pick up the fam's KFC order before it closes. Wanna meet me? I'll spot you a Famous Bowl

Maybe it's just exhaustion from what went down with Mom and me, or maybe it's the memory of him cheering in the crowd, but I find myself taking Zack up on his offer. I'm not so sure going one-on-one is the best way to resolve the tension between us, but since he reached out, I'm guessing he wants to apologize. I'm willing to at least try. If nothing else, it'll be an hour away from my mess of a family.

The KFC in the next town over is, as usual, dead as the hours whittle down before Christmas. Zack's already inside when I walk in, hunched over in a sweater that's more tinsel and puff balls than actual insulation against the weather we've been having. But he smiles at me when he looks up and pulls me into a hug. I realize then how much I've missed him.

"Business as usual at the Ito house, I see," I say, motioning to the KFC.

Zack laughs. "Yeah, can't get my dad away from his Japanese childhood traditions." We step forward in line, waiting as the cashier practically has to hit the register to get it to work for the next order. "How's everything with your family?"

My chest stings thinking about Mom and our last conversation. "It's okay. How's yours?"

Zack looks at the menu as he speaks. "It's okay. A lot of pressure with the losing streak, but . . ." He tenses and so do I. "We'll make it happen."

In the seconds as the cashier tries to get the register to work for us this time, I imagine a way this could all go down. I fix Mom's out-of-state issue the same way I fix things with Zack. I apologize for our fight, ask if Coach would let me back on the team, say we call it a mental health break.

But what would that even do? Nothing's changed. I'd still be treated like shit for being gay. Ostrowski would still be on the team, sabotaging me every chance he got. And then I'd have to abandon Amy and Christopher when I can see they're onto something huge.

When I've already filled pages of a notebook with ideas for our next event for Brianna. No way.

"I believe in you," I say instead, forcing my best smile. Besides, now that I know what goes down between Ostrowski's dad and the school board, I don't think I *can*.

By the time I shake myself out of my thoughts, Zack's deep into ordering for his whole family and my window to say anything else is gone.

It does feel really damn nice, though, when he remembers to throw in that Famous Bowl he promised me.

"I really miss you, man," he says as we sit down, waiting for Zack's giant-ass order to be finished. "I know what the team did to you was total shit. It doesn't feel right to me, and it never did. Like, I get it now . . . I get why you quit and I'm sorry I didn't before. I just wish that didn't mean we can't be friends like before. I'd do anything to get back to that."

I think about the way Zack cheered me on at the rally, despite being there with some of the shitheads on the team. About how he used to engage Amy more than me about social justice issues. Zack cares. I do genuinely believe that.

And I wonder if that's how I can bridge my worlds back together. Get him involved with Vote Squad.

"I've missed you too. I never wanted this to be between us. I saw you at the rally. Why don't you join Amy and me in Vote Squad? We could use a voice that's still on the team. You heard what I was saying about with Ostrowski's dad, right? All the shit he takes from every other part of the school budget so we can get fifty new balls we don't need?"

Zack furrows his brow as he leans in. "Wait, holy shit, man, that's not even the worst of it."

"What?"

"Last spring, Lochman's dad sold Mr. Ostrowski this expensive-ass retro Mustang. Like he hounded Lochman's dad for *weeks* to track down this car. Then he told Lochman how he never even sees Mr. Ostrowski driving it. You know how everyone would joke that Horvath must be running an illegal drug ring to afford a car as nice as he has? What does he have, Barcs?"

Oh my God. "He has some retro expensive Mustang."

I bet that's how Mr. Ostrowski is keeping the school administration and the board quiet about his travel agency team-travel scheme. Bribery. And somewhere out there, there's a whole car and paper trail to back it up.

I find myself smiling. "So not only is Mr. Ostrowski a piece of shit, but he's doing illegal stuff that could destroy him if we can prove it. I'm gonna do it, Zack. I'm gonna expose him at our next rally in January. Get him ousted from the board before anyone can even vote. It may be the one good thing that comes from this pep rally shit. And maybe you can help too, give Lochman the heads-up I'm coming to hit him up about the car."

But Zack isn't smiling when I look to him for a reaction. He looks more like I'm a train barreling toward him. "You're gonna tell everyone about *Mr. Ostrowski*? Dude, that's the quickest road to enemies. He's a powerful guy."

"He won't be when we take the power from him." I'm starting to sound like Amy. I kinda like it. "This bullshit has gone on too long. It's why we lost the championship last year, why Amy lost the spring play, why my grandpa . . ." I trail off. "He's not good for the town, the school board, or the team. I need to at least try."

"Barclay, I—" He exhales. "I don't know, man. Voting rights I'm all in on, but you saw the way everyone turned on you just for being gay. This is like, an actual reason for people to hate you. Powerful people. I only know what I'm going through trying to get basketball scholarships or scouts to notice me, but it feels like someone at like every school is watching me, waiting to check the box that I messed up. I—I still wanna have our dream, man. Going to the same out-of-state D-One school, partying together, being free to just be. And Mr. Ostrowski could end that for both of us *and* Lochman in one email."

He isn't on board with this. Zack, the guy who I thought stood up for principles. Once again, he's choosing staying quiet. Choosing the shitty team over me. And what future? How can I ever have a future with him as my friend if he still thinks like this?

"Well, my mom said I can't go out of state anyway since I'm not playing D-One ball, so that dream is over for me. But good luck." I stand up. "I gotta go."

"Wait! Barclay, please!"

But I don't turn around. This was a mistake. Zack hasn't changed at all.

After a shit Christmas Eve, I slog my way through Christmas morning and dinner. By December twenty-sixth, I think we're all exhausted from pretending we're a happy family without Scratch, and we retreat to our rooms. I shove my headphones on, playing music as I attempt to browse for a movie just so there's no moment I can possibly hear if Mom's back to crying.

Then I get a text.

From Christopher. I thought we seemed pretty wrapped up with the last Vote Squad brainstorm session we had with Amy a few days ago. I'm presenting potential speaker lists next time we meet. Why is he texting me?

Christopher

Did you get started on that movie list we put together?

Of course it's about that. Unfortunately . . .

Me

Not yet

Two texts sound off from my phone.

Christopher

Damn, Elliot! How am I gonna get background on you for this article if I don't even know your opinions on the classic cinema of our time?
Do you wanna watch 10 Things I Hate About You with me? Get the ball rolling?

Me

I'm stuck at home and can't come watch, you'll have to tell me about it. Is it good?

Christopher

It has Heath Ledger in it. Of course it is. And no worries; Netflix Party.

I can't believe he texts with semicolons. The next second, he has a Netflix Party link in my email and a second after that, he calls me.

"Um, yes?" I say into the phone as I watch the title screen for *10 Things I Hate About You*.

"Yeah, I want your live reactions, no bullshit. It's more like watching a movie together this way," Christopher says.

His voice seems a little more casual than usual. I wonder if he's in his room like I am. If he has nineties rom-com posters all over the place.

"Whatever you say," I say as I adjust my pillows and get comfy. But I'm grinning. With a set of old earbuds on, I'm sure that no one in the house can hear what I'm doing. There's something thrilling about that, having this special little moment with just Christopher—

—which isn't that special, since we're just watching a movie.

But as the seconds pass, even though I hate to say it, this is extremely entertaining. Christopher really *loves* this movie and spends half our viewing spouting trivia, gushing over his favorite scenes, and absolutely thirsting over Heath Ledger's character.

"So what do you think," I say through a smile I can't shake. "Should Heath Ledger have won his first Oscar here? Or are you just a total simp?"

Christopher gasps hammily. "How *dare* you! I can identify quality performances and happen to think rom-coms are generally short-changed in major awards."

"You didn't answer the question."

"I have *eyes*, Barclay!"

There's something about the way he says my name that makes my stomach flip. But I'm too busy laughing to dwell on it. "Yeah but, can we really definitively say that Patrick singing at the band rehearsal is the *best* grand gesture?"

"Yes! He rejected her, making Kat think that he was ashamed of being with her. So he *had* to do something embarrassing to show what ends he'd go to for her. Not to mention singing to someone is one of the most vulnerable, beautiful ways to express emotion."

"But then he has that bet and does like five other dick things. Why did Kat even want to be with him when he burned her twice?"

Honestly, the dudes in this movie are all kind of assholes. Romance shouldn't have to involve bets and trying to pick between a bunch of people. If Kat and Patrick were true love or whatever, why is it so hard?

"For the record, Patrick has *two* grand gestures. The second being when he gets her the guitar and recites the Shakespeare poem at the end. He shows that a great love doesn't have to be with two perfect people. What matters is that every time Patrick screwed up, he acknowledged his mistake and made right by Kat. It's romantic because it feels real."

Wow, Christopher really has thought about all this. And what he's saying is kind of really nice?

"I stand corrected," I say.

"So now that you know I'm a Heath Ledger simp," he says. "Who gets you going?" He pauses, and I swear I can *hear* him smirk. "Who, in the celebrity realm, at least?"

I glance at my walls. I don't have any posters, but the answer comes to me immediately. "Andrew Garfield."

"So sure of yourself. I can see it. Nerdy-hot."

I wonder if Christopher is ever called that.

Shit, no, no—

Christopher groans. "You're gonna make me watch his Spider-Man movies when it's your turn, aren't you?"

The ball of heat bouncing in my chest is so embarrassing, but I still find myself smiling. It's been so long since I could just sit and watch a movie with someone. "I guess so."

We hang up soon after. The heat doesn't dissipate as I shut my laptop, which is currently burning my legs. I'll, uh, have to invite Amy to that next movie night because I cannot be having these thoughts about Christopher. We're just friends. He even *said* he just wants more background for his stupid article.

Still, I keep thinking about him saying "your turn," like this is a thing we'll keep doing. I guess I never thought hanging out with him could be so fun.

CHAPTER ELEVEN

AND LASTLY," AMY SAYS, PURSING HER LIPS AS SHE STARES at her phone the first day we're back at school in January. "Let's get our pairs set for this weekend's door-to-door campaign. The election is in February and voter registration ends January twenty-second, so we've only got a couple more weeks to get new voters and get the word out about Brianna's platform."

There's about sixteen of us sitting in the quieter corner of the cafeteria, Tabby and Christopher included. Our numbers doubled after the first rally, much to Amy's unfiltered delight. Vote Squad has now become a daily occurrence as we consistently get together to talk strategy and check in with Brianna's team as she finalizes her platform. So far, Amy and I put together a selection of local activist speakers to go on before Brianna at our next rally, and I strategized flyer placement using the technique the team used to use during fundraisers to bring eyes to the cause. Tabby has been making baked goods for our meetings at least once a week, which is why Amy is currently crumbling a peanut-butter cookie in her hand as she thinks.

It's almost nice to be able to eat lunch and not have to yell to be heard or get yelled at by whoever is pissed about the Wildcats' basketball record that day (7–8). I've been told now that they've started winning more that I'm obviously not needed, and I wish that didn't still sting. But either way, I know I lose: if they lose more than three games, they can kiss the playoffs goodbye and I'm sure that'll be on me too.

While Amy ponders, Christopher, who's sitting close enough to me that his shoe has knocked against mine more than once this meeting, looks over to me expectantly. Lately, whenever he gets a free moment between us, he's either asking me questions for the article or digging for how we're going to get more actual proof of the basketball corruption. Which I was fine with, really, up until this morning. Principal Horvath called me in about the school board rally and said I should be careful about making such a stir. That I was lucky I didn't get suspended over "hijacking" the pep rally. As pissed as I was at Zack, he's clearly not wrong that spilling this could be used to destroy my chances of *any* college accepting me. I don't want to give in to that and go back on doing the right thing, but it's a lot to risk with no one else from the team backing me up. Again. Especially since Lochman is my only way to any concrete evidence and if Zack won't step up for me, I doubt he will.

So, I've been answering a *lot* of questions about myself while I figure out what to do.

Sure enough, Christopher leans over to me, so fast that one second he's sitting like normal and the next his breath is against my ear like we're in a classroom scene of one of those movies he loves. "Ready to spill for me?" My stomach sinks, but I just keep writing ideas in my notebook for the door-to-door campaign like I didn't hear him.

I glance over at him a few seconds later, and at least he's taken half a hint and returned to his place when I didn't answer. He's like a little shapeshifter in that way, going from incessant barnacle levels of drilling me for the articles to laid-back, teasing me about my TV taste and running his hand through his perfect hair. I want to tell him what I'm worried about, but I'm afraid he'll think I haven't changed again.

I look up and Amy's written pairs on her tiny portable white-board. I look for our names, but two down I see Amy's with Tabby, followed by *BARCLOPHER*. The other ten pairs have their names written like normal. I sigh.

"Do you have to write our names like that? I'm trying to lead this next rally and would love to be taken seriously," I say. I spent all day yesterday planning ways to incorporate Scratch's memorial into the rally. "You know people are going to assume Christopher and I are more than just friends."

I turn, expecting Christopher to back me up, but he's narrowing his eyes at me like I completely failed a gay lesson he gave me. "We're not even friends, Barclay, calm down."

"Yeah, but—" I say. "Wait, what do you mean we aren't friends?"

"It's not any different from straights," Christopher continues. "Haven't you seen *When Harry Met Sally*?"

"No," I say, flat.

One of the sophomores sighs. "Here we go again." He and the other members of the club sans Tabby and Amy start heading out.

"That's ridiculous; it's a classic. You have to watch it. Billy Crystal says to Meg Ryan—who's like, the best—he says, 'You realize we can't be friends because the sex part always gets in the way?' And they argue about if that's true. I mean, I know a number of gay guys up north and they all want to have sex with me."

I furrow my brow and Amy exchanges a look with Tabby. "Okay, Chris, it's probably time to—"

"So you're saying that a gay guy can only be friends with another gay guy he doesn't find attractive?" I say. So . . . does that mean he thinks I'm attractive or not? I honestly don't know which is worse.

"Oh my God, that's exactly what Meg Ryan said! And the answer is 'no.' Never. Because the sex thing is always out there, so the friendship is ultimately doomed."

Oh my God. Like, okay, I've thought about John more than I'm proud to admit. And sometimes, *sometimes*, I think Christopher is okay-looking and that I'd like to brush his hair out of his eyes, but it doesn't mean shit.

Does Christopher ever think about me like that?

Okay, I think I'm starting to see what he's saying. "Got it," I say, tossing an eraser between my hands. "So, it looks like we're never going to be friends. Can't take any risks. Glad to be on the same page."

"Sorry, Sally." He picks up his notebook, totally unbothered. "I gotta head to the band room. Meet me at Darling Street at ten a.m. Saturday. Don't be late."

That's it? I'm just supposed to stare up at that ship name Amy made after Christopher talked about us and sex in the same sentence and he's just gonna leave?

Once he and Tabby are gone, Amy pulls up a chair, turns it backward, and sits in front of me. "We need to talk."

"I know, did you see I emailed you an idea for a walk over to the stop sign to end Brianna's second rally?" I ask before the idea leaves my head. "It'd involve moving around when we bring up the stop sign during the actual speeches, but it should be easy to incorporate."

"That's great, Barc," Amy says. "But let's save that discussion for later."

"If it's about whatever just happened," I say, my face heating, "I have no idea what he's talking about."

Amy scrunches her face up. "God, no, I don't care about your sex life." Ugh, my skin's *crawling*. But it isn't the sex thing—well, not totally. It's like I've got this identity that comes with all these expectations for what I must inherently know about. That alone is just one tiny piece of the larger issue here; Christopher talks about being gay like I should know what he's referring to. But I just don't. I'm so disconnected from this community, *my* community, I'm trying to protect.

"Barclay, right now, we need to talk about you, Christopher, and the article. Why are you holding back on him? He's noticed and he thinks it's him," she finishes.

"I'm answering all his questions! He could probably fill out BuzzFeed quizzes for me."

"You know that's not the one I mean. The team corruption stuff. The one I'd really like to have so we can get Ms. Cho's approval and print it up for the second rally in just *a few weeks*," she says, holding up a palm. "It's not like everyone doesn't already see it. It's *obvious* that the basketball team can afford new uniforms and gear every year but even the other sports teams are still using stuff from the nineties. People *know* basketball gets favoritism, but they don't how deep it is. Barclay, look at me." I do. Barely. I look at the space between her eyes. "You wouldn't have brought this up to me if it ended with 'The school board supports basketball more than theater.' Or one suspicious trip to Orlando. What happened that surprised even you?"

That Mr. Ostrowski bribed members of the board and administration to approve the budget cuts that funnel business to his travel agency. It rings in my head, but I can't get the words to form in my dried-out mouth.

I throw my hands up. "I don't know what to say." It's the truth.

Amy snatches one of my hands, slowly bringing it back to the table so she can cover it. "It's okay to admit you miss basketball, you know. I know I talk a lot of shit, but I get that it's important to you. Are you *sure* this isn't about wanting to be able to go back on the team?"

"I do miss it." It's like a plug removed from a dam when I finally admit it. And suddenly I can't stop. "The game, at least. But if I'm honest, I don't miss the pressure. The relief from that has been amazing." I flash her a tiny smile. "For me, basketball has always been about more than just putting the ball in the basket. The team used to mean something to me, but now that I know that they don't feel that way too, it's just—and especially with—"

Suddenly there's a blast of sound from the hallway. I jump up and both of us look to the cafeteria entrance.

"I-to! I-to! I-to! I-to!" comes a cheer.

And there he is, back straight and a big grin on his face as he struts by with the other guys on the team.

I know why, I realize with a burning in my chest. Zack made the winning basket last game, keeping alive the team's hopes of hitting that .500 record and qualifying for the playoffs.

"It's okay to miss Zack too," Amy says.

I open my eyes, shaking off the heavy feeling. "I don't." I say it too quickly, but even if I do, I *shouldn't*.

How could I when Zack is still hanging out with the rest of those homophobic tools? The team draws slurs on my locker and humiliates Amy in public. And Zack says sorry, says he doesn't think it's right, but just lets that happen. Just like Mr. Ostrowski's corruption. He'll let anything happen as long as he gets to play.

Amy sighs, giving me a few slaps on the back. "Well, just think about it. You haven't picked up a ball in weeks and it's starting to freak me out. You can still take a stand without going on a complete basketball boycott. That's part of you too. But while you do, think about the article and what you can tell us."

. . .

It's so not a big deal, but I'm tense as hell when I pull a basketball out of the garage later that night, Amy's words ringing in my ears. Mom's working late as usual, so it doesn't feel like sad eyes are boring into me as I practice my form. I thought she'd calm down once I agreed to her in-state school plan, but she doesn't seem convinced I'm actually on board.

It's one of those nights where things are miraculously quiet, only the occasional sound of a dog barking in the distance. It makes the thud of my ball hitting the concrete ring in my ears. I start dribbling low, gradually adding more force until the ball is popping high above my head like I used to do with it as a kid. I mimic a passing drill, sending the ball across the "court" and running to the other side to catch it before it hits the grass. Within seconds, it's like the puzzle piece fits back into place. Muscle memory takes over as I turn around, dribble the most complicated maneuvers I know, mumbling:

"Elliot takes the ball from Ito, shoots." I shoot and—

"Score!" It goes right in. Nothing but net.

I laugh a little as I scoop the ball back.

There's stiffness in my muscles that comes from lack of conditioning, but it's like that magic something I always had is right back where it belongs. Once I'm back in my own rhythm, though, the bad stuff kinda comes too. What can I even do with basketball now? I can't go back on the team, but what am I without it? What future can I have if I'm not playing in college and beyond?

A click steals my attention.

I wheel over and see Christopher with his phone in hand, standing just within the gate.

"You're on your way to more paparazzi than journalist," I mutter.

He smiles at me. "Gotta pay tuition somehow."

I dribble the ball absentmindedly, wishing I could return my full attention to it. "I'm not in the mood for more questions."

Christopher shrugs. "I'm sure you're aware that Amy still wants the article about you whether you spill about Ostrowski and the team or not. But today, I'm just here to return your notebook. Grabbed it by mistake." I drop the ball and move over to take it, but he pulls it back. "Interesting reading. I love the walk to Scratch's memorial for after the rally and this door-to-door pitch is fantastic."

It's not like it's a diary, but it still feels like a violation. "You *read it*?"

"I thought it was mine and didn't realize until after I'd opened it."

He picks up the basketball I've dropped, setting the notebook aside. Without any prompting, he throws it up with one hand.

And it goes in.

I raise my eyebrows. "Wow, not bad."

"You shooting around by yourself feels a little tragic," he says. "I can play HORSE with you if you want."

I will not acknowledge the tragic bit, but I'm at least curious. *Do we have something in common?*

I start somewhere easy, an angle along the free throw line. Christopher's form is a little haphazard, but he makes it. I move on to three-pointer distance. He makes that one too.

"You wanna join JV?" I joke.

He pushes his glasses up. "I am decidedly mediocre and have no plans to impress or disappoint. It was easier to get Mr. Ndiaye off my back if I was at least proficient at one sport in gym class in middle school. Plus, who doesn't love a *little* Freddie Prinze Junior *She's All That* energy?"

"Just because I watched one nineties movie with you doesn't mean I suddenly know about all the other ones."

He shakes his head. "You have no taste. The nineties were the classic rom-com era and set everything ablaze for the 2000s and onward. It's like the only thing my parents and I agree on. Have you *really* never even seen *Sleepless in Seattle*?"

I practice my dribbling. "They never interested me."

"Well at *least* see *But I'm a Cheerleader*. That's just necessary gay culture."

We play like that for a while, with letters being accumulated every three or so shots and more movies being added to my list.

"Y'know, all the hype around you isn't just popularity bullshit," Christopher says as he gets to HOR. "You are actually that good." He looks over at me and I turn my gaze back to the hoop. "You miss it."

He says it like a statement, not a question.

I sigh. "Is this for the article?"

"Sure, but I'd like to know too."

"Yeah." In this place, with the ball feeling like an extension of my body, I can't fight it. "But it doesn't change the fact that I can't go back."

He shrugs, trudging around the court. When he stops, he does three full spins before shooting. "Not *necessarily* true. I gave up guitar for two years when I flubbed a rendition of 'Landslide' in a seventh-grade talent show so badly I cried and everyone posted it on YouTube."

Ouch; I wince just imagining it.

"But this year, I started playing open mics again, and even though someone taped it and called it 'sequel to the crier's last performance,' it's like I'm getting to do it again on my own terms." He looks at me mischievously and does one of those silly backward shots.

Makes it. I roll my eyes as he cheers.

He hands me the ball and brushes his hand against my arm. The hairs shoot up on the ends, the nerves firing for no reason.

"Listen," Christopher says as I set up to try his shot. "As much fun as I can tell you're having, from what I see in that notebook, I think you miss more than putting the ball in the basket. I think what you really miss is being part of a team. We can be your team too—me, Amy, Tabby. You just have to trust us."

I miss the shot and Christopher hands me my notebook, acting like he's getting ready to leave mid-game. "Hey, wait, are you—?"

Christopher laughs. That crinkles-in-the-corners-of-his-eyes laugh. "I gotta get going on homework. I had HOR and you had HO. Maybe we'll pick this up next time. I wanna hear more about your grandpa."

With that, he disappears as quickly as he came.

We can be your team.

I think about Amy sharing her CBD gummies with me between classes when I was nervous about tests that suddenly matter; the way Tabby always bakes for us and is setting up a watch party for the newest Marvel movie after the door-to-door campaign; the way Christopher smiled when I said I googled what exactly an oboe is. The way I'm in group chats with Amy and Vote Squad, where they do everything from send video game reviews at three a.m. to help me with my math homework, beyond the difference we're trying to make together. I was so convinced for so long that basketball was *the* team, my only team, that we had the only purpose worth striving for. That I could only exist and thrive if I was gunning for a championship. But now I'm in multiple teams, having fun trying new things, not hiding anything.

Is he right?

Maybe, but as I shoot solo hoops, all that's around to answer me is the silence.

CHAPTER TWELVE

BY THE TIME FRIDAY ROLLS AROUND, I'M TAKING ONE FOR my new team by covering for Amy at the diner. She tells me that she told Richard she was sick, but I'm pretty sure she and Tabby are trying to score Phoebe Bridgers tickets for the show that's rolling through Atlanta next month. Which I can respect. But it's game night and whatever way it goes will determine what kind of shift this is. No one's giving me dirty looks as I check in with Richard yet at least. Much as I don't really want them to succeed without me, if they do, at least maybe by the end of the year I can just be another guy trying to exist in Chitwood.

If I were on the team, I'm sure I'd be a ball of nerves, researching the rival players, searching every angle to get our advantage back on the road to the championship. But now, it all feels so . . . silly. No one does this for debate team or some other high school extracurricular. Yet the team still has this whole town, mostly full-grown adults, spellbound. I've seen the complicated diagrams people leave on desks in school, on tables at the diner, or countertops at the grocery store. It seems almost everyone is freaking out trying to figure out how to come back and win it all. And for what? Does a basketball team winning a championship make anyone's lives that much better?

I check my phone before I make my way front of house. There's a text from Christopher.

Christopher

Quick pick a guitar based exclusively off which one you'd want Andrew Garfield Spider-Man to be holding when you see him in your dreams

Three pictures of various brightly colored electric guitars follow. He's been texting me as he runs around doing errands with his mom in the next town over. I quickly text him back my answer, wondering if this is another personality quiz to help with the article or if he's actually going to buy one, but then put my phone on Do Not Disturb. Can't risk mixing up orders or bursting out laughing during Amy's shift, although I'm surprisingly looking forward to seeing whatever barrage of texts he leaves me next.

I'm rag cleaning a booth when the cheering starts. I'm looking down, but I don't really need to look up to know who's walked in.

When I do, I accidentally catch Zack's gaze. He and the whole team are making themselves at home in the biggest booth we have, not even consulting a sighing James, my coworker who graduated from Chitwood the year before I got there. And of course it's one of my tables. I slide over to James and lean in.

"I'll split tips if you take the basketball team," I say.

James seems sold even though my tips are essentially nonexistent, but Ostrowski motions Richard over. I watch their interaction hoping I'm wrong, but when Richard returns, he shakes his head and points to me.

"They specifically requested you," Richard says.

He says it with a tone I know all too well. We don't refuse customers' requests, no matter how ridiculous.

One of the middle-aged guys at the table next to them leans over into the team's booth as I approach.

"It's the final stretch," he says to them. "Box out every chance you get! Three or four of them on hulks like that Lewinski guy."

I remember when I used to get comments and game strategy like that, how I'd have to smile and nod along. I remember being like Lochman, nudging Kyle and whispering in his ear, giving a verdict on if it was good advice or not. Coach always used to say to ignore what the townspeople said, even the ones who are former Wildcats themselves. *The game changes*. Ignore everyone except himself and Scratch. I channel that advice now into ignoring everything but taking this order so I can get through serving them.

I take a long, deep breath, adjust my shirt, and walk over.

Ostrowski smirks at me as I approach. "Oh hey, butt boy."

I move to the other end of the table.

. . . Where Zack is. He looks up at me and smiles. A genuine one, like he's stoked to see me. Like we haven't been avoiding each other since the Christmas fight. "Hey, Barc."

"What do you want to order?"

Zack frowns, a divot forming between his brows. "Come on, can we please just talk? I've been trying to catch you in the hall, texting you . . ."

I just can't deal with him right now. I've seen the texts, yeah, I couldn't get myself to block his number again. But I resent the doubt he put in my head about what we're doing, the panic in his voice when he talked about how hard it'd be for both of us to get into college if I go through with exposing Ostrowski. I don't need to be around someone who thinks my only value is in basketball, who is too afraid to take a stand on anything else.

"I've been busy," I mutter, and move to Anthony sitting next to him. I know Zack's breakfast, lunch, and dinner orders here anyway.

Country fried steak, substitute the mashed potatoes for loaded baked potato. If someone doesn't order onion rings for the table, that too.

Thankfully, Anthony, Russell, Kyle, Derek, and Boris don't cause any trouble. Pat is noticeably absent.

But then, of course, I get back to Ostrowski.

He peers over the menu, like he really needs to read it even though it's the only diner in town and it's only changed *once* in our lifetimes when Amy said we needed to have a Beyond Burger and the cook said he'd do black bean.

"I'll do the hot dog. I know you guys have sausage tacos, but I don't think I can trust you to know anything about tacos," he says.

"Great," I say, not rising to it.

"But do you have any buns besides white? I mean, I assume you know a lot about the perfect bun to put your wiener in." A few of the guys are snickering, and I can't control my stupid face from heating at this. "Maybe *Christopher* can give me a bun recommendation. Can you give me his number?"

This joke isn't any better than the usual shit Ostrowski passes off as humor. It's not better executed, it's not something I haven't seen drawn on my locker time and time again. But there's something about him saying Christopher's name that hits my breaking point.

"You must feel like such a big man bringing Christopher into this," I snarl. "Like you're not shitting your pants scared what he's gonna do with all your dad's dirty laundry. Maybe tell him he ought to go bigger with the next car he buys Horvath; compensating for your defense should cost more."

I walk back to the kitchen without another word and pin up all their orders, including *fucking hot dog* on the bottom of the list for our cook. For a few moments, I linger back there. Despite the heat from the stove, despite Richard in there checking inventory sure to ask what I'm doing any second, despite the tables filling up out there, it's a shelter from what I know will be waiting for me. I watch the window, expecting one of the players to poke their heads in to complain about me like a Karen in training.

No one does—but a few beats later, there's a crash.

Stomach clenching, I peek my head out as Richard jumps out the door to investigate.

The team's table is pushed several feet from the booth, and sugar and jam packets litter the floor. Ostrowski has launched himself across the booth space, toward Zack. He throws a punch that lands right between Zack's nose and left eye.

Richard, for all that Amy and I hate him, does manage to gun his way into the scuffle and intervene like a champ, screaming for them to cool it. It ends the event pretty quickly and Zack immediately rips away from the group. I think, for a fraction of a second, what would happen if I went out after him. But soon some of the other guys do instead and my moment comes and goes. I try to tell myself that I don't know it was about me, and instead I take a deep breath and turn back to the kitchen. Guess we can take their orders out of the queue. I reach for my little sheet of paper as Richard drops back into the kitchen.

He glares at me, nostrils flaring. "What did you say to them?"

I shake my head in disbelief. "What? They just started fighting. I was back here with you!"

Richard edges closer to me until he's right in my face. "After *you* took their table. Don't think I haven't noticed the way your little temper has been interfering with my customers. This is your last warning, Barclay. I should've fired you after what you did at the pep rally. I'm done with your stirring up—"

"But I didn't *do* anything. And where were you when Ostrowski was harassing me? Or any of your other customers for that matter."

"You're a *waiter*! If a little heckling is really setting you off, you're in the wrong damn business."

Heckling? Screw this.

I pull off my name tag. "I quit, then."

An itchy feeling nags at me as I head out of the diner, but I swallow it down. Before I can second-guess it again, I'm pulling out my phone and texting Christopher.

Me

I can tell you how Ostrowski's dad is influencing the school board to decide where the budget goes. It's definitely not legal. I'll tell you more in person.

I don't care if this torpedoes my college plans. I'd rather work another year at somewhere like Beau's and go to community college with the truth out than try to escape the guilt if I don't.

I get home early, expecting a silent house. Sure enough, Mom's still at work. But I can hear Maggie typing on her laptop from the couch in the living room, even though I'm pretty sure she should be at one of her art clubs. She's hunched over, hardcore into whatever she's doing. A half-eaten frozen meal sweats on the coffee table and her headphones are in, but she's not moving her head in a way that suggests she's jamming to anything.

Perfect time for a little sneak attack.

I creep up behind her, but just as I'm about to reach over and grab her shoulder, I catch a glimpse of her screen.

She's in Mom's email. I know it's easy to get into—Mom leaves all her passwords on a piece of paper in her bedroom—but why the hell would Maggie be on it?

And then I see it.

SUBJECT:
MARGARET ELLIOT - FAILURE NOTICE - URGENT

Maggie? Straight-A student, special feature at art showcases since she was in kindergarten, perfect attendance record Maggie? For a moment, I wonder if this is all some elaborate prank. But the harder I look at the email, the more I stare at the official logo of Chitwood Middle, it hits me.

Maggie's failing school and no one's mentioned it once.

"Failing?" I exclaim.

Maggie jumps so hard she nearly falls off the couch, clutching her laptop as it almost launches out of her grip. "When did you—?"

"How did *you* get Fs?"

She narrows her eyes. "It's not exactly hard. I wasn't even trying to slip up at first. It was impossible to concentrate on anything I liked with Gramps gone. Then when everything happened with you and you quit, it felt like why shouldn't I too? I mean, what's the point? It's not like Mom even cares anymore."

What is even happening? How could we have not noticed Maggie doing this? God, the thought sours inside me. Is this why she's been home so much?

"Do your friends know about this? I thought you were all like, nerd cheerleaders for each other or whatever."

Maggie glares at me. "What friends? The moment I stopped

wanting to sketch *all* the time, my art friends stopped inviting me to sleepovers and extra events. They said it was so disappointing that I missed the deadline for the winter art show. Even Emily stopped talking to me a month after Gramps died. She said I was too sad all the time."

"Why didn't you say anything?" I ask, incredulous.

"It wasn't like I even had a chance to. You've been taking over the drama for weeks. Devin has all his new college friends. Mom is always working again. Now that you threw basketball away, she has to work even harder for any chance of you not going into massive debt for college, which is all she can talk about when she is here. Or have you not noticed?"

The room jolts like someone suddenly turned while driving on the highway. "What do you mean? Yeah, Mom has been gone a lot, but she was just making up for . . ."

"The funeral? It's so much more than that. Haven't you heard her crying, like, every single night? Gramps was helping with some of the bills and now she doesn't even have that. She's had no choice but to push herself back even faster." I hang my head, but then she swallows distinctly, hard. "We *all* lost Gramps, you know. It's sucked for me too. But Mom told me not to freak you out about money because she thinks *you're* going through so much. So where does that leave me?"

I open my mouth to say something—to defend myself, to blame Mom. Like an asshole. I open my mouth to say something brotherly, to assure her that everything isn't as bad as she thinks and that she should relax and everything will fall into place. But none of that is right. Everything she just said—*that's* right. I've been so used to being single-lane focused whenever basketball season starts that I can hardly see anything around me. And even without it, I still couldn't see what was going on. Even when she's clearly struggling so much. It's so obvious now. The redness in her eyes, whether from crying or staying up too late. The way she's always shut up in her room.

And Mom—I squeeze my eyes shut—she's been so focused on making sure Maggie and I have a future that she isn't here to see what's going on with us now. But maybe that's on me too. When she said I couldn't do out of state, she meant tuition. I can't *afford* out-of-state tuition without basketball scholarships, not that I'm not good enough at anything else. What else have I been missing?

"Maggie, I'm so sorry," I say. I try to make eye contact, but she won't hold it with me. "I'm sorry Emily and your art friends are being such huge dicks to you. I don't know if you want to try to make up with them, but I'm here to help if I can. I'm sorry we haven't been paying attention to how you've been dealing with losing Scratch. I guess with basketball being our thing, I got wrapped up in how it was for me."

"He used to brainstorm art ideas with me when I had blocks, you know. He encouraged me to even try in the first place. Art was our thing. It was nice to be around him because *he* was the only one who really saw me. And now that he's not here, I don't know what to make art about, but it hurts so much to not be able to do it. I don't know what to do," she admits.

He was the only one who really saw me. God, do those words feel familiar. And I had Amy, Zack, and Christopher to fill the void. What has Maggie had?

"I get it. You feel alone right now and like it'll stay that way forever." I pause. "But I'll be here a lot more. I quit the diner and I'll have more time to spend with you. There's a show I really wanna watch with you. Maybe I can help you find a new muse for your art."

Maggie throws up her hands. "That's *worse*, you idiot! Now you have no money coming in to help Mom! Are you going to quit *everything*?" She jumps to her feet. "Why would I ever depend on you? You think you're so much better, but basketball was the only thing that made you interesting. Now you're just like me."

She runs off, shutting herself in her room, leaving her laptop behind. I wish I could go in there and fix this, but I clearly have no idea what to say. So I sit, eyes on Maggie's laptop like a bomb, waiting for Mom to come home.

I wait hours. I prepare what I'm going to say, plan out where we should sit when I break the news. I try to account for every variable. When Mom does finally come home, though, she looks positively beaten. All my strategies fly out the window.

"Hey," I say as she walks in.

She doesn't even seem to hear me. Just goes right for the fridge, places her keys in there, and pulls out a pan of leftovers. She sets them on the counter and just drops onto a chair.

"Do you want me to heat that up?" I ask her.

"What's that, honey?" Mom says, finally turning to me.

"Dinner. Do you want me to heat it up?"

"Oh, sure." She gives me a weak smile. "Thank you."

Something tugs at me, says, *Do it later*. But Maggie can't wait anymore. I grab a spatula, carve her a square of the lasagna she made, and stuff it into the microwave.

As it hums, I take a seat beside her. "Did you know Maggie's been dropping out of all her art stuff and is failing school?"

I open up the laptop and pull up the most recent conversation that Maggie didn't have time to log out of. "What?" Mom straightens back up as she takes the laptop and reads. I tense, waiting in the seconds that feel like hours for her reaction. For her to freak out, charge into Maggie's room demanding answers and starting a screaming match.

But all she does is drop her head into her hands. "How could I have let this happen?"

"Maggie told me about the money stuff. I have more time now, I can . . . do more work around the house, or get another job." I can't tell her about the one I just quit, not now. "But about Maggie. What can we do to help her?"

Her eyes and mouth are soft, but her expression is almost desperate. "If you really want to help me out, you'll go back to the team." She puts a hand on my shoulder. It burns. "Where you belong. I'm sure they must all be over this by now. If you get a scholarship, I can be home more."

I keep thinking someone's snapped the last straw, but this time, God, when the straw breaks, I collapse too. She's my *mom*. How could she think this could possibly be a phase? That this part of me is something for people to get over?

"Basketball won't fix what's wrong here," I say as I shove Maggie's laptop into her still-shaking hands. "And it really fucking sucks that you still think that."

She whirls around to face me, her expression twisting in anger that somehow seems inevitable. "Oh, really? Tell me, my sixteen-year-old son, what your plan is or how you would've parented better?"

"Maybe Maggie and I have needed you for other shit these past few months. Maggie says she gave up on art because Scratch used to be here to help her. And you've been so focused on me and basketball you didn't even notice that we were hurting, especially Maggie. I came out because—"

"You came out in a spectacle! You opened yourself up to . . . It could've gone so much worse than it did, Barclay. I thought you *knew*. Sports, even in a progressive-growing state like Georgia, it's not welcoming to gay players. Especially not programs where you're the first one. I am so proud of you for trying, but if you had come to me before, I could've prepared you! We could've gone into this situation *together*! We could've found a way for you to be yourself and keep basketball. But how could I have ever tried to help you when I had *no idea*? You didn't give me the chance until it was too late!"

Is she trying to pin this on *me*? "*How* could I talk to you? You spent every day after he died in your room crying! The second I came out you were at work! I needed to be out right then and *you* weren't ready to be my mom then."

She stares at me. Really stares at me, X-rays through me, as I find myself shaking. But seconds pass and the anger that sprouted falls away from her soft, worn face. It's almost scary how much older she seems in the few months since we lost him.

"I know," she says, her voice soft. "I know I failed you as a mother. I failed Maggie and Devin too. And I'm so sorry." She pauses before looking over to me with all her weary strength. "I've been just trying to get by and keep everything afloat. I had a good job and there weren't any more threats about a sudden new round of chemo for Dad since he was doing so well." She winces along with me. "But then the funeral, Devin's college starting, and especially when basketball season rolled around." She looks away. "Plus"—she pauses this long, painful beat—"your dad has a new girlfriend he moved in with in Canada. He's stopped sending child support." Those last two sentences come out like gasps, tapering off like a deflated balloon until she's not breathing anymore. She's crying.

And not just a few tears spilling down her face that she'll swipe away and pretend I didn't see. Red-faced, body-trembling, spit-dribbling-onto-her-hand sobs that she tries to muffle so Maggie can't hear. I can't help but think this is what she looked like all those nights I stayed in bed. All those years I let Devin comfort her after Dad left.

Jesus, Dad has a girlfriend. This is about so much more than money. Like, look, personally, any guy who runs out on his family when his oldest kid isn't even out of high school isn't worth much space in my mind. He was always sulking and picking fights with Mom and Devin, anyway. The house is more peaceful without him. As far as I've been concerned, I had my grandpa and Devin. I didn't need another male figure in my life. But more than that, I had Mom.

Maybe that's why it's been so hard to feel like I didn't. But it never occurred to me that years later Mom was still affected by the Dad stuff too. I feel myself not knowing what to do or say, like always, but I won't let it stop me from trying this time. I hug her, envelop her in my arms like I'm the adult here, and I hold her until her sobs fade away. Finally, she pulls away and takes my hand.

"Barclay, I love you with every fiber of my being," she says, strength returning to her voice. "There is nothing you can ever do to change that. Every new thing you discover about yourself that you feel comfortable telling me I will embrace. I'm sorry you felt like you had to navigate coming out alone. I'm sorry I made you feel like I cared about basketball more than your mental health." She takes a deep, shaky breath. "I was so focused on the future, but I'm going to be there for you kids. For you, now. Whatever you need me to be, I'll do it."

She really means it this time. Just the thought of having her back, of having her asking us about our days and trying to brainstorm solutions to problems again, feels almost as good as thinking about times when we still had Scratch. A normal I never let myself really miss.

It could be a new normal now, I guess.

"Okay," I say. "I'll help too. I'm sorry for being so selfish. I get it—there's so much more going on. You've been dealing with so much more than I ever thought." And even the thought of trying to help Mom scoop up all the balls she's juggling makes my throat tighten, but I have to do something. "I'll take the college stuff seriously and I'll help with Maggie." I pause, guilt twinging inside me. "Even if, well, I just quit my job."

She sighs and squeezes my shoulder. "We'll make it work."

The next morning, I wake to Mom and Maggie in the kitchen. All of Maggie's school stuff is spread out along with folders and highlighters and planners. They're both so intent, mumbling about some academic rescue plan, that I grab my breakfast and tiptoe back up before I disturb them. Already, Mom's fulfilling her promise from last night. I have no idea how to start on mine, though.

I think about it over breakfast until my phone dings, breaking me out of a trance. It's 9:58 a.m. Who could be texting me?

Christopher
I'm outside.

He's *where*?
Oh my God. It's door-to-door day.

Me
I thought we were meeting at the corner?

Christopher
Lmao didn't trust you to actually make it.

Me
Didn't trust you to mind your own business so I'm not surprised either

Shit. I don't have time to shower. Even if it's Christopher, I can't smell like I just rolled out of bed. No, *especially* because it's Christopher I can't. I refuse to be dunked on for five hours straight. So I settle for mouthwash and doing the ole baby wipe and body spray routine. I have short enough hair that I can get away with it like I styled it to be messy at least. I shove on the voting T-shirt Amy got me, basketball shorts, and I'm off. I sneak my way past Maggie and Mom and open the door for Christopher.

He's wearing the voting T-shirt, bright cherry-blossom-print shorts, and white sneakers. "The latest in Japanese fashion?" I ask.

Christopher furrows his brow a moment before looking down, then whipping his gaze up to meet mine. The playful look shines in his eyes, today a little more green than gray, and I know he remembers the jeans he sent me too. "Australian, actually."

We start walking to the neighborhood pocket Amy assigned us. Even though I was up so late with Mom last night, I have the energy of several cups of coffee I didn't drink. "So I'm thinking we can add a little strategy to this. There are a ton of young families and they won't want to be interrupted until the kids are settled. The teens won't be awake until twelve anyway. So we start with the senior citizens, maybe changing it up if we see people on their porches not doing anything interesting."

Christopher laughs. "Should we be doing a team chant to get our heads in the game?"

I refuse to respond to two *High School Musical* references in less than a month. "And we start with Berry Street because the blue house on the corner had a Black Lives Matter sign."

"But then wouldn't they have already voted?" Christopher asks.

"Maybe, but even if they did, they have a kid who's a senior at Chitwood. He might not have registered yet." Despite himself, he nods, impressed.

We pass Amy and Tabby along the way. Both are wearing the T-shirts, though Amy has hers tied at the bottom so she's showing a slice of stomach. Tabby's holding a batch of cupcakes. I seize up, waiting for the lashing from Amy for abandoning her shift yesterday, but she must not know yet. She just gives me one of her signature unenthusiastic waves. Tabby, on the other hand, crosses the street and holds out the cupcake container for us. These are chocolate, all spelling out "vote" with one letter on each cupcake. Like fancy Hostess cupcakes.

Christopher smiles as he takes one. Before I can grab one, he takes a bite and throws Tabby a thumbs-up. "Wow, Tabby, these are great," he says. "You figured out how to make the hollow in the middle for frosting!"

And Tabby lights up like a Christmas tree. "Thanks, Christopher! Yeah, I did. That video you sent really helped."

He presses his thumb and index finger together in the *perfect* gesture. I grab a cupcake, determined to say something nice this time, but as soon as I have it in my hands, Amy motions for Tabby to follow her. I never thought about Tabby spending all that time trying to learn and perfect something for the rest of us. Even now that we've been hanging out a little, I still hardly know anything about her. Just like Maggie.

I look to Christopher, who's studying me. "Everything okay?"

I nod my head *yeah*, even though it isn't.

Christopher follows my advice, and we go to the blue house first. He knocks distinctly, three hard raps, before pulling back, cinching his hands together behind his back.

A woman answers the door. White, bottle blond, maybe in her forties, and distinctly *not* part of the family I thought lived there. I look back and realize the BLM sign is gone. My heart speeds up. I'm hoping Christopher won't know the difference.

"Morning, ma'am," Christopher says. "Could we have a minute of your time to talk about voting?"

The woman visibly sighs. "Just give me the flyer."

But Christopher doesn't hand a flyer over to the woman, like he knows she's just going to trash it. "We're hoping to bring awareness to more of the local issues on the ballot. After all, what does voting matter if it's not making tangible change, right? We have a school board election coming up too."

"Please, kid, I'll take the flyer. I have to get back to—" the woman says.

"They're even voting on an alternate emergency response team," Christopher says quickly, bringing up something I've heard Amy mention, but never thought would be useful for us. "It would create a way to deal with noise disturbances and neighborly disputes more fluidly and quicker."

This actually gets the woman to lean forward a little. "Really?"

"Yeah," Christopher says. "And registration is easier than ever now."

"I haven't re-registered since moving here from California," she admits.

Christopher smiles. "Well, welcome to the neighborhood. Your vote can bring some of the legal weed and gay rights of California here, just with some Southern charm."

I don't even have time to start having a panic attack before the woman laughs. "Well, when you put it that way, I'm in."

Christopher finally hands her a flyer. "Plus, print out your registration and you can get a free entree at Grand Street Cafe."

It's only once the woman closes the door that I turn to Christopher in utter disbelief. My heart's finally slowing down. "Wasn't that a little risky?"

Christopher laughs. "Barclay, friend, straight girls don't wear rings on their middle fingers."

What?

"I . . ."

He smirks, holding up just his middle finger knuckle. "Or have two interconnected woman symbols tattooed on said knuckle."

I look at my own bare knuckles, remembering how I used to be the one catching a game-changing detail like that.

We might actually get somewhere.

The next few houses fly by way more smoothly than I could've ever expected. Not everyone takes our flyers the way the first woman did, but no one slams the door in our faces. When Christopher's in the zone, he's *in the zone*, as dedicated to getting his way as he is with my interview. And I take all the skill I used for analyzing defenders for weak spots to get around them for my shots and turn it to persuading people. Every defender had something visible in the way they stood, the way they moved their bodies, how they'd look at me and what they'd say to me that revealed their strategy. Turns out, even annoyed middle-aged Chitwoodians will reveal their openings too—sports hats and shirts with slogans, children-at-play signs outside their homes, stuff that indicates what they think is important. Between the two of us, well, we make a pretty convincing pair. Not that I'll ever tell Amy.

By the time we're onto a new block after getting through our first, I'm feeling pretty good.

But the feeling, well, it doesn't last. Because, as I realize from the name on the mailbox, the next house on our list is Mr. Durkin's.

Mr. Durkin's hardware store is a few plots down from the diner. He used to wave to me as I biked to school every morning, even hang a big sign in his window with my name on it. That sign was in a dumpster when I left the first game.

I'm rooted to the sidewalk, but Christopher is already up the driveway and knocking on the door before I can warn him.

Mr. Durkin opens the door just as I get there. I'm hoping he'll just slam the door in our faces like we're annoying traveling salesmen or Jehovah's Witnesses (he's a strict Baptist). But he looks us up and down, slowly. Like he has all the time in the world to deal with us and not because he's interested in what we're peddling. His nostrils flare when he gets to Christopher's bright shorts.

"Afternoon, sir," Christopher says. "Could we have a moment of your time to talk about voter registration?"

"No, you may not and that goes for the rest of the houses here too," he says. "This is a *family* neighborhood."

It's not unexpected, but it still stings. Christopher seems unfazed, though. He just adjusts his glasses and keeps going. "It really is a great family neighborhood, I agree, sir. But seeing as Barclay and I are merely standing on your porch, I'd say we're fitting right into that parameter. Standing around while being gay isn't any less family-friendly than standing around and being straight."

"This isn't New York or LA or any other liberal cesspool," Mr. Durkin snaps. "We have decency down here. You choose to be like that and I can choose to get you the hell off my property, by any means necessary."

My head's swimming, a million thoughts flying through it that have all combined into a sludge I can't understand. I grab Christopher's shirtsleeve.

"Come on, Christopher, let's go," I say.

But he won't budge. In fact, he doesn't even look nervous. I run my hand through my sweaty hairline as I attempt to save Christopher from being punched for the first time in his life. "I'm sorry, Mr. Durkin," I say in my waiter voice. "We didn't mean to upset you. You know me from basketball, so we just thought—"

Nothing in this man's face is readable, but apparently, it's not Christopher's shorts that set this man off. It's basketball, because at this his icy veneer finally cracks. "Is this really what you do to make your mother proud? She loses her father, then you abandon the team that was counting on you just to go be a fairy with this little fag and try to get more fairies elected to ruin our schools even more?"

Christopher touches my chest, quick, almost imperceptible. A *stay still* sign. "If you want to refer to our sexuality, just 'gay' will suffice. But as we were saying, voter registration is a few weeks away and every vote counts, especially for bipartisan issues being brought before the school board, and—"

What happens next happens incredibly fast. Mr. Durkin opens

his door a little wider, exposing an end table right by the door. An end table with a pack of cigarettes and a shotgun.

He doesn't reach for the cigarettes.

The barrel of the gun goes right into Christopher's face. My heart's hammering so hard I swear it's going to burst out of my chest. We have to get out of here. Now.

But Christopher is just staring down the barrel like it's nothing.

I grab the back of Christopher's shirt and give it a tug.

He takes a step back, but first he puts a flyer on top of Durkin's gun.

"We'll just leave this with you, I think we've done what we came here to do," Christopher says.

I count the steps it takes for us to walk down Durkin's driveway. Out of his yard. Behind his fence. Down to the next house. I can't even bear looking back to see if he's lowered the gun. But I don't hear footsteps behind us at least.

Once we make it to the next driveway, I don't stop there. I force myself to keep walking on jelly legs. Way down the block.

"Hey! Barclay, we missed this house!" Christopher calls.

"Nope, nope, nope," I mutter to myself.

I stop at the end of the block before my legs all but give out. The corner house has a stone fence, so I drop onto that. Holy shit. We could've—we almost—and Christopher—

He approaches, bobbing his weight back and forth like he was just on a jog. "What gives? We're not done."

"Were you not fucking scared?" I demand, my voice *almost* cracking for the first time since puberty.

"Well, a little," Christopher admits. "Guns aren't meant to be friendly. But messed up as it is, I kinda doubt that that guy would blast away two white boys in the middle of the day in front of the whole neighborhood." He wrings his wrists and there's a long pause until he finally speaks again. "And . . . well I'm just done not standing up for myself. When I first came out to this guitar teacher I was working with, he said he couldn't work with me the next time I tried to schedule an appointment. I just pretended it never happened, bombed the talent show, and the guy is still in business. I can't sleep sometimes thinking he's crushing the soul of some other queer kids. I wish I'd stood up for myself. For all the kids who come after me. So, I made a promise to myself not to be intimidated by who I am. Not by anyone."

Every time I think I understand Christopher a bit more, he just adds another layer. Somehow Christopher, this skinny pasty guy who plays the oboe, has a John McClane side. I just don't know, though, how Christopher's kind of bravery can exist.

I ask before I can stop myself. "But how? How does it not bother you what other people think about you? My thirteen-year-old sister calling me uninteresting still burns."

"Well, it does burn." He holds up his palm. "But you know what? We're the ones who have to live with ourselves in the end." I expect him to launch into another story, but Christopher's stomach rumbles instead. Finally, he says, "We can talk more, but after lunch."

Live with myself. It was so hard to live with myself when I was closeted, every moment a kick in the back reminding me that I wasn't being the real me. But now that I am the "real me," it's not like I've felt any better—but I guess I haven't really *been* living.

"Do you just have these speeches ready to go?" I ask.

"Yup, just in case there's ever a pep rally without any drama," Christopher adds with a smile.

• • •

Christopher and I don't go back up into the neighborhood, not yet. Instead, we end up at the park. We both go to Mr. Hafeez's halal cart without even discussing it. He has been saving up money for a brick-and-mortar restaurant for a decade now, which of course Christopher already knows. Mr. Hafeez gladly tells us that he's only a couple thousand off from his goal now. Christopher hands him a pamphlet as I focus on fishing out a decent tip and finding us a bench to catch some sun. It's barely gotten any warmer since this morning, and all Mr. Hafeez sells are ice-cold Cokes.

Once the two of us sit on the bench, I can't help but notice that we aren't on opposite sides. We're a normal distance apart. Maybe six inches. Friend distance. Distance that we could steal bites of each other's food if needed.

As we eat, I find myself flipping what he said over in my mind again and again. There's so much of Christopher's story I don't know. I wonder what made him come out. Would he have done what I did, considering how open he is with his sexuality?

When I open my mouth, though, that's not what spills out first.

"My mom and I got into a fight last night." Christopher looks over to me, still chewing. "We fixed it, but we were talking about how I came out. She basically said I rushed into it and didn't think enough about the consequences. And I found some stuff out about my sister and her and it made me realize there's so much else I wasn't seeing too. Do you think she was right?"

Christopher takes a swig of Coke before answering. "I think you can never really know how people will react or what's right for someone else. But I also don't think I would ever have come out at a pep rally. That's a *lot* of variables."

"I know but—" I exhale, trying to ignore the way my throat's suddenly itchy. "Scratch meant everything to me. He was like a grandpa, dad, and best friend all in one. I got myself through the grueling extra training we did over the summer after our loss in the championship by thinking of his face the next time I could take home that trophy. It was all for him and then—" I pause, blinking through the stinging in my eyes. "—then he was gone. He was the kind of guy who'd cheer the loudest at games, defend anyone who needed defending, even if it insulted his friends. Hell, he saved two guys in his platoon back in Vietnam, dragged them a mile to safety. He was so untouchable, you know? I thought I'd have all the time in the world."

Christopher's gray eyes get watery. I swallow the lump in my throat.

"I thought coming out the way I did would be the bravest thing to do," I continue. "To honor how brave *he* was. But it didn't fix anything. It didn't make me feel better about how I didn't tell him. It didn't make the school a more accepting place. It didn't even fix anything with my family. I just lost more people and now everyone hates me."

"Okay, wait," Christopher says. His hand falls to my knee. I think it's just to get me to stop, but all it does is send a shock through my body. "Why do you think *everyone* hates you? It seems like some people have been totally cool with it."

I look to him, skeptical—hasn't he been listening? It almost overpowers the tingling of his hand on me. He sighs.

"Not the Ostrowskis or the Durkins of the world. They can choke," he says. "I mean someone like Tabby; she's had your back, right? And even someone like your friend Zack. Have you talked to *him* about it? Like really talked since that day? Maybe there's stuff he's realizing he didn't see before too."

Christopher pulls his hand away as my leg muscle twitches under him. "I did talk to Zack. He told me I was selfish because I didn't put the team first and then he was all chickenshit about doing anything that might hurt Ostrowski, but didn't care about hurting me."

Christopher cocks his head at me. "But that doesn't sound like he hates you. It sounds like he just doesn't understand. But that doesn't mean he can't, especially if you're willing to have the hard conversations. And look, I get it. Straight cis people don't have to do this and you shouldn't have to try this hard. But some people aren't hateful; they just . . . don't know how to react in the moment. It doesn't make it right, but sometimes they can blossom into amazing allies. I don't know anything about this Zack guy besides that he plays basketball, so maybe I'm wrong, but I know you guys were close and I hate to see you think that just because coming out wasn't awesome that it can't get better. We're out here because we believe that we can change people's minds—get them to care. Maybe he's one of the ones that can change." His words hit deep, like they're pressing on a bruise. I try to process them, but I don't know what to say.

Christopher sighs. "I know, you probably think I still don't get it. But I haven't been totally straightforward about my coming-out story with you. I had a boyfriend at the time, and we were really careful about who we were out to. My parents knew about him, but his didn't know about me. None of his friends either. It was really need-to-know. But at some point, rumors started circulating about us being a couple. It was just a group of idiots, not like the whole school, but I figured we'd be better off just coming out. Someone rumored to be gay is gossip, but a gay kid just living his life is boring, you know?

"So we wrote up this really cute matching coming-out post. I posted mine, but I waited and waited and his didn't go up. I texted him, but he didn't answer. I got scared, but my mom made me go to school." He pauses. "When I got there, the guys who'd started the rumors were all waiting by my locker with the photo from the coming-out post taped up on it. They all accused me of being a creepy stalker and told me to leave my boyfriend alone. When I confronted him later, he said that the bullies cornered him and asked him if were dating and he got so scared that he reflexively told them that I was just obsessed with him."

God. "Christopher, I'm so—"

"Obviously, we broke up. I transferred right after and then we moved down here. But my side of the story was just"—he shakes his head—"lost. I don't want anyone's stories to be lost like that again."

I find myself shaking my head too. "All that happens to you and your response is to come out immediately in Georgia? To stick up for people just like you? Just like that? And I thought *I* was being brave."

"Hey, don't put me on that pedestal. I've been keeping that inside me. I never told anyone else that and I haven't dated anyone since. And for what? Don't be like me, Barclay. Holding in the pain doesn't make it go away." His hand returns to my knee. But it doesn't jolt me this time. It's warm. Assuring. Steady. "Maybe it's time for you to stop running from your pain. Maybe the brave thing you needed to tell people wasn't just that you're gay, but that you're grieving. I know that awful feeling of hiding bubbling up inside you until you can't take it anymore and you just have to say it. I can't imagine what it must've been like to feel that *and* feel like you couldn't talk about your grandpa. It's not weak to admit you need support and ask for it even if you feel like you shouldn't have to. And you know what? It's *brave* to give people a second chance in spite of that. A chance to do better."

Two months. It's been two months and no one has said anything remotely like this to me. It's like he's soothing wounds I'd hacked shut, forming proper stitches.

I don't say anything for a bit. Christopher doesn't need me to, though. He just rubs his thumb against my knee, and neither of us try to move. We could sit this way all day.

But then I remember Amy. The team.

"I have a lot to think about now," I say, cracking out a smile. "Are you gonna write all that down for the article?"

Christopher smiles back. "I just might." He takes a deep breath. "Speaking of the article, maybe this is a bad time, but are you sure you want to follow up on the lead about the team funds? I got the feeling that was an emotional decision."

"I am," I say, no hesitation, but it feels different than last night. "This isn't revenge anymore. It's just what's true."

"So what've you got?"

"Well, you and Amy know how Ostrowski has been moving funds from the performing arts and other clubs to basketball so his travel company can make our tournament arrangements—"

Christopher huffs. "It sucks, but it's not illegal. The school can hire a local parent's company."

I smirk. "Yeah, but buying Horvath a car so he'll agree to adjust the school budget to use his company is. That's why the stop sign wasn't fixed up either. The money wasn't just taken from clubs, it came from everywhere. And I'll bet anything the rest of the board got pricey 'presents' too."

Christopher's eyes go wide first, then a smile slowly creeps onto his face. "Ho-ly shit."

We finish our lunch and get back to our route, discussing possible leads as we go.

A month ago, a week ago, hell—a couple hours ago—I would've never been able to get up and get back to work like this.

But somehow Christopher keeps finding ways to surprise me into doing more than I think I can.

For the first time in a while, I think maybe I don't have to accept how things are. If I'm going to make myself a better, brighter, stronger future, I can't hold all these grudges. I just have to live my life, really live it, and maybe people might see the real me like I've been wanting. Or maybe they won't. But that part, at least, isn't on me. And even though I have no idea where to start, I feel lighter just thinking it.

CHAPTER THIRTEEN

THE WILDCATS LOSE ALL THREE GAMES IN THE FIRST TWO weeks of January. Meaning they now need to win every game left, including the Panthers rematch in three weeks, to make the playoffs. And the Panthers have been doing amazing this season off the momentum of our disastrous first game. It's grim all over town. Last week, that would've probably had me wanting to skip school and hide in my room, but come Monday after the door-to-door event, I'm feeling great. Even the people hissing in my direction for once just feel like nothing to me.

After grabbing my books out of my thankfully not-defaced locker, I head over to Amy and Christopher at his. The two of them are already smiling and Amy wheels around to face me, slapping me on the shoulder.

"Here's my transformed Wonder Bread king," she says.

Christopher snickers. "She's just pumped because Brianna's team sent us a great update."

"They got almost *double* the web traffic they usually get this weekend and a bunch of young voters registered! We're really making a real impact. Not to mention *all* our ideas are officially listed on her platform online."

Christopher throws me a smile. "Almost makes getting threatened with death worth it."

Amy shoots Christopher a warning look, although I don't know if it's from Christopher joking about the situation or not running away. "But meanwhile, we've got some key dates to prep for. I really want to try to get the students here more involved in the rally at the end of the month, but it's hard when we're not an official group."

"Do we have any update on if Ms. Cho is going to put your Brianna profile in this week's paper? It'd be great to start the publicity early," Christopher asks her.

"She'll probably need me to soften it for the admin, but maybe if I frame it like a 'meet the candidate who wants to save your clubs' and we pair it with your profile on Barclay? We can angle it with the same interview format so it seems like an assignment, not us spewing opinions. I bet Ms. Cho will let me interview students about the budget cuts to the arts to make it more student-centered."

She points at Christopher. "Now you, how's the misappropriations from the school board article coming? Ms. Cho says it's last pitches today for articles to publish before the election. If you have real evidence, she says she'll have ammo to try and publish it."

"I finally found a place to start," Christopher answers, shooting me a knowing smile. It sets off a spark inside me.

"Great. Let's follow it up fast, then. If we can get it out the week of the election, it'll be fresh in everyone's minds and give them something to show their parents."

The bell rings and we break as if we were in a pregame huddle. The sense of purpose from it all shifts how I walk through the whole morning period. Whereas the past several months I've been looking down, so hyperaware of eyes on me, today I start to notice what's going on around me. I'm on time to all my classes and I actually have my homework done. Some of my teachers smile at me now that I'm

171

trying harder. But even better—they're smiling at me and I know it has nothing to do with a game. No more pity, no more tricks, no more favors. When they compliment me on a good answer, it's genuine. Jake even jokes with me when we bump into each other after English. But mostly it's just normal, neutral. It's starting to feel like the pep rally was drama and that drama faded, for everyone but me. They don't seem to *hate* me so much anymore. Maybe they never did, really.

When we have a lab for chemistry and we're asked to pick partners, I find myself rushing over to Tabby instead of waiting for everyone to pair off. She seems startled at first, but as I ask her if she can fill out the handout while I mix the chemicals, there's no forgetting the grin on her face. And she totally has me cracking up as she shares stories about her and Amy literally *dancing* to convince one of the Chitwoodians to register to vote.

I'm still riding high as I take my weird cafeteria pizza to the newspaper room, ready to see how we can get started on everything we talked about this morning. But as soon as I arrive, I see Amy's pacing outside. And not Amy Thinking pacing. Amy Is Pissed pacing.

I approach Christopher, who's unwrapping a sandwich while leaning against the wall.

"Aim, come on, at least don't waste your energy," Christopher says.

"What happened?" I say, pushing my way into the conversation.

Amy takes a deep breath before turning to me. "Christopher and I just got back from the principal's office. We've been removed from the school paper for being 'too political.' I *tried* to ask how encouraging students to become aware of issues in their community and exercise their rights was *too political*, but Horvath said that was just his 'final decision.' Fucking bullshit. One article that hasn't even come out yet, and he even removed Ms. Cho as the advisor! Newspaper is screwed!"

No. No, this can't be happening. Ms. Cho has been a lifesaver in our fight to get the truth out with newspaper, going to bat against the administration. So many students said they found out about the rally through the newspaper. It was our best source of getting our stuff out there. We can't let Brianna down. Not now. Not this close.

Amy pauses, fuming. "At first I thought they figured out about Vote Squad. But we haven't exactly been hiding that. It doesn't make sense."

She slams her fist against the door for good measure. I wince. I don't know what Amy thinks happened, but whatever is left of my good mood plummets when I realize I know. The fight at the diner didn't just end with Ostrowski throwing a punch at Zack. He went and punched right where it'd hurt us.

"So I don't think I told you I pissed off Ostrowski at the diner last week . . . ," I say.

"You did *what*?" Amy turns to me with white-hot intensity in her eyes. I'm like eight inches taller than her and I still balk.

"I mean, Barclay egging him on or not, it's not surprising," Christopher says. His voice is still even, but this isn't Calm Christopher. His fingers are digging into the soft bread of his sandwich, his back ramrod straight, like when he was staring down Durkin. "We were afraid the school board was going to intervene eventually. So plan B. I'll just make a blog and publish our Brianna and corruption articles along with Barclay's finished profile before the rally." He winks at me. "We'll blast it all out on social. None of us are going to be silenced; that's the whole point of our project. I'll start teasing the article at my open mic next week so people know to look for it."

"Wait," I say. "That's great, but it isn't enough." Amy and Christopher look to me expectantly. I don't know if they've done that before. "I think we need to go for the jugular and call him out at the rally itself. The article will have all the facts to cover our bases, but we should make sure everyone knows what he's been doing before the election." I stand up straighter. "And I can be the one to say it. They'll know I had access from being on the team, at least some of them should believe I'm telling the truth." I look to Christopher, who's gotten some color back. "As for where to start, Lochman's dad is the one who sold Mr. Ostrowski the car. He seemed confused that Mr. Ostrowski wasn't the one driving it, and he also happened to love telling Zack and me how efficient he is since he started using the same password for his home Wi-Fi and all his email logins."

Christopher and Amy exchange a conspiratorial look before Christopher says, "I'll have it ready by the rally."

Despite the new setbacks in Vote Squad's reach on campus, Amy is ready in full force to get back out there. She breaks our meeting before lunch ends so she and Christopher can start digging, and I find myself walking the mostly empty halls. I'll have to prepare a really kick-ass speech to get everyone fired up and invested before the Mr. Ostrowski reveal. How could we promote this rally to get more people there? We got a lot of Chitwood High people last time, but there are parents at the lower schools and local adults to target. Maybe there's some way to advertise within town?

That might even be a nice way to involve Maggie. She can make us some really amazing promo art. The idea of pitching this to Maggie brightens the usually drab view of the halls as I walk through.

I quickly find myself passing by the gym, where I hear Ostrowski's yells from within. The team doesn't usually do practice at lunch, but I guess they're in emergency mode.

As much as I want to linger, to get another tendril of information, I keep going. I'm by the lowerclassmen lockers when I see Pat of all people standing in front of his.

Against all my better judgment, I stop. "Why aren't you at practice?" I ask. "I could hear Ostrowski shouting from down the hall."

When Pat looks over to me, I hold back showing my surprise. He looks like he's about to cry. "Coach made Ostrowski captain."

Of course. "Not Chase?"

"No. Not that it'd be much better with Chase." He rubs his eyes, although they're still dry. "I get why you did what you did. Being on the team was basically hell."

There's something so small and pathetic in Pat's voice as he speaks. Something I wonder if everyone else saw in me. "Was—?"

"Ostrowski made my life a living hell playing. I couldn't do anything right. He never passed to me during the games and then said it was my fault for being lazy on the court. And my dad believes it. So I decided I'm done too. I'll find some other way to get to college."

God, and Pat didn't even have a few years of padding before hitting the same rock bottom I'm at. He didn't do anything to deserve dealing with this. He's so talented. It's such a waste that he didn't even get a chance to prove himself. He shouldn't have to give it up.

"Hey, wait." I can't believe I'm saying this, but I continue. "You love basketball, don't you?" He nods. "So don't let them take it away from you. Ostrowski will be gone by the end of the season. So will Chase and Boris and Kyle. You'll see, the team will keep shifting, and you'll have more influence next year too. It's worth sticking it out for if you love it."

Pat looks away from me. "Then why did you quit?"

It stings. "Different situation." I pause. "But you know I'm right."

Pat takes a deep breath. "Maybe. I still wish you hadn't."

As I watch Pat walk to the gym, I realize it's the first time some-one has said this not to guilt me or use me. And maybe that's why for the first time I let myself wish I hadn't too.

Vote Squad ends up switching our planning session that day to the diner after school, since Amy's convinced Horvath has ears every-where. She still gets her discount and I have to admit that I still really like the food here. Plus, Richard isn't around today to glare at me for my sudden departure. (Or for me to beg for my job back.) In the wake of the last Wildcats loss, Richard has increased the "Wildcat" discounts on the special board. With fewer wins to celebrate, I guess it's the only way to keep people coming in during the usual season surge. This week's is titled WILDCAT ALUMNI GAME DISCOUNT — 50% OFF ALL APPS 5–6 PM ALL WEEK.

Christopher types away while Amy and I inhale sandwiches. I notice his tongue sticks out when he's concentrating hard. It's kind of adorable.

Adorable?

Since when do I find Christopher adorable? Is this some kind of slippery slope to cute? I can't think Christopher's cute. The next step from cute is handsome which leads to hot which—

"Can I have a fry?" Christopher asks, eyeing my plate.

But instead of shoving the basket toward him, for some reason I pluck one out and hand it to him. Salt transfers from my fingers to his.

"Thank God for this alumni game special. Fries taste even better when they're fifty percent off," Christopher says.

His foot brushes mine under the table.

I try to focus on what Christopher said. The alumni game, right. "I love—loved—the alumni game."

"Really? What is it?"

"It's been a tradition for decades. Basically, during an extended halftime, the current team plays a set of team alumni who volunteer. Sometimes it's college guys, but usually it's middle-aged and grandpa-aged guys, so it's more the teams joking around for half an hour. Scratch—" My throat's starting to tighten a little, so I focus on selecting a fry for myself. I prefer them crispier, but I got a softer batch. "It was our thing."

"Why don't we go?" Christopher suggests.

"No way. If I ever decide to attend a game again, the last thing I need is more people there."

Christopher shakes his head. "Come on! It's good for the article. It's important to see you in your once-natural habitat. Besides, you gave up the team, but that doesn't mean you have to give up ever *seeing* basketball again." He shoots me a grin. "Your jock head would explode."

The idea of it forces its way into my brain. Christopher and me in Wildcats gear. Christopher and me sharing a box of popcorn. Maybe I'd get to see him smile when I tease him that basketball is way more than just HORSE (which we haven't had a chance to pick up again, but I want to)—

—and I need to stop thinking about this. "You sure you need any more? At this point, you've been working on the article so long I don't know if blogging will still be a platform by the time you're done."

Christopher chuckles. "Oh, I'll know when it's done. Don't you worry." He knocks against my foot again. "But for real, let's just go to the game."

I think back to what Christopher and I talked about in the park. If I'm living my life for me, then I would want to go to this game. Plus, if I'm ever going to go to any Wildcats game again, this should be it. "All right, I'll go."

Christopher looks to my other side where Amy's sitting. "You coming?" And I can't even say how much relief floods through my body. *It's not a date.* It's a "friend" group outing.

"Nope," she says. "Your flirting is cute and all, but I'm not interested in this *particular* date concept."

The relief, well, it's gone.

"It's not a date," we say at the same time, jumping and stumbling over each other's words.

Amy gives a coy smile. "Yeah, whatever, boys. Have fun."

Christopher picks up his phone and boy do his eyes pop. Even more so than at the suggestion of the date. "I gotta go. I'm gonna be so late for my sound check."

For seemingly the first time in my life, I find myself kind of bummed that Christopher has to go. And apparently that thought takes a couple brain cells out with it because I stand up. "I could come with. Pass out more of our voting flyers. Build some buzz."

If I'm honest, I'm mostly painfully curious to see Christopher play. I know about the pain he's gone through to perform. But I've never actually heard him do it. There've been so many sides of Christopher I've seen lately and I'm dying to see this one in action—and to see if he actually bought the color guitar I picked. Plus, it's about time I get to observe him without him observing me.

He looks me over, a hint of confusion between his brows, but he doesn't question it out loud. "Yeah, sure, let's go."

When we get to the dimly lit coffee shop he's performing at, there's already a decent-sized crowd. Teenagers and college kids are all sunken into ratty red lounge chairs or sitting cross-legged on the floor as they hold instruments or pieces of paper I assume they're going to do readings off of. It's a relief to see a small business in Chitwood that hasn't plastered itself all over in Wildcats stickers. There's only one on the cash register with the caption GO WILDCATS, where someone's written *Not This Year LMAO* over it in Sharpie.

Chitwood has always had a decent enough arts scene, so it's not that surprising that this place is pretty crowded.

No, the surprising part is watching a couple people from our school jump to their feet the moment they see us walk in.

And rush right up to Christopher.

"Ah, the headliner has arrived!" one of the girls says.

The crowd here is a lake of familiar faces from school, Catherine Finney included, which makes my heart sink. It's almost funny how I'd been so secretly desperate for her to leave me alone, but now her cold shoulder makes me miss her making eye contact with me. Though if I'm being honest, I can't bring myself to blame her when I let her crush on me for years.

The crowd around Christopher swells with such excitement I wonder if he's been lying to me about being a secret celebrity or something.

I start handing out flyers, hoping it'll distract me from my sweating palms. I can't even quite figure out what feels weird about it.

I get that Christopher said he didn't have a particularly difficult time coming out here because he was new and not all that popular. But these girls, some of the same ones who gave me the cold shoulder, aren't just ignoring him or pretending he doesn't exist. They're *supporting* him. They *love* him.

I spot Tabby and beeline over to her, and Christopher swerves over too. "Hey Tabby! Thanks for coming!"

"Wouldn't miss it," she replies, smiling.

"You have quite the adoring fanbase," I comment.

Christopher glances back at Catherine and her people. "Oh yeah." He rolls his eyes as he heads toward stage. "Half these girls just want a gay best friend."

I don't get time to think more about it, though, because all thoughts melt away when Christopher starts to sing. He has one of those rich voices, a little raw and unpolished but just, I don't know. There's something about the way he clutches his pick and lets his hair fall in his face as he's concentrating hard. The way he wraps his legs around the chair and leans close into the microphone. How he smiles a little as he sings.

But I think mostly, it's the emotion. His notes ache with it. So much more than they need to at a small-town open mic. But he's just going for it and people are leaning forward to listen. *I'm* leaning forward to listen. Like he's wide open and inviting us all in. I wonder what that's like.

I guess I have felt that, though. The flow I get while playing, like I got while shooting hoops the other night. That freedom of nothing but me, the ball, and the silence surrounding us even when there's a full crowd. And in this moment . . . I let myself miss it. He lets me miss it.

Christopher moves into a rendition of Foo Fighters' "My Hero." It's been so long since I've heard it. One of those songs that would come up on the radio or Amy's random Spotify playlists on long drives. It feels timeless in a way.

But not Christopher's version. Christopher's version burns through the buzzing, caressing my ears. It feels specific, locked in this particular moment as he belts out *"Kudos, my hero leaving all the mess*" looking around the room. Looking at me, for a skin-tingling second. I log each note the way Christopher sings them, so this'll be the first version of the song that plays in my head. Christopher's voice, Christopher's hands on the strings, Christopher's dark eyelashes soft against his skin as he closes his eyes to sing. In this moment, I feel like I could write an article about him. I'm so lost in it that I almost don't realize the song is over until I hear him say—

"And don't forget to support Vote Squad by registering to vote by January twenty-second! Rally that Saturday!" when his set ends. "Brianna Collins is here for all students, so let's get her on the board! Follow Vote Squad on the link in the flyers for more information and check out or blog coming soon. We've got a *doozy* of a reveal coming up in the next few weeks."

People even clap when he finishes saying that too.

Later that night, Christopher and I are the last ones in the coffee shop, breaking down his equipment and picking leftover flyers up off the floor. Even though his set ended a while ago, that odd electric feeling from watching him is still coursing through me.

"You were really good up there," I say. I want to say "amazing," but at the last second I chicken out. I don't want to make it weird.

Christopher waves away the compliment and studies me. "I can tell something's up with you, so spill. I know it's not my melodious voice that spellbound you."

My ears get hot. I can't tell him the truth, so instead I ask the question that was buzzing through my brain before his set. "Why do the same people who want a gay best friend not want a gay basketball captain?"

Christopher works on securing his guitar case a moment. "I think it's because people want a gay sidekick, not a gay hero. It fits their idea of what a gay person is. An elite basketball player . . . doesn't." Christopher shakes his head, his gaze on me. "Everyone coming up to me, even if it feels kind of good for a night, wants me out of the spotlight by tomorrow."

I think about the gay best friend on TV. The one who can give fashion and dating advice to the manic pixie dream girl main character while making sexual innuendos about a life that the cameras will never show. The caricature that bigots will point to when they say they're not homophobic as they call every real, complex gay human a groomer and write their oppression into laws.

I frown, regretting even asking the question as his expression falls. "Wait, wait, wait. You are *not* a sidekick! For God's sake, would a *sidekick* be successfully running a campaign to change the culture of a whole high school?"

"Amy's doing that."

"*You* and Amy are doing that." I think about Christopher's singing, about what he had to go through to get there, to give a performance like that. "And it's not just that! You're a kick-ass journalist and a super-talented guitarist, getting up there after everything you've been through. You do more and take more charge of your life than anyone I know. That's protagonist shit."

Christopher smiles faintly, but I don't know if he really believes it.

"One day someone is going to see all the parts of you that I see. Some people may not want that character now, but they won't have a choice. And when that day comes, it will be because people like you dared to be themselves—your whole self."

My fingers wrap around Christopher's hand as I finish what I'm saying. Loosely, like a burst of wind from the front door opening could make me lose my grip. But our hands are still boiling hot and Christopher stares at me, speechless. We've never been this close, and his gray eyes are unreadable.

He's the first to pull away.

"Can we go back to how good you thought I was? Like just okay or really superb?" he asks, grinning. "Worthy of a music major in the future?"

"That what you wanna do?"

He shrugs. "Music, film, journalism. All of them. I like having options."

The moment's gone; I'm both relieved *and* disappointed for reasons I can't name. "I gotta go, but uh, you were way more than okay."

As I walk away, I wonder if Christopher's hand is still tingling like mine.

CHAPTER FOURTEEN

I TRY TO TELL MYSELF THAT THE ROYAL-BLUE T-SHIRT BRUSH-ing against my skin as I step down the stairs Friday night to leave for the alumni game is just that—a T-shirt. It being a Wildcats shirt is just a way for me to fit in. But I'm headed to a basketball game, my first one since leaving the team, and the feeling is like an itch on the back of my neck, making the shirt somehow feel like a target instead of camouflage. Still, I promised Christopher I'd go. *I* want to go.

"Where're you off to, honey?" Mom asks as she puts away dishes.

I pull at my shirt. "Um. I'm going to check out the alumni game."

I brace for her eyes to *light up*. To take it for more than what it is, but she smiles like I said I'm going to the movies. "How exciting!" she says, then gets a mischievous look. "Is it a date? That boy you were out with at the door-to-door campaign is a real cutie. Don't think I didn't see him when you two came back."

God, *nooo*, please. Even my *mom* ships me and Christopher now? "It's not a date!"

She shakes her head, still smiling. "*Okay*, sweetie."

An idea—not a good one, but an idea—pops into my head. "What if you come to the alumni game too?" Then she'll *definitely* know it's not a date. I'll take the risk even if she has my baby pictures on her phone. Plus, maybe it'll help her get her groove back, no pressure for me to be spotted by any scouts, just cheering on a team like we used to do all together when I was little.

But Mom bites her lip. She looks back at Maggie, who's working on some poster designs for the rally I asked her to do. It's only been a day with her drawing out ideas, and she's already working on her third iteration of one I'm super stoked about. Plus, she says she has another idea she'll share if it works out. "Oh, I'd love to, but Mags and I already have plans tonight."

I can't deny how good it feels to see them both with plans. I can roll with this.

I call to Maggie as I go. "Don't watch the next episode of *Glee* until I'm back!"

Fifteen minutes later, I spot Christopher looking at his phone near the gym entrance. His hair is windswept, clearly unintentionally, and he looks weirdly casual in just a blue T-shirt and jeans. I suspect it's as close as I'll ever get to seeing him in pajamas. *Not that I want to see him in pajamas*, obviously.

"Ready for the alumni war, Elliot?" Christopher asks as I get closer.

"Oh, hell yeah!"

Christopher sighs. "I can't believe I'm associating with someone who takes *basketball* this seriously."

Both teams are stretching and the stands are filling by the second when we walk in. It's loud, that perfect mix of chatting, balls bouncing against wood, sneakers screeching across the floor. Pom-poms are being thrown into the crowd, and the gym still smells more like fresh popcorn than sweat. Students in the stands yell, "Beat the Bulldogs!"

"So, savor this because it'll never happen again," Christopher says.

I laugh, until the view stirs up memories. "My grandpa played this game practically every year after I was born. Some of my favorite memories were coming here as a kid to cheer him on. It's so weird not see him here."

Christopher drops his fingertips onto my leg, just long enough to say, "It's sweet he participated for as long as he did."

When he pulls away, the heat lingers.

Then, as the Wildcats start their warm-up drills, I stop thinking about it because the weirdest thing happens. My hands actually twitch to mimic the motions, practically feeling that weight of a ball beneath my palm. I ball my hands in fists to stop it and keep my eyes face forward as we pass the court on the way to the stands. If I can go this whole game without being harassed, it'll be a miracle. Maybe I should make a bet.

"Barclay!"

I only look up because there's no way the hoarse voice that calls my name is a teenager. Sure enough, it's Marvin, one of my grandpa's old teammates. He straight up hugs me like always. I don't know why I figured he'd just ignore me without that connection to bridge us, but he doesn't.

"It's so great to see you; we'll talk after the game," he says to me as he squeezes. With his old-man aftershave, I almost believe I'm in Scratch's arms for a second.

I pull away, heat creeping up my neck, remembering Christopher is right here. He's smiling to himself as we climb the bleachers.

"You better get used to old-people attention, slick," Christopher says. "Twunks like you will be attracting old gay men for the next ten years."

People are looking at me, but I barely notice I'm laughing too hard. "I feel like you just sorted me into some dystopian faction."

Christopher raises his eyebrows. "I mean, not entirely inaccurate."

We find some seats just as the pregame announcements start. Coach Ferris, who looks a little redder this game than usual, gives his usual talk about the importance of tradition and honoring history and legacy. Stuff that I *do* still believe in, even if this team doesn't live up to it.

"We'd also like to take tonight to honor Archie Elliot," Coach says.

Archie Elliot. The name sinks in slowly in the seconds after Coach says the words.

"Archie was a forward on the Wildcats. His hard work and talent took the team to a win at the 1973 championship. After the war, he attended University of Georgia, where he played forward for them. After graduation he returned to Chitwood, where he worked in construction management until his death a few months ago. Scratch, as we all knew him, was always involved in Chitwood basketball and an avid supporter of sports all over this town, including founding the local pool hall that gave him his nickname. To honor his legacy, we'll be retiring his number."

Retiring his number? There's something so huge, so final about it. But also . . . this is the kind of decision I should've been a part of. I'm sure if I'd stayed on the team, I would've been. But they didn't even invite me as his grandson? Did they even tell Mom this was going to happen? I'll have to ask Mom later.

I roll out my shoulders and Christopher scoots in closer. At least I'm here for it. At least I'm not alone.

Before I know it, the game's started. And from the moment that

Zack starts executing a flex warrior play the two of us had down to an art, I find myself practically digging the soles of my shoes into the bleacher, as if it'll keep my body from wanting to spring onto the court.

Then, as the minutes tick by, I don't know about the rest of the team, but I'm fully aware that the Bulldogs *suck* this year. In fact, they're leaving entire sections of the court wide open. It's like watching a bunch of middle-aged people try to plug in an Xbox when none of them knows what an HDMI cord is. Yet somehow, the Bulldogs are within just two points of the Wildcats as we close in on the end of the first quarter. How could they not be seeing the opportunity here? A gift-wrapped game and they're missing it. It's no wonder they're one game from a losing season.

"Zack! Your left is wide open!" I find myself screeching before I can think too hard about it. Others are cheering and cajoling too, so I'm not completely embarrassing myself.

To my surprise, Zack actually looks up. But with his attention on me, I realize I can't be that guy taking his head out of the game. So I cheer. "Zack Attack! Zack Attack!" The same cheer I would've given him from the bench if we were both on the team. "The Bulldogs better watch their back!" I'm grinning by the time I finish saying it.

Zack refocuses but he uses his open left, and drives the ball to the basket until it swishes in. Game tied.

As the half presses on, and the score slides back and forth like a game of tug-of-war, I keep cheering. I keep calling out plays and stamping my right foot four times when the Wildcats miss a layup, an old team superstition.

"Oh my God, I've never heard you speak this much," Christopher says, laughing his ass off.

I check the scoreboard as the half ends. The Wildcats are winning by five when halftime hits. They start the transition to the scrimmage.

Out of nowhere, Marvin makes eye contact with me on the sidelines.

"Hey, Barclay, get over here!" Marvin calls.

I head over, hoping they won't ask why my mom isn't here. No one gloms on guilt like grandpas.

"So the boys and I had an idea," Marvin says, throwing an arm around his teammate. "You *are* technically an alumni of the team now. Would you like to join our side and play? It'd even things out since we always get our butts kicked."

An instant *no* bubbles in my mouth. But I find myself wondering why *no* feels so instant. I'm literally vibrating with the tension from watching this game and not playing. Isn't this what Christopher and I were talking about? Doing things because I want to and not because anyone says I should or shouldn't? Plus, the idea of playing alongside Scratch's friends feels like a connection I've been waiting for. I'm not going to get another chance like this.

"Yeah, let's do it," I say.

Danny Adebayo, the resident hype guy for the team, gets set up as the team jogs back onto the court. Just as I'm trading my T-shirt for an alumni game shirt and throwing my old one to a bewildered but grinning Christopher, he starts introducing the alumni.

"From the class of 1980, we've got Wesley Goodman, the man so good at defense that he could play it while giving your dog a teeth cleaning!" Danny says.

Wesley runs up to a wave of cheers.

"From the class of 1973, we've got Marvin Klein, the man, the myth, the menace. Marvin's a maverick on the court, delivering three-pointers from half-court like it's his job!"

Marvin goes running up, grinning and waving to the crowd. I'm cheesing harder than any other time during the game.

"And as a surprise last-minute addition . . ."

Oh God, no. I look to Danny, suddenly terrified of what he'll say, but he isn't looking at me. I force my gaze on Marvin rather than the current team, who still haven't quite noticed I'm down here.

"We've got basketball prodigy and the only guy who eats the gross pizza in the cafeteria, Barclay Elliot!" Danny finishes.

Danny seems . . . genuinely pumped.

"Oh shit, I didn't know you were into *older men*!" Ostrowski lobs from the other side of the court.

It's only then that I look over. Everyone on the team is silent, brows furrowed and eyes on the alumni like they're still processing how this is possible. Zack's jaw is on the floor.

I turn away and volunteer for tip-off. Ostrowski must too because he gleefully hustles over to face me.

And, even without weeks of practice, as soon as the ball hits the air, I take it. I take it with ease and a smirk on my face. I'll show all of them what they've been missing.

The ball feels perfect in my hands as I swerve around the court. Zack's the first one who comes to guard me as the team scrambles to adjust. Cheers and jeers shake the bleachers.

"What are you doing here, man?" Zack asks, laughing.

"Kicking your ass, Ito." I grin, and it feels like we're playing at the park again for a second.

I punctuate it with a fake and an easy layup. Two ahead for the alumni. I'm grinning so hard I can almost forget the small pull in my side. *Noted: I'm a little out of shape.* But whatever. I head back on defense, and before long Wesley rebounds a missed shot from Zack, shooting it over to Marvin. Instead of just dribbling down the court, Marvin the Menace lobs it into my hands.

By about three plays of the same, I realize it's not a coincidence. They're just feeding me the ball whenever they can. Which starts as a great idea, but only a few minutes in, my out-of-shapeness becomes a lot more apparent.

I line up for a shot from the three-point line, one that I've been making consistently since eighth grade. I square up, but I'm breathing hard and I can feel my form is way off before the ball even leaves my fingers.

It bounces off the basket, right into Zack's hands. I hustle with the other alumni to get it back. But that three-pointer isn't even the worst shot I take. I miss layups I haven't missed since I was ten too. The whole thing becomes embarrassing. I'm not in shape and it's becoming clear that *wanting* to play basketball is not the same thing as actually being able to do it.

I try to block it out as Wesley gets the ball back to me yet again. I pivot, positioning myself to take another three-point shot.

"You sure about that move, Elliot?" Ostrowski jeers as he makes his way over to guard. "You haven't made a single one of those shots all night!"

For once, he's not wrong, but I use the opportunity for a fake and fly past him to go for a layup . . .

Which gets stuck in the space between the rim and the board. I jump up to dislodge it, but Ostrowski does at the same time and we end up colliding.

The buzzer keeps us from going at it any more, though.

191

"Shit, man, Scratch could've played better than you and he's dead!" Ostrowski says.

I practically see red, but unlike last time I was on this court, I hold my ground. I'm not gonna punch a guy on a night meant to honor my grandpa. I'm not going to give him the satisfaction, not again.

A whistle blows and I exhale as Ostrowski takes his attention back to Coach, who is calling a huddle.

Meanwhile the alumni huddle around me, all cheers and back pats, even though we lost 20–30.

"Sorry about not being much of a secret weapon," I say.

Marvin slaps me hard on the back, delighted. "Are you kidding, we lost by *way* less than usual."

As everyone heads to the sidelines, I take a minute to look around. Because there's no way in hell I'll ever be allowed back on the court after sucking out there like that.

But when I look up, Christopher is cheering from the stands, not caring at all how many shots I missed or made. I shake off the feels and smile for the picture with the alumni, who hold up Scratch's old jersey, and then turn to head back over to him.

But before I get there, Zack steps in my path. "That was wild! God, I miss playing with you, Barcs."

My heart warms even as it sinks, because it's about playing again. *Second chances,* I remind myself. I'm the one who's been ignoring Zack, but he's talking to me, and basketball has always been one of the biggest things connecting us. Maybe this is just him trying, like Christopher said. "Yeah, for sure. I've missed you, man." But my skin's crawling at the thought of doing some gushy friendship makeup in public after already putting myself out there in front of everyone with the game. Besides, I'm here with Christopher; I don't want to keep him waiting. "Can we talk after the game?"

"Sure, man." But Zack doesn't run off to join the team. He waits, face twitching until he blurts out: "Come back."

It's like the whole world pauses.

"What?" I sputter out.

"Come back to the team. And before you say it, no, not for me or for scholarships or for anyone else at all in this stupid town. Because you *love* the game. Look how happy you were out there!" He pauses. "I thought maybe you didn't care about it anymore. But now I know you do and for you to give up something you love this much because of us, because of me." Another pause. "It's wrong. I'll have your back," he says. "I can't fix what happened or how badly I reacted or even change anyone's mind, but I will stand by you if you come back. And I know for a fact more of the team than you think would feel that way. We aren't the same without you."

For a second, I picture it. After-school practices and drives in Zack's car that always smells like McDonald's. Reopening the door to the future I never really stopped wanting. Winning that championship game that meant everything to me for so long.

It all seems so real, but that *if I come back* snags in my mind like a jutted nail. Zack may not believe it, but I *know* I can't come back to the team. It's like Mom said, like Christopher said, no one is going to cheer for a gay team captain here. And it would be stupid to think that a second time. Even though I don't want it to, anger snakes up my spine at Zack for making me want it again.

"What planet are you living on?" I sound angry. *I shouldn't sound angry right now.* "Ostrowski just tried to body me again in a onetime scrimmage. Didn't you hear everyone cheering for all my misses? You're delusional."

Zack scowls at me. "I can't believe you still can't trust me. Ostrowski isn't this whole team. I am literally telling you half the guys want you back. Hell, Pat told me you convinced him to stay on the team!" I scan the crowd. I need to find Christopher and go. This game is over for me. Basketball is over for me. "I didn't say it was going to be easy, but you never used to care about easy. I guess quitting when things get hard is your new thing, though. I'm done trying."

And that's it. Zack goes and joins the rest of the huddle as the Wildcats prepare for their second half. I stand there for a few seconds, watching where he once was like the words are stuck in the air and I can rearrange them to form what I wanted him to say. But I don't even know what that is.

My muscles are quaking and the gym is suddenly boiling and I want out of this stupid fucking T-shirt and away from this gym and everyone in it.

At least the exit isn't that far away.

I settle myself out by the bikes. It's one of those crisp nights as the weather settles into winter. Quiet, too. I'm aware of a soft ringing in my ears and the tremor of every muscle that hasn't been used in months. I sigh and start stretching out my back.

Christopher runs out soon after, my shirt dangling off his hand. "Everything okay?"

I'm startled by his tone before I even see his face. When I look over at him, I recognize the look. The softness of his features, the way his hands are tensed up as if he's unsure of where to put them. He cares. Even if we "can never be friends," he cares.

"Zack was . . . still trying to get me to rejoin the team, pretending it was for me. Between that and Ostrowski trying to insult me with a Scratch death joke, I just . . . couldn't handle it," I say. There's a lump in my throat, and this time it doesn't go away no matter what I try.

"Barclay, I'm so sorry." I haven't heard him say my name like that. I wish I could record it until I memorized how it sounded. "I shouldn't have pushed you to go."

"I just wish things were different," I say. My words shove against each other to get out around the lump. I don't know why I trust Christopher with all of this stuff, but I do. And I don't care that I do.

I think about the future I can never have. The future where I kiss my boyfriend at the postgame diner celebrations. The future where that boyfriend . . . has glasses and wears patterned shirts and his hair falls in his face and he loves nineties rom-coms and is nice to my sister and has the balls to face the barrel of a gun. Who shoots little looks while playing guitar that I know are just for me. Who listens to all my stupid questions about being gay. Who must think I'm so pathetic and wouldn't love someone like me if we were the last two gay guys on Earth.

Slowly, Christopher slides a hand onto my back. It travels up my spine like an electric bolt. "Hey, hey, it's—it's going to be okay. Good, even. Coming out sucks. The period where the world needs to adjust to you sucks. But you'll get through it, and I can just tell the person you're gonna be is going to shine. You already do and—" His chest hitches. "There's still time for things to be different."

I stare at him. Christopher, who knows exactly what I'm going through and sees a not-impossible future for me.

"Can I kiss you?" The words fall out of my mouth. It feels like there's a hook in my chest pulling me to him.

Christopher leans closer, so close I can see the lines in his eyes, like little supernovas. He chuckles a little, biting back a grin. "Yes, of course."

As I lean in to Christopher, I'm shaking like this is my first time again. Like I'm staring down a cliff and have to just plunge off or I'm never gonna do it.

So I do. I throw myself into him, clutching him to me. Our lips meet, snug, smooth, everything I could've imagined. Skin to skin, our mouths moving together as we inch our bodies closer. He's so . . . cozy. I never knew kissing someone could feel like sitting in a roller coaster when it stops, when the adrenaline is still floating around inside you. I never knew kissing could feel secure. I never knew it could flood into my head, almost making me forget the physical parts, so unlike John, where sensation stuck to hands and lips.

But wow.

I pull away after what must only be a few seconds, suddenly aware of where we are.

"I, uh," Christopher says. Red rushes up his cheeks like watercolor. "Thanks. I'll, uh"—he smiles and looks away—"see you later? To maybe do that again?"

My stomach swoops. *Maybe do that again.* "Yeah, definitely. Thanks for coming with me."

"All worth it."

We stare at each other for a minute, and I wonder if he's thinking what I'm thinking. That I wish there was a way to keep going. To find somewhere that can be all ours. To be together and talk and laugh and have nothing get in the way. To start a bright future now.

But in the end, we both end up just waving goodbye.

CHAPTER FIFTEEN

'VE NEVER THOUGHT I COULD BE A ROMANTIC GUY. NEVER allowed myself to really take the time to imagine my wedding, or fan the flames of that particular pull when I saw couples sharing milkshakes at the diner. Never let myself see a hot guy and wonder what he'd want for Valentine's Day.

But as I park my bike Monday morning, I think I finally get it. The feeling of being wanted and wanting that person back, it's addicting. It's not that people do all that lovey-dovey shit because they feel like they need to. Or, at least, I won't. I just close my eyes and think about Christopher and I *want* him to feel as good as I feel with him. I want to make him laugh. I want to put my arm around him as we share food at the diner. I want to find him the perfect new notebook when his current one runs out. I want to watch and discuss nineties movies with him, play HORSE with him in my backyard, then go upstairs and kiss him until our lips are numb.

I want to see how much farther we can go beyond kissing.

And it feels possible. With the second rally this coming Saturday, I won't even have to try to see Christopher; we'll just be working together all week to get registration up before the January 22nd deadline. We're going to destroy Mr. Ostrowski together. Nonstop time to listen to Christopher rant about politics I'm trying to understand, and sneak stolen glances as we set up the stage hoping Amy doesn't catch on and tease us. And after we're done, he can come hang out with Maggie with me when we watch *Glee* together. We can go visit Devin where we don't have to worry what anyone is going to say or think (he's already stoked to meet Christopher after I texted him about the kiss last night). There's so much we can do.

But part of me wonders if I'm jumping too far, too fast. If it's going to be the same when we see each other. As much as he said there would be a second kiss, I was too chicken to text him this weekend and he didn't reach out either. Did I do something wrong, or am I too inexperienced for him, or did he just feel bad for me and he doesn't actually want to date me? Or what if he comes up and just kisses me in the hall? I don't know if I'm ready for that yet.

I take a deep breath as I open the school doors. I'm not going to run from it. We just have to talk.

But one step inside and it's obvious something's gone down. There's a humming of voices traveling through the hallway, like everyone's talking about the same thing. I shake the feeling off, though, even as the hair on my arms stands on end. At least Christopher will probably tell me the latest Chitwood tea. Maybe it's just everyone talking about the game, but the Wildcats won, so they're still hanging on to the possibility of playoffs. Why isn't everyone just pumped about that?

That's when I notice the staring.

I'm walking past freshmen I've never met huddled around each other and snickering at me; sophomores I share Spanish with stare, only looking away when we make eye contact. Is everyone pissed I played at the alumni game? God, if it is that, I don't have time for it. In fact, it seems trivial and boring and nowhere near as interesting as finding Christopher. So that's what I focus on.

My heart leaps as I finally spot him.

But the leap is cut off at the knees as I see the look on his face. The watery eyes, the tightness in his neck, the ruffled look of his hair like he's been raking his hand through it. And I think, for one moment, that Christopher regrets a night I was so sure was incredible.

"Barcs, please don't freak out," he says with a tone in his voice I haven't heard before. Panic. *He's panicked.* Christopher Dillon, who looked down the barrel of a gun, is panicked. "It's—it's just par for the course. Everyone here's a dick and—"

"What is it?" I demand.

Christopher pauses, then pulls up a TikTok. My ears burn as the snickering gets louder around us.

It's a video of Christopher and me kissing. An image that, on its own, if I'd consented to filming it, looks exactly like those rom-coms Christopher loves. Like seeing my favorite memory over and over.

But there's voice-over. Ostrowski, attempting a shit Steve Irwin impression. *"And here we see two homo homoluses, a subspecies of the inferior Neanderthal. After a brief mating ritual in which the jock homo homolus informs the nerd of his phallus size and confirms whose asshole will be wrecked, the two homo homoluses peck the lips to secure the—"*

It feels like a bad dream, that sinking, falling, grabbing-for-nothing sensation. Maybe if I squeeze my eyes long enough, I'll wake up in my own bed, the whole thing never real. This is something I couldn't have even *imagined* in a nightmare, though. I try to force air in, but my throat closes. Out of control. I've never felt this out of control before. I can't be here.

But then I spy Ostrowski himself, standing with Chase and Boris, smiling from ear to ear with his orthodontist-perfect teeth.

I run at him, raising my fist to get a clean shot at those stupid fucking teeth.

But two hands pull me back by my shirt. Christopher. "Barcs, please, this isn't worth it. The school has a zero tolerance policy. You've run out of free passes."

I don't give a shit. Even if I have to go be homeschooled. Ostrowski's the one who's run out of free passes now.

But Christopher doesn't relent. He wraps his arms around me to hold me back.

It's like someone's locked me in a box. A tiny, windowless box where I can only hear people's voices from the outside. And everyone has seen and now I'm in his arms again and they're watching and it's like I'm right back up on that stage all over again. . . .

I can't take this. So I break the box this time.

I wrestle out of his arms, shouting, "Don't touch me." *I don't want you to get hurt.* "I'm not your boyfriend." *You can find someone better, somewhere better.*

I storm out before I can bear to see the look on Christopher's face. I know even without seeing, though, that the words have hit and I can never take them back.

This time I'm the one who made our future impossible.

CHAPTER SIXTEEN

I NEVER THOUGHT THERE WAS A LOW TO HIT AFTER THE COM-
ing out went so badly. But it turns out, coming out is the beginning of a nail-strewn road you have to walk barefoot. It turns out,
you have to keep coming out, and every little thing that happens to
you just solidifies the idea that *no, people won't stay just as bigoted as the
first time you say anything*. Maybe they'll get worse.

I catch Mom right as she's heading out the door to work the next
morning. Maggie's already out working on some surprise for the rally
with her morning art club, the one extracurricular she's felt ready to
rejoin with Mom's help. Mom should be having a stress-free start to
her workday, but here I am, miserable and still in my pajama pants and
Devin's Georgia Tech shirt.

"Can I stay home today?" I ask her.

She doesn't tighten her jaw or look at her watch. She just frowns.
"What's wrong, love?"

Embarrassment floods me as I even consider talking about
the video. Talking about the video will involve talking about the
homophobic shit Ostrowski's been pulling, and how I couldn't stop
it myself. Not to mention it'd involve saying that the alumni game *was*
a date for Christopher and me, so much so that we kissed. And that I
ruined it. It's all too much for right now.

"I . . . they actually retired Scratch's number at the alumni game. It just finally hit me really hard this morning," I say.

Mom's expression softens. She approaches me and wraps me in a hug. "Just for today. Get Amy or Christopher to get your homework for you. Do you want to talk about it when I get home?"

I shake my head. She kisses my forehead, and walks out.

I sit at home playing video games for the rest of the day, thinking about how Christopher is never going to forgive me and shouldn't.

No one even seems to notice or reach out. Not until Amy drops by.

She knocks at the door right at 3:10 p.m. I try to ignore her, but she's rapping so hard with no signs of stopping that I'm going to have to take her to the minute clinic when she breaks the bones in her fist if I don't answer. So I do. Her look is on the extreme end of punk today, like she's trying to appear scarier than usual. But it's not the chunky combat boots, raccoon makeup, or 1800s widow dress that's making her seem terrifying. It's the look in her eyes.

"You going to hide in here forever?" Amy asks as she lets herself in. Her tone is harsh, but it still takes me a second to realize she's angry *at* me this time.

"You really gonna victim blame?" I reply.

She laughs humorlessly. "Don't you dare angle it that way. I've been a burning sun of pissed at Ostrowski. I egged his precious convertible with the top down inside and out. But when I look at this situation, I can't help but notice that there were *two* people in that video. Two victims, and you might've even thought to ask the other person in that video how they were doing. But no, you decided to attack him for trying to stop you getting expelled."

Amy's close and frothing. I want to take a step back, but no way am I just going to let her spout that shit at me. Everyone already knows Christopher is gay and doesn't care! Girls flock to Christopher *because* he's gay. He faces down guns; this is nothing to him. But it's not *nothing* for me.

"You don't get it. Things were finally getting better and now they all see me as just a stereotype. A nature experiment. The only two gay boys in school can't keep their hands off each other."

Amy rolls her eyes. "Jesus, fuck that, Barclay. The only *stereotype* you're becoming is a boy who's so wrapped up in toxic masculinity and insecurity that you'd rather hurt the guy you love than face an ounce of struggle or vulnerability."

"I don't *love* him!"

"God, you're so insufferable! I'm done listening to your complaining when all you care about is how people you don't even know see you. You know what, I didn't even come here to lecture you. Here."

She slams her backpack onto the couch and removes a pile of leaflets.

"Not that I even want you around if you're going to be like this, but you also don't deserve to get off that easy. You're folding these leaflets for *your* rally you planned. And remember, *you're* scheduled to drop the Ostrowski bomb with all the details we uncovered. You know, about the corruption on your bigoted team you *should* be mad at instead of Christopher. In case you forgot what's important right now."

"I—" There's no way I am getting up in front of this whole town again now. No way.

"I'll see you then," Amy says, shoving the leaflets into my hands. She glowers at me like she can hear my thoughts. "No excuses."

And she just leaves.

My phone pings. Finally, a response from Devin.

Devin
That sucks so much, man. This tool is gonna get what's coming to him at the rally. But check up on Christopher, ok? You've got so much better shit going on and don't let this ruin it! Focus on that. Plus that looked like a pretty good kiss . . .

"Fuck!" I scream. I can't do this. I can't do this and I can't believe Amy and Christopher and Devin really don't see why.

I'm so tired. I'm so tired of convincing myself that I'm the kind of person who can head a rally, let alone one that would make a difference. It was a delusion. Better to end it now before they have to watch me flop onstage again and take their dreams and months of hard work down with it.

I shove the leaflets under the sofa and crawl onto the couch to sleep.

I bribe Maggie with Pop-Tarts into calling me out, and I skip the rest of the week. And when Saturday arrives, I stay in bed. My phone, though, is extremely busy.

Amy
9:02 A.M.
Don't forget the flyers.

Amy
9:15 A.M.
Barcs, if you overslept, HERE'S YOUR WAKE UP CALL YOU COW

Amy

10:13 A.M.

I might be able to forgive you if you get here now.

Amy

11:45 A.M.

IF YOU DON'T GET YOUR ASS OVER HERE EVERYONE
AT SCHOOL HATING YOU WILL FEEL LIKE A TEA PARTY
COMPARED TO ME

Amy

11:59 A.M.

You're such a disappointment, you know that?

Yeah, that's the one thing I do know. What else is new? The
phone dings again and I'm about to just shut it off when I see this one
isn't from Amy.

Christopher

12:02 P.M.

So much for a team huh

If Christopher still thought the "team" could accomplish something after all the evidence otherwise, he's an idiot.

I force myself back asleep.

When I wake up, it's to Christopher again. This time, though,
he's sitting in my desk chair, with his windswept hair and his voting
rights volunteer shirt that he always makes look good. He's wearing
that stone-cold disappointment face Amy was giving me. A look that

confirms what I already knew, that there are no words to make this better.

Amazing how I'd imagined being shirtless in my room with Christopher before. How it had looked so different back then.

"How did you get in here?" I ask.

"What the hell is wrong with you?" Christopher says, ignoring my question, an edge of pain in his voice. "Amy was freaking out the whole rally. She had to scramble together *your* speech at *your* event. And you know what? The crowd started leaving when they heard it. They didn't believe her. It mattered that *you* be the one to talk about the corruption that happened on *your team*! And Brianna was furious. You let everyone down."

Despite my instincts to burrow farther under the covers, I sit up. "Because this whole town let me down. All my speeches have ever done is rain fire down harder on me. It wasn't going to be worth it, no matter who said it."

Christopher huffs. "No, I'm so tired of you not seeing this. What happened was shit, but you turned it into 'everyone against Barclay' again, when it was *just* Ostrowski. Every time someone doesn't agree with you, you just bail. And I don't know if you remember, but *I* was in the video too. You know what I did? I turned to my friends, who comforted me when all I wanted to do was lash out too." He runs his hands over his face. "And shit like this is an old wound for me, which you are the only person who knows. But I got through it. *We* got through it together. The group would've had *your* back too. And we needed you."

My body goes ice-cold, but I shake my head. "I just—you don't—"

"No! I'm not finished. God." His mouth tightens. "It's actually meant a lot to me to hang out with another gay guy here, to put everything just out there. Do you really not feel the same way?" *I do.*

206

"And it's made me realize—the only way you fight this stuff is with *joy*. With being happy with all the good that comes from being gay, like that. I've had more fun writing this article about you than any fluff culture review I've done, and I *really like* small-town attempts at ballet and avant-garde theater. Because I've seen the parts of you that you thought you had to hide and they made me like you more. But you'd rather self-destruct just like they want you to and hold on to every negative instead of that joy. So you're not walking on water anymore—so what! I thought you would've realized by now that no one can, but I guess not."

Joy. He thinks I can find *joy* in the past few hellish months? School feels like walking into a ticking time bomb. I have to live with the fact that people who've been tormenting me will get scholarships I need. Every time I get even a sliver of a good thing, it just gets smashed down like my happiness is the universe's demented whack-a-mole. And just holding Christopher's hand is supposed to wipe all that away? Now who has the ego?

"It can never happen," I say. "I'd rather have it snatched from me now, while I don't believe in it. Nothing will make this town less of a bigoted shithole, nothing is going to make it possible for us to be anything, and no stop sign will bring—"

My eyes widen as the rest of the sentence I wasn't expecting to say hangs in the air. *Scratch back.*

Christopher swallows. "Okay. I . . . Barclay, I know your grandpa meant so much to you and—"

"Don't," I say, my voice far harsher than it'd been in my head. "You *don't* know. You could never know, and whatever you think, you don't know me. Just leave. Now you don't have to finish the stupid article about me that you never wanted to do in the first place. No one was ever going to change their mind about me. Not even you. We were kidding ourselves."

Christopher gets up, eyeing the door, but doesn't take the steps toward it. "The article's finished, why don't you read it and judge for yourself if I changed my mind about you? Though I don't know if I even recognize the person I wrote it about right now. If you want to hide in here, that's on you. But this time, I think you have to ask yourself: Are you acting like your life is over because some people in Chitwood are homophobic and don't like the real you, or because you have no fucking idea who that is without your grandpa?"

As Christopher leaves, my phone dings.

It's a link to his blog.

But I can't read it. Because I have no idea who he wrote it about either. No idea who I ever even thought I could be.

CHAPTER SEVENTEEN

BARCLAY ELLIOT: THE STAR THAT NEARLY LOST HIS FUEL

By Christopher Dillon

[Continued from page 1]

Even as his activism is on the upward swing, one can't help but notice the way Barclay still looks at the Wildcat trophy display and the gym when basketballs can be heard bouncing along the wood floor. The fact remains that Barclay, despite attempts to deny both at various times, is both a young gay man and a basketball player. He should've never had to choose between the two at all, especially in such a vulnerable time in his life where his town should've embraced him.

After all, why do people stay in Chitwood, move to Chitwood, value the small town? It's because, at least as the community wishes us to believe, there's a stronger sense of humanity amongst a group of people who take the time to know each other. Working adults commute out of town to bring enhanced salaries back into their neighbors' small businesses. Small business owners chat with increasingly isolated senior members of the communities and volunteer their time and resources for local school functions to benefit the foundations of the town's youth. And the town's youth, who dedicate portions of their lives to activities such as basketball, not only perpetuate success back into the community, but give the town something to look forward to, to pour hope and joy into.

Barclay Elliot was and has been a fully committed member of this community. For most of his life, he was ready to give his all to the Chitwood basketball effort, physically and mentally. He would fight through injuries, fatigue, even grief, so the Wildcats wouldn't suffer, and shoulder the blame for losses he did everything to prevent. Yet all it took was one little vulnerability for people who've known Barclay since he was a baby, who told him daily that they'd always look out for him and support him, to drop him. Something he can't control, something that has nothing to do with basketball and shouldn't erase what you loved about him.

Yet Barclay is still giving back to Chitwood

even after they turned their backs on him. He still loves his town, even if the town doesn't deserve that love. He loves basketball but wants other clubs to have the budget and opportunity to shine too. He wants a school board free of corruption even though it benefited him. He's fighting for protections for everyone, whether that's keeping stop signs visible like the one that led to his grand-father's death or making a safe space for kids who haven't been able to come out like he has.

Speaking of which, while that coming out has been much maligned in every possible way—too public, too grandiose, too selfish, too naïve, too early, too late—in spending time with Barclay and trying to understand why he did it the way he did, when almost anyone would have certainly told him how it would go, the one thing I can say is that it wasn't any of those things. It wasn't rooted in popularity or ego, but in love, in a desire to share himself with the people he loved and believed in—all of you—after losing the chance to do so with the person he loved best, his grandfather. If believing in the love that was shown him was naïve, well, I think that says more about us than him.

Barclay's situation also highlights issues that go beyond him. If a person like Barclay—basketball prodigy, favorite son, destined to make Wildcats history and redeem a team and town—can't love who he loves without giving up his sport and his community, what is life like for the average closeted Chitwoodian? While Barclay Elliot is helping change that, it's imperative that we all remember why. And it's not just his job, but our job to make sure no one else will go through this in the future—years from now or tomorrow. There's always room to restore the love in a community and there's no time to heal like the present.

CHAPTER EIGHTEEN

STARE AT THE ARTICLE FOR A LONG TIME AFTER READING. Reread it, sit with it again. Phrases pop out, making me wish I could highlight them for the first time in my school life. Of course it's not a vanity piece; he told me it wouldn't be. But this is better. It's—God, it's like Christopher has taken all the pain I couldn't say out loud and laid it across the page.

I settle on that last little paragraph. I'd wanted Christopher to want me, but I never even thought about how I wanted him to *see* me. This feels like it, though. He saw me as a whole person. For a time, anyway, he liked that whole person.

And I messed it all up.

Registration is over, the election is just weeks away.

The season could be over any game now.

We're over, before I even gave us a chance to begin.

Before I realized his is the only opinion I care about.

There's no time to heal like the present.

I have to hope maybe he still believes that.

The hallway is quieter when I arrive Monday. People are all staring at their phones, craning over each other's shoulders reading something. But I keep my head down. When I do accidentally make eye contact with people, they don't glare. They just kinda furrow their brows and look back like they're studying me. But I hardly give them a second glance. I have to find Christopher and Amy.

"Hey."

I wheel around, braced, but it's just some sophomore in my math class.

"I, uh, I read the article about you," he says. "The stuff they said about your grandpa really hit home for me. My grandpa passed away last year and I had a really hard time. I thought maybe it was stupid to feel that way." He smiles this tiny smile. "But now . . . I think maybe it's not."

My cheeks go pink. "Oh, thanks. I'm sorry."

"I hope they get the stop sign fixed."

Wow. I don't even know what I was expecting, but it wasn't that.

Tabby approaches my locker next, a tin of cupcakes in her hands.

I take the tin, but only so I can hug her.

"Hey, Tabby," I say. "Hope you had a good weekend. Sorry about missing the rally."

Tabby shrugs. "It's okay. I had no idea about what you were going through with your grandpa. People should be giving you more kindness anyway." She takes the cupcakes back from me and opens the lid. "I know these didn't come out that pretty. . . ."

I pluck one out. "Hey, don't beat yourself up. It takes major skills to put *any* picture on food. You're a master baker."

Tabby grins ear to red-tinged ear. "Wow, thanks, Barclay."

"You know it. See you in chem?"

"See you then!"

I watch her walk away with this soft feeling inside me, like I finally made something right. I can't wait until I can make Tabby smile like that again.

Even if I don't know if I can make it right with Christopher and Amy, I'm trying.

I'm on my way to lunch, rehearsing my apology to Christopher and Amy, who I couldn't find before class, when Zack stops in front of me, right in the middle of the hallway, forcing everyone else to rush around us to get to the cafeteria. He's looking pissed. I don't think I have the energy to deal with figuring out why.

"Give me a second," he says. I wait nervously, unsure of what exactly he means. He takes a deep breath, shaking out his hands like he's about to enter the big Panthers rematch a week early. "What Christopher wrote is a great article. Don't get me wrong. And I know you don't want to talk to me, but I just, I have to get this off my chest." His eyebrows knit together. "Barcs, why did you let him write the entire town turned their backs on you when you weren't what they wanted?"

"Take it up with Christopher. I didn't write—"

"But you think that. I know you do."

I pause, trying to find the words. All that comes out is a nod, though.

"Well, I just want you to know that I feel the same way sometimes. About you. I'm sorry I couldn't be what you wanted right away, but I apologized. I was wrong and I knew it and I tried and I tried to fix it, but it really sucked when my best friend since we were kids saw one thing and then assumed the worst of me every time after."

It rocks me, the way he says that. For once, I can fully imagine the tables turned because here I am hoping Amy and Christopher won't judge me by the stupid mistakes I've made, my bad reactions.

"Zack . . ." I still don't know what to say.

"I really do care that you're okay." He puts his hand on my shoulder. "What do you think I was fighting with Ostrowski about at the diner?" I think of the moment where I could have gone after him, the one I just let pass by. "I've been battling with Ostrowski and all his bullshit. Pleading with Coach to talk to you, to talk to the team. Trying to show you that I wanted to be your ride or die again. That I got it, that I could learn what I didn't get." He looks to his shoes. "I wasn't alone either; a bunch of the guys felt like shit after you left. We want you as our captain, but we *need* you as our friend. I know we're the reason you believed everyone turned their back. We all could and should have reacted better that day and made mistakes after, but I wish you'd given us a chance to prove you wrong too."

Before I can reply, really reply, Zack walks off.

I spend the day alternating between trying to find Christopher and Amy, or Zack, without success. It takes waiting outside the gym after school for my chance with Zack to come.

And in between, I finally figure out what to say.

I spot him walking with Lochman, who peels off in another direction before even seeing me. But Zack's eyes lock onto mine immediately, like how we could always spot each other in crowds when we were best friends.

"Can I speak first this time?" I say, "I mean, apologize first."

This gets Zack to stop. He drops down onto the ground and we both lean against the outside of the school. A winter breeze blows in our faces, knocking his long hair into his eyes, and he tries to flip it away without success. It'd be something I'd tease him about if we were good.

"You were right," I say. "About a lot of stuff. Starting with what you said about the article. I did ghost you. I was angry, I was dealing with shit I've never dealt with before, that I'd been holding in for too long. But it was wrong of me to assume the worst and never give you a real chance to talk it out. Friends shouldn't abandon each other so easily. We never did before that and I hate that it happened now. I should've fought as hard as you fought for me. I should've seen that you were fighting." I pause, forcing myself to look him in the eye. His expression is unreadable, making me sweat as I keep going. "Everything just got so messed up quickly and . . ."

Zack sighs. "I should have told you to come back to the team because I wanted to play by your side, not just because of the scholarship or the scouts. We were both caught in our own shit." Then he smiles, reaches over, and punches my shoulder. "I forgive you, Barcs, and I'm sorry."

And that's it. I let out a sigh of relief. "Shit, let's not do that again."

"Eh, I'm sure you'll be telling many more hot guys about your feelings. It'll get easier."

I laugh, flipping him off as I do. The air lightens around us.

"So were you on your way to practice?" I ask.

Zack shrugs. "Yeah. Coach has us practicing every minute we have free. We managed to claw our way to a chance at the wildcard spot. If we win out, we might be able to turn all this around. We still have about a week before our Panther rematch, so I have hope. We turned our train-wreck friendship around, after all."

I exhale. "I hope you're right."

"You know, there was one other thing I noticed from the article," Zack says. "I know it's complicated and that you've been saying that you're fine without basketball, but . . . this article was

217

a lot about basketball. Basketball is a part of you and that's not going to go away. It shouldn't *have* to. I know you've talked about how much it sucks that you had to hide being gay to stay on the team. But at the same time, I hate to see that you think you have to hide the badass basketball player I know you are to be out."

He smiles. That sheepish, cheesy smile.

The feelings aren't less complicated than they were at the alumni game, my answer to that question isn't so simple, but it's also different now. For the first time in so long, I let that idea light a flickering heat in me. Excitement. The idea of playing again *does* excite me. I am done with pretending that's not true. I don't know how it would be possible, but I didn't think fixing us was possible either. I also know he's not going to ask this time. This time I have to be the one to say it.

"To come back to the team . . . I'd have to start training again," I say, fumbling. "You saw how I played the other night. And even if I could do it that quick, Coach won't take me back. Not this far into the season and not after all that's happened. I can't be a distraction again."

Zack scrunches his face. "Let me worry about the guys. Coach cares about winning more than anything." He nudges me. "It's worth a try, right? And I'll have your back. One hundred percent."

I think about the other complication, everything Amy and Christopher have uncovered. "I'm also not going to stop what I've been doing about the school board stuff. I'm dedicated to Vote Squad and taking my work with the campaign all the way. And that will include exposing Ostrowski's dad and the corruption with the team budget." I'm not backing down. If I can't be all of me—gay, basketball player, advocate—then I won't settle.

Our first new hiccup. Zack's eyes widen. "Damn, you found the evidence?"

"Christopher did. But it has to come from me."

"Okay."

"Okay?"

"Yeah, okay. Mr. Ostrowksi isn't the one shooting three-pointers at the games, and his son isn't exactly a big help. If we're good enough to qualify for the tournament, we'll do it without favoritism and whatever shady shit they do. Do whatever you and Amy and Christopher have to do."

As I look at him, the last objections finally fall away and I feel it all. The adrenaline from that night on the court. The rubber on my fingertips. The steadiness of my muscles when routine and discipline is injected into my life. The swish of the net. The feeling of that number 56 jersey on my back. I look up at the sky and think of my grandpa beaming down at me.

I just want to do this for myself, even if it's hard. I don't want to prove anything to anyone, don't want to even be the best. I just want to be whole. I'm choosing joy, finally.

"Let's do it," I say.

CHAPTER NINETEEN

AS MUCH AS I LOVE BASKETBALL, MY FIRST DAY ON THE varsity team as a freshman haunts me late at night sometimes. Even though everyone from Coach Ferris to Scratch insisted I *belonged* on the team, I still walked into the gym with my braces and Slenderman limbs and got half a dozen glares from upperclassmen who'd just finally gotten onto the team and a bunch of the JV ones who hadn't. I should've straightened up and just played, but I cowered and tried to stay invisible for the whole practice.

Walking into practice with Zack the next day feels an alarming amount like that first practice ever. My calf still twinges from the alumni game and I can't shake the thought that I'm going to suck, if I even get the chance to play. Or that if I get a chance to play, I won't be able to make a difference.

Zack pats me on the shoulder blade right before we open the gym doors. "It'll be fine, man."

Right away, though, every player stares hard at me. Yeah, great start.

Coach is the only one who doesn't look utterly shocked. He's gone right past that, into his tight-jawed, narrow-eyed look. My mouth goes dry.

"Coach, could we have a word?" Zack asks, thankfully.

I clench my fist at my side, mentally preparing. If he says no, it's not like I've lost everything this time. My future doesn't have to depend on basketball anymore—it's in my grades, in my work with Amy and Christopher, or something else I haven't even tried yet. And it isn't about lifting up the whole town, taking on all their worries and expectations. This is just for me to do something I love, because I love it. There's a world outside this gym. This isn't going to be the only thing that defines me anymore.

"My office. Make it fast; I don't waste the team's time," Coach replies.

My insides wriggle at the way he says "the team" pointedly, drawing a distinction.

There's a robotic nature to us all packing into Coach's office. He opens the door. Zack and I take our seats. Coach closes the door. When he sits back on the opposite side of his desk, I lean forward, waiting for him to say something first, but the silence stretches.

"Are we just gonna stare at each other?" Coach finally asks, gruffly.

I take a breath. "I'd like to ask your permission to return to the team." I hold my hands out, trying to pause Coach before he can start in. "I know I've been gone a while. I don't expect to start or even to play. I know I'll have to work twice as hard to get back in shape." I make eye contact with him, but his expression is stony and gives nothing away. "I'm not apologizing for what I did at the pep rally, because I still believe things shouldn't have gone down the way they did, but I also shouldn't have run away. I'm not here because I'm ready to hide or swallow down anything about myself." Coach's face twitches. "I'm here because I love basketball and being a Wildcat. I want to finish what I started."

Coach stays totally silent. Zack's gaze flits from me to Coach, but I shake my head. I said my piece and Zack doesn't need to add to the argument. Just getting me here was good enough.

I'll be okay without basketball, but I know I'm better with it.

Finally, after what feels like a lifetime, Coach speaks. "I thought you'd be more loyal than you've proven you are, Elliot. Really, you don't deserve to be on this team. I'd never do this for another player who pulled *half* the shit you did. Which you believe you shouldn't apologize for." He pauses. "And if someone else does something to upset you? Will you just leave again? Do you think we could survive you leaving again before a game like this?"

"I won't," I say, swallowing that being "upset" and being harassed aren't the same thing. It's clear I'm not going to change Coach's mind or who he is. Just like I won't let him change who I am.

"Why should I believe you now?"

I pause. Every answer to that question doesn't feel like it's in words. It's in the raw determination buzzing in my chest, the ache in my limbs to play, the hope that walking on the court gave me.

Before I can even try to find words, the door to Coach's office opens, loud enough to make me jump in my seat. I wheel around to see Lochman scrunching into the doorframe.

"I would just like to say"—he puts his hands up, playing it remarkably sheepishly for having just barged into a tiny office— "that I fully believe Barclay should be back on the team. He had great captain vibes and we definitely need that going into the next few games."

Coach takes a deep breath, steeling his gaze on me instead of Lochman. "Okay, thank you, Lochman. Now get—"

"Coach," Pat's soft voice says. He's gotten in front of Lochman. Wow. "I agree with Lochman. I was getting really frustrated with our new captain, and Barclay kept my spirits up. Even without being on the team. I'd love to play with him again."

"OUT!" Coach exclaims. "This is a *private meeting*! Everyone who isn't Elliot out *now*!"

It takes everyone a second, but they head out. Zack gives me a little pat on the shoulder as he goes too. For a few seconds, Coach and I just sit there again.

Finally, he exhales. "Ultimately, I want this team to win. I know how much this means to everyone on this team, and in this town. To Scratch. We have to win the Panther rematch *next weekend* to have any chance at participating in the tournament. Every game after that will be for the championship too. It's not much time, but if you're willing to put in the work, I'll let you try."

If I ever win the lottery, I don't think it'll feel as good as this victory. I can't believe this is happening.

"Thank you so much."

Coach scowls. "Thank me after we win."

When we step back onto the court, I can see the whispering and smiles between the guys who stood up for me.

"Attention, everyone. Barclay is being reinstated onto the team for the remainder of the season," Coach says, hardly any emotion in his voice besides maybe impatience, like he'd like nothing more than to get back into routine and yell at us where we can't yell back.

And, judging by Ostrowski's red face, someone really wants to yell. I hold back a burst of laughter in my chest just as he lets loose.

"No way! I *refuse* to play with a fairy like him," Ostrowski snarls. He motions with his arms as wide as they'll go. "I'm captain and I say *we* won't play with him."

Some players start moving toward him. Boris, Kyle. All chiming in "No way!" like whining toddlers. But that doesn't hurt that bad, it's expected. No, what really hurts are the guys like Anthony and

Chase who don't move but still refuse to look at me.

I remind myself to focus on the good. Not the ones who are against me but the three quarters that aren't, at least not totally.

Coach just shrugs off that chasm he's opened up. "Scouts won't be discovering you this late in the season if you're not in the championship circuit, but if that's your choice, your funerals."

Ho-ly *shit*. I mean, it's no zero tolerance policy, but he's not giving in. And despite their furious looks, no one leaves, not even Ostrowski.

"Well, now that *that's* over, let's get moving, boys," Coach says.

I know I'll never be close to Coach again. He's shown his colors, severed any ties that once really mattered. I think I'll miss him in the way I miss my dad. I'll miss more the possibility of closeness, notice the empty space. But it's not like I don't have other people to take his place. It's just made his role in my life smaller. He's just a basketball coach and that's all I need from him now.

As we get in formation to run laps, I slip Zack a high five and start running as hard as I can. I started conditioning after the alumni game because I hated how it made me feel, but there's so much more to do. I'm determined to keep improving.

Ostrowski, however, wastes no time in approaching me as we run.

"Congrats on your return," he says, sneering. "Finally done giving little speeches about things you don't know shit about?"

"I'm just getting started. I've got plenty more to say." I speed up, passing him, refusing to let him get under my skin. "On *and* off the court!"

Zack fist-bumps me as I catch up to him.

We move into a shooting drill first. I can feel his eyes on me, unwilling to let it end there, but I take a deep breath and focus. I'm ready to get my famous jump shot back. My heart speeds up as we go down the line, balls flying off nearly as much as they make it through the hoop. Zack's the one who finally tosses a ball to me.

For a moment, I realize how much I missed the feeling of these new, perfect basketballs where you can still feel every ridge. But it's out of my hands in seconds. Sailing through the air, and—

—in.

I smile, circling back and passing the ball to Anthony.

But as we move through the drill and my record goes from 1–0 to 3–0 to 5–0, the exhilaration isn't coming from whether or not anyone's paying attention. It just feels so good to be playing again, and playing *well* again. Any cheers or captain titles or articles written to gas me up are just bonuses. The rush already feels different, whole.

It's not that Barclay Elliot is back. I think I'm here for the first time.

By the time practice ends, I'm exhausted. Muscles I forgot existed are screaming, and I'm walking-is-ten-times-the-effort sore. Still, despite the tension, I feel *good.* Lighter, like just that practice alone knocked some of the rust off and I can move better. I even can't wait to get back to my backyard. Christopher would—

—*would nothing*, I think with a pang in my chest as I unlock my bike. He'd feel nothing because I made sure we would never be together, never be friends like he said we couldn't be. I sigh.

Even though I couldn't find them today, I can't stop thinking about them. I want to know if Amy broke it off with that senior after he got caught making out with a sophomore behind the bleachers. I want to hang by the band room and watch Christopher clean his oboe. I hate not bantering with Christopher about movies or surprising Amy by knowing an obscure indie punk song she was humming before class. I hate not knowing how they're doing.

Having the basketball team back is amazing, but it feels wrong without my other team. I can't go back to the way things were without them.

So I have to find a way.

I hop on my bike and immediately my thighs burn. I kind of regret not asking Zack for a ride, but I'd been convinced that biking home would be a good cooldown.

I start pedaling and while my muscles are sore, it's nothing a hot bath or some hot and cold pads while watching TV with Maggie won't fix. Thank God Mom made spaghetti and meatballs last night because I'm aching like I've never ached before to throw several scoops of meatballs into a leftover baguette for a sandwich. Maybe two. Not that it'll help get my six-pack back, but that can be a tomorrow problem.

Headlights bounce off my mirror, pulling me out of my thoughts. They're *bright*. I squint, instantly moving to the side so the car can pass. Mom's only taken me out practice driving a few times since we just have the one car, but I know Zack comes up with new swear words and then some whenever he gets trapped behind a bike, and I don't want to be that guy.

But the car doesn't pass. In fact, it veers to the right and stays there behind me. I take a deep breath. Home, meatball sandwich, bath, *Borderlands* until I fall asleep.

The car speeds up. Follows closer. I pedal a little faster to give us some room. I want to look back, to see if it's some asshole texting or what, but I don't, not even when we stop at a stop sign together. I wait, poised, and take off again, hoping they'll turn left or right.

Instead they go straight, right after me.

Then they speed up again.

I tense and pedal harder, but it's obvious my bike is no match for their acceleration.

The engine roars in my ears, painfully now. I swear I can feel its heat. My muscles protest, even as my brain tells them to keep going. Faster, faster, until this guy turns and this all becomes some weird story I'll tell at practice tomorrow.

But they give the gas pedal one last tap.

The car lurches forward.

And knocks my tire.

The bike is sucked under with a horrifying screech and I'm launched off it like a video-game character, up in the air one second and tumbling to the ground for what feels like a drawn-out eternity between one and two. Eternity where I wonder how much it'll hurt. If it'll be a mercy or a death sentence if it doesn't hurt. If this was how my grandpa felt in that car. If he knew that he wasn't going to survive. Setting that countdown clock was so stupid because I could never prepare for something like this.

Then my body slams into grass somewhere next to the road, and I didn't have to worry about it not hurting because it does, big-time. It's not the local sting of a bad cut or a headache. It feels like my whole body is on fire.

A second passes, then two, then three. I squeeze my eyes shut, trying to focus on the poke of the grass on my skin instead of the pain underneath.

Then the pain begins to fade away. Well, softens, at least. Enough to clear my head and feel the gentle breeze of the night and the vibration of the car engine.

Whoever did this is still here. I don't dare to move until I hear the laughing.

Ostrowski's laugh.

I watch him drive past me at a snail's pace. His anger is gone, replaced with a disgusting, cartoonish sneer. "I better not see you at the game this week, Elliot, and I better not see you giving speeches. Or next time, I won't miss."

My body shudders as his car disappears from view. I look around and realize I've landed on the grass on someone's front lawn, but none of the lights are on. I start to move all my fingers and toes, and find luckily they still work. My legs shake when I try to move them, but they do move. I force myself into a sitting position and once I do, I see that my bike's an unrecognizable hunk of metal sitting in the road. My stomach lurches thinking that's what I could've looked like. I can't believe Ostrowski is so determined to keep his captaincy and bury the shit his dad's done that he was willing to risk maiming me, maybe even killing me.

I pull out my phone, which is scratched but working, and I use the light to survey the damage. A lot of bruises and a couple stinging cuts. Nothing too bad.

Still, I don't want to walk back alone.

Amy would probably come help me, but I can't call on her when I wasn't there when she needed me. Same with Christopher. I don't want Zack to get worked up and go after Ostrowski. He needs to stay on the team.

Which leaves only one person.

I think Mom would be holding my hand if it weren't for all the visible cuts on it. It's something you just kind of pick up when you're with a person long enough. The way she usually rests her hand with her fingers flat, but now they're a little curved.

228

"If I tell you what happened, will you promise not to freak out? Or can you just . . . listen first? To the whole thing?" I say as she starts up the car.

"Yeah, of course." She pauses. "I'll try."

I take a deep breath. "I mean, it's not like the team hasn't been doing stuff all along." I think about Zack and the guys who supported me today and amend. "Well, some of them. Mostly Ostrowski and his goons have been calling me slurs, drawing dicks and defacing my locker, harassing me at work. But it was all just words then, I guess."

"Barclay—" I catch Mom's glance and she stops talking.

"I lied about why I stayed home from school that day. Christopher and I kissed after the alumni game"—God, I'm burning saying this out loud—"and Ostrowski recorded it. He made a TikTok narrating it like it was a nature documentary and the whole school saw it."

Mom's eyes are wide in horror. "He did *what* to you and Christopher?"

She says "you and Christopher" like it's the most normal thing in the world. It'd make me so happy if it were any other circumstances.

"I . . . didn't react well. But I decided I wasn't going to let it stop me from playing anymore. So I practice with the team tonight, and then . . . they brought it up a notch, I guess," I continue. "I . . ." I tense my jaw, then slowly release it. "Mom, I thought they were gonna run me over. I've never been so scared in my life."

I don't even realize my hand is shaking until Mom does reach out and take it.

"I tried to put everything aside and not let it bother me," I say, my voice shaking as hard as my hand. "I wasn't good at that for a long time, but now I really don't care what they think. How can I ignore *this*, though?"

Mom's thumb runs over my knuckles, her touch extra gentle on the stinging cuts. "You *shouldn't*, Barcs. None of us should be. What those boys did to you is . . . sickening. Evil. Jesus Christ." She pauses, blinking back tears. "None of this is your fault. Please know that."

Not my fault. The words float around me, not quite reaching in and settling yet.

Mom tries to take a deep breath, but her chest hitches and it comes out shuddery. "It's this school's fault and they've been silent far too long. I'm going to change this *right now*. Once we get home, I'm filing a report with the police *and* the school."

It feels so relieving to have her taking charge. "You're not alone, Barclay."

I take her hand. "I know. I have you and Zack and . . ." I trail off.

Mom parks the car in the driveway and finally I feel safe. While I ease my way out of the car, she moves to the trunk to grab the remains of my bike.

When we catch each other's eyes, the words I've been thinking spill out. "You don't have to do it alone either." I should have told her that when dad left. When her dad died. She needs to know too.

She bridges the gap between us, enveloping me in her arms and holding me tight. I find myself squeezing her back, hoping she understands. I'm here for her too. And it feels like someone else is there for us as well. It opens something up inside me.

I never answered Christopher's question out loud about whether basketball or being gay came first. The answer was gay at eight, basketball at eleven. But in those years in between I was convinced my family would hate me if I wasn't athletic, manly, *normal*. In the years after that, I still pushed myself to the brink with basketball because I thought I couldn't be loved if I was just okay and gay. That they'd only love me if I was gay and *amazing*. I know finally that Mom, my siblings, and my friends love me even without basketball. But even if I hope, even if I believe, I'll never know with—

I turn to her.

"Do you think Scratch would've still loved me?" I ask quietly.

"Barclay, honey. Of course. He loved you so, so much."

"But how could you *know*?" I'm trembling now.

Mom pulls away, sighing. "You know, I really love my job. I know I make it seem like it exhausts me, but I do love it." She pauses. "I was even planning to open up my own real estate agency. But it was going to be such a huge leap financially and I was so scared that Dad would tell me I shouldn't right now. That he'd knock the dream out of me." Tears pop into her eyes. "I never got the chance to tell him because I spent so long agonizing over what he would've said." She looks to me. "I'll never know what he would have said, but I know what he always taught me. To believe in and trust myself. So I know he'd say the same for you, and he'd be very proud that you have."

She wipes tears off my face. Tears I didn't even know were falling. "Do you think he knew?"

She laughs a little. "Well, Dad did know pretty much everything. Including that you're going to win the championship this year." She kisses the spot where she mopped up my tears. "And even if not, he would've fought tooth and nail for you the moment he learned. No homophobic asshole would've been spared."

We share a laugh as we walk into the house together, where Maggie greets us, concerned.

When I've convinced her I'm okay, I settle into my room for the night, and find myself doomscrolling through my phone. I end up in my photos. One of the last ones I took was of Christopher and me cheesing around at one of the Vote Squad planning meetings. The happiness is palpable.

My mom's words settle in my head. *He would've fought tooth and nail for you.*

I know this, somewhere deep inside me. But I also know just as deeply that I haven't fought tooth and nail for Christopher and Amy. If I want to apologize and show them how much they matter to me, I can't just run into them and try to explain myself. I have to really *show* it. But it can't be like what I did at the pep rally, over-the-top and flashy. There has to be a perfect middle ground somewhere. I know voter registration has ended, but I bet I can still pump up those who have registered to vote for the right person, to stay fired up about the issues even after they vote.

My eyes fall to the box of leaflets that I shoved under my bed after Mom found them under the couch. I find myself running into Maggie's room.

She's sitting on her rug, surrounded by homework, and I toss a pile of leaflets in front of her.

"Wanna take a break?" I ask.

She practically throws her pencil and papers aside. "*Yes.* What's up?"

"So your flyer artwork turned out really great." I dig my hands into my pockets. "Think you can do one more on the fly?"

Maggie's eyes light up. More than I've seen in so long. "What do you want it to say?"

I sit down beside her, and she and I form the first step to my plan.

CHAPTER TWENTY

I HAVE ALL MY HOPES PINNED ON A READ RECEIPT. I TEXTED the invitation to Amy and Christopher begging them to meet me here Thursday at 5:00, and I'm already pacing by the time it hits 5:02. I know there is a high chance that this will be a flop, but that read receipt of Amy's keeps my hope alive.

At least, if Christopher and Amy don't show up, a lot of other people seem to have. I only had a few days to get the word out, but with Maggie's incredible design on both the flyers I handed out by the hundreds as well as the beautiful surprise mural that she got Mr. Welles to let her paint onto the blank wall of the Chitwood pool hall building (pool balls forming Scratch's basketball number along with the phrase *Never stop fighting*), we seem to have gotten people's attention. It's way less organized than our other rallies, and I'm working with a battery-powered microphone and a podium I snagged out of the band room, but a crowd has formed outside the school nonetheless. Right next to the stop sign where he died.

I try to resign myself to the fact that they aren't coming, but in my one last scan of the crowd before starting this thing, I spot Amy. Ripped band shirt, black shorts with all the patches on them, look of absolute murder in her brown eyes. I should be cringing, but I just feel relieved, being in the same space as her again. Because even if she's pissed, she's here. Even if Christopher . . . is. I'm floored when I see him grabbing something out of her car. He doesn't make eye contact as he approaches, instead he just looks at something on his phone.

Their expressions have my heart sinking, but I take to the "stage." They're here. That's all I needed from them. I've got the rest.

"Hi everyone," I say, careful to keep my face the perfect distance from the mic. "Thank you so much for coming out to this little event. As many of you know, my grandpa, Scratch, was killed by a driver at this intersection outside the school. The driver should have been paying more attention, but they also didn't see the sign, since it was covered in overgrown plant life." I take a deep breath, steadying myself. I'm really gonna do this. "And I know this seems like a driving issue, but it's more than that. This stop sign is on school property, and is therefore supposed to protect everyone, from students to staff to members of the Chitwood community. It's usually part of the school budget to hire gardeners and maintenance to keep the plants on the grounds trimmed. But the budget was slashed by the school board. They heard numerous complaints about this stop sign's visibility, but still they didn't do anything."

I know I could leave it there, but I look into the crowd, at Amy and Christopher, and press on. It's time.

"This wasn't just negligence. This was active corruption. The board member who led the initiative that cut that budget was Grant Ostrowski. He advocated for taking money from other vital areas of Chitwood High, including both student organizations and the upkeep budget, to funnel it all into the basketball team, specifically its travel budget. The basketball team uses Ostrowski's travel agency, you've seen the 'sponsored by' on the back of our tournament shirts, and a lot of fans do then too. It's always been a perfect means to keep his business booming but also to secure his own power and his son's spot on the team."

People are leaning in, enthralled. My heart picks up, but not in a bad way.

"It's not just that, though, it's also how that budget got passed. He didn't just convince the board to support what should have been a wildly unpopular initiative, serving only fifteen people, like me. He *bribed* them to vote his way. Trips, money. He even bribed Principal Horvath with a new car to not raise a stink about the budget cuts and to suppress students speaking out about it. So everyone who wasn't an Ostrowski or a Chitwood basketball player or a school board leader suffered."

Mumbling grows from my crowd. We even have local press here whose eyes seem to be lighting up.

"But I'm not here to talk shit." I'm so into this now I don't even care if Mom is in the audience and scandalized by my swearing. "I'm here to give everyone a constructive way to make a difference. Do you want the budgets to go back to where they belong, to where they're needed? Then you must vote Ostrowski off the board in February! We can make a better future for Chitwood and give *every* kind of student— artist, athlete, scholar—the support they need. We just have to elect someone who isn't out to serve simply their own interests. Let's make sure that this is the last memorial to a beloved Chitwoodian we ever have to make."

Heart pounding, I pull the tarp off the stop sign.

It took hours, but I managed to clear the brush myself. I rearrange the flowers I set down at the base. Blanket flowers, which were my grandma's favorite.

It looks like a real tribute now.

One worthy of the cheering that explodes from the audience.

For a moment, I bask in the way everyone's enthusiasm falls over me. I smile thinking of people marching out to the polls in less than two weeks, of the joy Amy and Christopher will feel when Brianna wins this election. Even if they never forgive me, that'll make it worth everything.

Still, I do what my grandpa would've done. After the event ends, I find them in the crowd to apologize in person.

Amy's eyes don't look quite so murderous. In fact, she's kind of smiling as she crosses her arms. "Pretty impressive."

I chuckle. "Damn, never thought I'd hear that from you." I hold out my arms, testing to see if I can get a hug. "I was a total dick to you and let you down. Can I keep pulling triple my weight to prove how much this and our friendship means to me?"

For a second, I think Amy's going to flip me off. But then she scoots into my hug. It feels so good to wrap my arms around her. "You're on probation."

"I'll serve my time. I won't let you down."

When we pull away from our hug, the two of us look to Christopher. His thumbs are jamming across his phone screen, a deep furrow between his brows, but he nods. "Pretty good turnout." When he looks up at me, a piece of hair falls into his eyes like usual, but then he turns and walks away.

He didn't smile at me. Not exactly. It's more like something crosses over his eyes. Like a ghost of a smile or something. And he definitely didn't wait for my apology, so it's not enough to dream that we can pick back up where we left off, but for the first time in so long, it feels like at least I did this right.

I tell myself that I can work through the pain like always. But I've never been run off my bike before, so this pain feels different. I swear my limbs ache before I even walk into practice.

I'm the first one in, as I've been trying to be ever since rejoining the team. I want to show the guys every second of every practice that I'm dedicated to the team and our success, whatever they might think of me. And I've been trying to stay optimistic, but the team just isn't in sync. We have all the skills we need to win, but we won't get ahead with all the holes in our defense. I try to think through solutions as I use the extra time to stretch on the nearly empty court. I inhale the faint cleaner smell and stretch out my ankle while the cheerleaders pack up their mats. It didn't take the brunt of the hit earlier this week, but even the littlest jostle can flare my old injury if I'm not careful. Catherine surprises me with a sympathetic smile when we catch each other's gazes.

But my peace goes pretty fast.

Anthony walks onto the court next and takes his sweet time looking me over. Almost an uncomfortably long time.

"What're you doing?" I finally ask as I pull myself from one stretch to another.

"Is what everyone's saying true?" he says. "Did Ostrowski really hit you with his car?"

Something presses onto my chest. It's not that I didn't think the rumors would spread. Mom filed her report with Horvath, but while his assistant tucked it away to collect dust, the student office assistant listened with wide eyes, and we went to the police next. I heard whispers the next day. I know Horvath is going to say it's not the school's responsibility since it was off grounds, but his isn't the only opinion that matters if the story is deep in Chitwood gossip circles already. I guess the best I can do is own it. "Yeah, he did."

Anthony starts to stretch out his own left leg. "Such a dumbass. Like we don't play a game that involves our *bodies*. If it wasn't psycho enough on its own, it's like he'd rather torpedo the team just to feel like a big man."

"Here." I stop my stretching and help Anthony stretch out his leg.

Anthony, who was neutral at best to me throughout this whole coming-out fiasco, is now taking a side. Mine. Is this one of those enemy-of-my-enemy-is-my-friend things? Does it even matter?

As we stretch, more people run onto the court. Zack, Pat, Lochman. Kyle, Chase, then Russell. Even after a handful of practices working together, two groups still form, people still either gravitating toward me or away.

"Hey, man, killer speech last night!" Zack gets to me first, slapping me on the back. I can't hold back a wince. "You feeling any better?" Even through all the pain, it was nice to be able to text Zack about what happened after. Like old times.

Lochman leans against one of the poles, glaring at the locker room door. "I can't believe Ostrowski would sink to that level. And for what? Does he really think the team is gonna side with him now?"

"What happened?" Pat asks. I guess the rumor didn't spread to everyone.

"Oh, nothing. Just a little attempted vehicular manslaughter," Lochman says before raising his voice toward the other group. "Tim Ostrowski, team captain, tried to *run Barclay over* in his car to stop Barclay from telling the town the truth about what a piece of shit his dad is!"

Chase rolls his eyes as he starts pulling out balls.

"Can we not get into drama right now?" Russell says. "I have a scholarship riding on these next few games."

"Tell that to our captain!" Zack shoots back. "Who isn't even *here* yet."

Coach isn't here yet either. I shiver, unsure of whether I want him to hear or not. I still have no idea how he'll react to that or what I did yesterday.

"Calm down, Ito!" Kyle groans. "I'm so tired of everyone's shit. Barclay has to take over a pep rally, Ostrowski's trying to kill people—"

"Do you not see the *killing people* as worse?" Zack snaps back.

I stop stretching. Much as I appreciate it, I'm done letting Zack fight my battles for me. I'm done with all this bickering too. I'm also more than done with Ostrowski dominating the conversation when it needs to be about strategy for winning the next game. "Guys, stop it. I'm fine. If he wanted me off the team—"

That's the moment Ostrowski decides to pop into practice, Boris by his side. His gaze lands on me like it's got physical weight. My heart starts to race, and I swear I can feel the wet sting of fresh grass on the cut on my cheek.

But that's as far as I let my body go. "—he didn't accomplish it," I finish. I make eye contact with him. His eyes are blazing with anger. "Didn't even get close."

Ostrowski runs at me.

Every instinct in me tells me to run, to avoid, even flinch. But I hold steady as he gets in my face. "Wanna say that again, Elliot?"

"I've said all I need to say. This bullshit has to stop, now. Go be a captain to your team."

He gets even closer to me. Unnecessarily close. Close enough to smell his mouthwash and see the sweat beading on his upper lip. "If you thought it was bad when your little kissing video got leaked, you have no idea what's coming for you now. That car can go pretty fucking fast and I won't miss next time."

He's saying this just to me, but he's certainly not lowering his voice. I look beyond him, at the way Russell, Kyle, and even Boris have their eyes on the floor, exchanging glances with each other.

I step away from Ostrowski, and just to piss him off more, look beyond him to his friends. "You do realize what he's threatening, right? Are you gonna let him murder me for real this time?"

Ostrowski laughs. "God, Elliot, can't take a joke, can you?" He turns to the cheerleaders stretching on the other side of the court. "Right, ladies? You're still coming to my party after the game, right?"

Catherine Finney exchanges a look with her friend Emma. "Yeah, not gonna happen."

Immediately after, Emma says, "Fucking psychopath."

Just loud enough for the whole team, including Ostrowski, to hear.

"Yeah, people are really taking it as a joke," I say. All the guys look to me. Some start inching toward me.

When Coach shows up, none of us say anything, but as practice starts, everyone starts feeding me the ball a lot more. And every pass brings us a little closer back into sync.

CHAPTER TWENTY-ONE

WITH A FEW MORE DAYS BEHIND ME, MY CUTS AND bruises are mostly healing, but a new sickness has overtaken me. My stomach is churning so hard I could've mistaken it for food poisoning, but it's not. As I look on my phone, a PANTHER REMATCH! notification pops up, not that I could forget. I'm just nervous as all hell. More nervous than, honestly, I've ever felt before a game.

I slowly push myself out of bed and glance at the countdown clock. The number hardly registers, though, as I make my way to the bathroom for a quick shower.

It doesn't matter that I'm not as well conditioned as the other guys, I tell myself, or that I haven't been part of every game up until now. I have to trust that I'm a great player, that Coach let me back onto the team for a reason. I know it's not the end of the world if we lose, but like the countdown clock says, I'm not done yet. It's not our time to stop.

My shower is short. I hardly remember putting on clothes, and I can't feel my feet when I step downstairs. Just the thud of my heart, almost as loud as my steps hitting the wood.

It's so loud I almost don't notice that Devin's downstairs. He's wearing his old Wildcats T-shirt and grinning at me.

"What're you doing here?" I ask. I feel like he told me he had exams next week.

"What do you think, loser?" Devin says, grinning. "I'm here to cheer you on!" As I approach him, he rubs my shoulder. "Plus, I know this game isn't gonna be easy. We're going all out today."

I raise my brows. "'We'?"

Devin opens the front door like he's a cheesy stage performer. A cheer seeps in from outside, revealing Mom, Maggie, Amy, and Zack all out on the stoop. They're decked out in all the Wildcats merch and school colors, makeup streaks across their faces and everything. (Well, except Amy, who's in her usual getup with one pom-pom.) It's exactly what I need to melt the anxiety knotting inside me.

But I can't help noticing that Christopher isn't among everyone.

I push away those feelings as best as I can. I still want to make things right with him, but for now I'm surrounded by people who love and care about me and that has to be enough.

It hasn't felt this way before a game in so long.

I clap my hands together. "Let's go!"

We head off together, and I find myself thinking that there's this thing about expectations that keeps surprising me. I always have these clear ideas of what milestones and happiness are supposed to look like. How it was supposed to be thunderous applause the moment I came out at the rally. But as I walk into the gym with my friends and family by my side, I realize, wow, *this* is that happiness I've been fumbling for for months. It's so far from what I ever imagined it would be. The wounds from that wrong turn are still there, but it's like I can feel them healing. Feel the new skin forming stronger.

Better.

And it doesn't matter anymore how I got here. At least I'm here, with them.

The locker room is surprisingly non-antagonistic, and I can't help but wonder if Ostrowski truly ended some of his key alliances at our last practice. But it's also silent and when Coach calls us out, I stay back. Zack pulls on my arm as the last of the team heads out to face the crowd accumulated in the gym.

"C'mon, it won't be like last time," he assures me.

I take a deep breath, and think about Mom, Maggie, Devin, and Amy.

Don't think about Christopher. Not now.

The hairs on the back of my neck stick up on end as Zack and I hit the court. People are whispering. More people than were talking before. I catch my name over and over again.

I look to my cheering section. Amy and Tabby have huge grins on and are both holding Amy's single pom-pom for maximum effect. They're such weirdos. My weirdos. I tear my eyes away at Coach's whistle. Time to warm up and get my head in the game.

Christopher would die if he knew I just thought an actual *High School Musical* lyric.

Stop.

We get started. I force myself to keep my breathing even as Ostrowski skips me in the passing drill. No fights this game. I'm here for the people who need me today. Including myself.

The drills end without any more issues, and Coach huddles us up.

"Now, for starters," Coach says. "Ito." I high-five Zack.

He then names off four other players. Not me, which burns, but

I shake it off pretty quickly. That's what I'd expect for any player who ditched out on part of the season. The more interesting part is that *he also doesn't call Ostrowski.*

"What the hell, Coach?" Ostrowski demands. "I've been starting in every winning game this season and—"

"Can it, Ostrowski."

The stony look on Coach's face says it all. Ostrowski drags his feet to the bench and plops down, hunched over like a dying plant.

Within the first eight minutes of the game, we're down by as much. My feet are tapping, and my mind is racing as I note the weaknesses in our play and theirs. We're playing like we're scared of the other team, passing but not getting any closer to the net. I glance at Coach, wishing I was in a position to share what I'm seeing with him. But I keep focused, writing out strategy in my head if I get an opportunity. I'm in the zone. So in the zone that I only hear Coach the second time.

"Elliot! Get the hell out there and don't fuck it up!"

Here we go.

I jump up and tag in at the buzzer. I focus my attention on Zack. It's time to get some shit done. Zack inbounds the ball to me.

Almost all that rust from the alumni game is gone. It's just me, the smoothness of the court, the electric connection between my fingertips and the ball, and navigating my way past these huge-ass Panther players.

I catch Zack's eye and smile. Good thing I've got the best teammate in Georgia.

I don't even notice the reaction of the crowd. I head toward the basket, and a couple huge Panthers come up on me.

"Haven't seen you in a while, fairy," one guy says. "Too busy crying over your boyfriend?"

But Zack sails in, setting a pick that causes the two idiots to go colliding into each other. I sink the ball for two points. It's a better feeling than any *fuck you*. The crowd roars with each basket the team and I get. Soon, we're *having fun*. That lightness I was searching for with nothing holding me back on the court, I finally have it.

The minutes tick away, until we're slowly inching our way back to a tie. It's tough, though; almost whenever we score, the Panthers swarm in and get two right back.

Within ten minutes of me going in, Coach lets Ostrowski in and subs Boris for Zack. Almost immediately, we fall out of sync. One of the biggest Panthers practically walks past Ostrowski to put up a three-pointer.

Thankfully, he misses.

I run in and grab the ball. No way they're getting another chance to back up there. Not right now. I dribble it back out across the half-court line.

But the moment I get the ball across, the Panthers descend on me, working a double-team just like a wall, trying to trap me on the sideline. There's no way for me to take a shot. I look for who I can feed the ball to, but I can't see anyone waving for it even though someone has to be open.

With no help coming and the ref counting the seconds, I pass in Boris's general direction, but one of the Panthers intercepts. He barrels into me as he does, so hard I end up shutting my eyes as I'm thrown to the floor.

The impact isn't as hard as the other night, but it knocks my teeth. For a moment, I swear I almost taste the wood. But I force my eyes open, stare into the bright lights, and remind myself where I am. Cheers along with groans sound from the stands. One of the Panthers of all people is the first to offer a hand to get me up.

By the time I've shaken off the fall, the Panthers have already scored an easy layup that sails clear over Ostrowski's and Boris's outstretched hands. On our possession, I barely get the ball to the three-point line before I'm descended upon by a wall of Panthers again. By now, they get it—no one up front is coming to help me.

"Oh hey, gay boy, what happened to your team?" one sneers.

I try to see through the gaps of the bodies, but with my options down to nothing, I fake to get some room and take an absolutely ridiculous jump shot, pushing myself as high as I can possibly go—

—and the Panthers' center knocks it down, like he's playing against a child. They drive down for another two.

"Time out!" Coach screeches, and the ref whistles.

We run to the huddle. "Guys, you gotta decide if you're playing with Elliot or you're not," he says. I don't think it's just the cardio making my heart speed up. "He's getting the shit beat out of him. And, Ostrowski, you haven't set a decent pick all night."

"Tell the homo to hit a shot."

Coach shakes his head. "Bring it in." We all join hands in the middle. "Elliot is playing. He's your point and he's calling the plays. You all need to get used to it, especially if you want to take home a win tonight. Or your season ends tonight. If you can't handle that, get on the bench."

Thankfully, Coach sends Zack and Lochman back out there with me, a balance for Ostrowski and Boris. And we give it our all. My muscles are straining, and my head's swimming a little from the lack of water I should've replenished during the time-out. But the Panthers' wall isn't so solid with Zack and Lochman flanking me. We score, but I know this game can't be won by Zack and me turning every Panther rebound into points for us. We need to stop them before they even get the chance to shoot.

The half ends 36–26 in the Panthers' favor, and I know something bigger has to change if we're going to keep the season alive.

Once halftime starts, we all leave the sidelines with a little less wind in our sails than I'd been hoping for by this point. I rub my sore arms, hoping Coach has one of his famous pep talks ready to go. It's not only me who could use the boost, I realize as I watch Zack stretch out his back and groan.

But when I go to enter the locker room, Coach is hunched over, talking to someone by the doors. The sight of the two together is so weird that it almost feels like some kind of fever dream I would've made up. This person is in a Wildcats shirt with a backward hat that is so *not* his look, but he makes it work, as with everything.

Christopher's here.

And talking to Coach?

But before I can do or ask anything, Christopher waves at me and runs off, I hope back to the stands to watch the second half.

I head back to the locker rooms like everything is normal.

But everything in the air changes.

Ostrowski looks right up at me as I enter.

"You used to be better," he says with a sneer.

"You didn't, but at least you used to try to set a pick," I reply.

A few *ohhhhs* from the team do knock a little spark into my chest.

"Maybe I don't want to set a pick for a fag," he says, approaching me. But without his car, I'm not about to be intimidated or goaded into a fight by him. I wave him off and walk away.

"Are you actually as stupid as you sound?" Zack is stepping

between us before I even realize how fast Ostrowski's charging at me from behind.

"All right, all right, get away from each other!" Coach snaps as he enters the room.

I move over to Zack, hoping I can convey my gratitude with a look. He nods.

But Coach's silence after this, his *dead silence*, isn't helping. In fact, he just stands there in it. As the seconds pass, the confusion turns to dread. Has he, what, given up on us?

"I know a lot has gone down these past few months"—he looks pointedly at me—"but this is your year. And on paper, you can beat this team. On the basketball court . . . you're going to have to decide. Are you going to put that on the court or are you going to keep fighting each other?"

Ostrowski's jaw flexes. "Well, if *someone* would—"

Coach wheels around to Ostrowski, and I've never seen fire in Coach's eyes like right then. Even I jump a little. Ostrowski, well, he looks like he's about to melt. *"Not you, Ostrowski."* The whole team freezes. I swear time itself freezes, all eyes on the way Ostrowski's face goes red. "I've just been shown video footage of you running your teammate off the road in a vehicle. You are *off this team*."

Holy shit. How? Wait, Christopher—is that what he was doing? Where did he find footage? It's not surprising considering how resourceful he is, but—*shit*. I feel like I'm sitting through the cutscene after a boss battle in a video game, where all the good guys win and the tightness and adrenaline finally slow down in your neck and shoulders.

"What are you talking about?" Ostrowski sputters. "You can't just—I didn't do anything more than just playing around. He's fine—" He grits his teeth, getting up in Coach's face. "Don't forget what I bring to this team."

Coach doesn't even flinch. "You're already a senior, so it's not like I was expecting much generosity from your father next year. Plus, I have it on good authority that his support will be ending soon. The funding we need, we'll earn from winning the championship. But we can't do that if one player almost *kills* one of the others. If you think that's just playing around or acceptable hazing, then I've got to make some big changes to the discipline on this team."

The whole team pales. I may never know why, whether it's the shock of watching someone stand up to Ostrowski, or the prospect of what *more* discipline could mean. Maybe both.

A second passes. Two, three as we wait for Ostrowski's next move.

And like all the babies of the world, he goes running out and punches a wall.

But even when he looks back through the window, Boris, Chase, and the other seniors don't move.

"You all have two minutes to sort everything out before the game resumes," Coach says, leaving as quickly as he came in.

The elation fills my chest like a balloon. Ostrowski, truly gone and out of my hair just like that. It happened finally and everyone's looking to me like I should be making some huge speech. But, you know what, I'm not captain. Not anymore. Someone else deserves that.

I turn to Zack. "Floor's yours, man," I say. "It should go to the guy who made us a team again."

Zack gives me a hug, the sun shining through his eyes he's so happy. I can barely get him to pull away to give a speech. He clears his throat, shakes his shoulder tension a bit, and starts to speak:

"Guys, we are down ten and everyone in here knows we can make that up in four possessions. We know them. They play the same way no matter what year it is. Boris, you need to push the ball. And Lochman, we need you to box out and get every offensive rebound. We are only going to win if we get those second-chance points. Look, gay or straight, Barclay is our best shot. You don't have to sleep with him to feed him the damn ball. Let's do this."

But then Zack looks back at me and I realize I do have something to say, one last thing to put it all to bed. "I know I made it about myself at the pep rally. I don't regret telling y'all who I am because"—I swallow—"a team is a family and you should be yourself with your family. I meant that. But I also know this game and the season aren't about me—they never were. It's about all of us playing together. No stars, no perfection, no championships. Let's play for the Wildcats. Don't even think about the Panthers tonight."

I tense up, waiting for the same glares and eye rolls I've been getting for so much as mentioning the pep rally. But that's not what the guys do.

Lochman claps his hands together, slapping sound through the silence. "Hell yeah, guys! Wildcats until the end!"

From there, it's instant. All my teammates start smiling—Derek and Pat. Russell and Anthony. Even Ostrowski's so-called friends Boris, Chase, and Kyle. Everyone's nodding along and exchanging grins like the season just started over.

Then Zack breaks into the chant. We end up all but singing it, bouncing around and pumping ourselves back into the zone. It's almost beautiful. *This* is why I love being on a team. This is why I love basketball, what I missed those months without it. This game, win or lose, will be the mixing of all our talents, strength, and fortitude. And when it's fourteen people instead of one holding up a burden, even the biggest ones can suddenly seem small.

Right now I can't even feel it.

Finally, we're ready to get back out there.

The nervous excitement as we return to the floor is palpable. The Wildcats have won a lot of games from behind, but we rarely find ourselves down ten going into the second half and it feels like everyone knows it. I shoot a glance at my cheering section. Christopher is there like I was hoping. I watch him laugh at something Amy whispers to him, but I can't help but ask myself why *did* he go to Coach with that video? How did he know and . . . what does it mean? But there's no time to ask now.

Around them, Willie the Wildcat shoots T-shirts into the crowd. The fans are going wild. The cheerleaders are giving the best performance I've ever seen them do.

Every extended Wildcat is ready to fight with us.

And from the inbound we go in like charging bulls.

We trade sharp passes around the Panthers. There's no more hesitating, no more waiting around for openings and cowering at bad defensive walls. Lochman and Zack pass and steal and block like I've never seen before. The Panthers start exchanging long looks with each other, throwing up frustrated hands as we steal ball after ball. The game goes along in harsh bursts instead of a volley like the first half so that by the time we reach five minutes to go, we've clawed back to a five-point deficit, 61–56. Coach huddles us up and even he can't quite hold back the smile that the rest of the team is passing around.

"We've got them right where we want them," he says, rubbing his palms together. "We are in our house, down five with plenty of time. Remember, make the extra pass and take the high-leverage shot. They are going to double Elliot and when they do, that's going to leave Lochman open under the basket. Let's flip the script." He looks to Boris. "Harris, you get it in quick to Lochman, let their defense collapse on the middle and we feed Elliot or Ito at the arc. Ready? Let's go."

The Panthers can't double all three of us and it works like a charm. We sink three unanswered baskets in a row and take the lead. Two strong Panther possessions later, though, and they've taken the game back. It's whiplash speed, but these five minutes feel like hours, shoes squeaking so hard on the wood as we change directions that people in the audience cringe. The fans have been maintaining cheers for what feels like ten minutes without stopping. I'm huffing for breath, my body just *waiting* for a buzzer that I don't want to buzz yet. Not until we are on top.

By the time we hit twenty-three seconds remaining, the Panthers are up two and it's their ball. 72–70.

Coach calls for one last time-out. Before he starts talking, I shoot a glance out at the crowd and I catch Mom. I catch her smile like a lucky charm and stow it close to my heart. A reminder for the future—*We can get through anything together.*

"Let's change it up again," Coach says. "We've been zoning them all game, so let's jump to man. They're going to try to feed forty-two and hope we foul. Let's give them that look, then back off, and double before he gets to half-court. Elliot, you gotta get that ball."

"Got it," I say.

"Then they're going to expect us to call a time-out. But we push the ball. Let's tie this up."

As we take to the court, the Panthers look confident. They're seconds away from another win against the favorite Wildcats.

But this isn't like last time. I may never get the jeers or homophobic comments to magically go away. But I'm here anyway. Playing anyway. Zack's got his hand on my shoulder, and I can see what's ahead of us. I want that future of a championship and being able to run into Christopher's arms to celebrate. Maybe. If I'm not too late. I want to play on a college team. I want to bring a future husband and kids back to this town and proudly show them the trophies I helped win for us.

And all that starts here. I'm grabbing my future now.

Ball inbounds.

Lochman fronts the ball handler, then backs off, and I sneak around back to make the steal. I charge down the court, then feed the ball to Zack.

Zack pushes the ball up, catching the Panthers off guard as they look to the sidelines for the time-out whistle they're expecting.

"Let's go!" Coach screams from the sidelines.

Our cue. Time to show this gym what we're really capable of.

Eight seconds left. Zack swing passes the ball to Lochman.

He fakes and kicks it out to me. Four seconds. Zack covers me. I dribble around his screen. Two seconds.

I'm back behind the three-point line. I could make the shot to win, not tie. The Panther who called me a fairy, the brick wall one, is launching himself at me. Still, I could make the shot.

But someone else is back here too. Someone who's wider open and needs it more.

I throw it to Zack.

Two, one—

Zack shoots.

The buzzer rings

and *it*

goes

in.

It's like the seconds before a dam breaks. Silence, then a sudden flood. I run to Zack, slamming my body into his as everyone dogpiles on him. The crowd is screaming, so loudly that I feel it more than hear it.

We did it.

I think about my countdown clock. So much happened in just four seconds on the court, I didn't even notice them ticking by.

I guess it's not so important to know how much time you have left, if you live every single moment like it could be your last. I got so worried about my future, I forgot it's what you do with the present that matters most. My life changed forever after that pep rally. But now, I have the courage to live it.

Yeah, these people cheering my name again might only all love me while I'm winning. All this game has done is saved us from being immediately disqualified from playoffs, after all. We still have to win every game left in the season to make it to the championship again. But I'm back with the team, doing what I love, and scouts or no scouts, I've won.

The team peels away from each other, just in time for Mom, Maggie, Devin, Amy, and Tabby to approach. No Christopher, but I do my best to shake off the sting of disappointment.

Mom wins the race to get to me, enveloping me in a hug so tight it makes me suddenly aware of my aching muscles. "Scratch would be so proud of you. *We're* so proud of you, every bit of you."

"For the record," Amy says, "I like you the exact same amount as before."

Tabby elbows Amy, who actually *blushes*. "But she will admit that that was pretty exciting."

I laugh as Maggie approaches next, hugging me. She doesn't say anything, but the way she snuggles into me says more than any speech. Devin runs in next, straining to pick me up and twirl me around.

"Coach Neptune himself will be back after him by next game," Devin says. "Forget his *scouts*."

And then, like that final music-swelling scene in the romantic comedies he loves so much, Christopher's the last person in front of me. He removes his hat and runs his hand through his hair. My heart seemingly grows three sizes.

But Coach calls us to the locker rooms for postgame before I can talk to him.

Hopefully he can find it in him to forgive me not only for what I've done to him, but making him wait a few extra minutes.

CHAPTER TWENTY-TWO

GET HERE EARLY FOR NEXT PRACTICE," COACH SAYS AS we all exit the locker rooms. "We've still got a long road to the championships."

I hear the words, I know they're true, but it's like my brain's padded and the words can't *quite* break through yet. The world feels a little brighter, like I'm looking through an Instagram filter—lines sharper, colors bolder. Zack jumps onto my back once Coach turns his. I stumble, surprised at the move, but I catch myself.

"You hear that, Barcs?" Zack says. "We still have a *ton* of games to blow people's minds."

I laugh. "Want to switch off next game so I get at least one winning shot?"

"Only if there are no Duke scouts there."

Devin's and Zack's words echo through my head. And suddenly, it doesn't feel scary or impossible like at the start of the season. I take a deep breath as I let Zack off, looking around at the team. It's not all on me, we'll get there together.

"Wanna hit the diner?" Zack asks. "Some of the team's going and Amy said she's 'considering.' I think she may not hate me anymore."

I look around the now-empty gym, nothing but popcorn stuck to the bleachers and loose confetti. My heart sinks a little when I see Christopher isn't here. Then my gaze moves to the jersey now hanging from the rafters by the gym doors. My throat tightens, but I don't want to swallow this feeling down just yet. I think maybe I need to just sit with it.

"I'll catch up with you," I say.

I wait until Zack's shut the gym door behind him and the echo bounces off the massive walls. The walk to the memorial feels longer than it is as slow breaths fill my lungs.

It's nothing too flashy. Below where his jersey hangs is a plaque with his name and year on it, two black-and-white photos—one of him in his basketball uniform and one of his team jumping up in victory at the championship game. Tears well in my eyes, and I don't blink them away.

"I know you would've loved me whether or not we win the championship, but I hope you're proud, Gramps," I say to the photo. My fist clenches at my side, wishing more than anything to be able to feel the peaks and valleys of his bony hand in mine. "I know it took me so long to come back to basketball. To believe people could love the whole me. I feel like if you were here, you would've knocked some sense into me months ago, but I think I did okay." I swallow. "I miss you so much. I don't think I'll ever stop missing you. But that's how it should be."

I wipe my tears again, straightening back out. I kiss my fingertips and touch the photo.

Then I turn to leave.

And there's Christopher, standing on the front-row bleacher bench. "'Gay Saves the Day.' That's going to be the headline of my first article for my internship at the *Chitwood Gazette*. Moving us on up in the world."

"Ah, still so humble," I tease, but my heart is hammering.

Christopher jumps off the bleacher. He strides over to me, more at ease than I think I've ever seen him. "I know I'm the writer, but you, mister, have a flair for the dramatic."

I shoot him the finger, my cheeks heating. "That was for my *grandpa*—"

Christopher puts his hands to his mouth, almost as if *he's* embarrassed. "No, no Barclay, the *game*."

Oh my God. Now we're both a little redder than before.

"Thanks for the save with Ostrowski and Coach," I say.

Christopher grins. "Shit, if you thought that was good, you should see what I sent Brianna's campaign. You and Lochman were right—his dad really doesn't change any of his passwords."

"Holy—"

"If that doesn't get Ostrowski straight-up removed from the ballot, there's at least no way he's winning. The editor for the town paper is also pro-arts and snatched up my article before I could finish pitching it. 'Brianna Collins Wins School Board Election in a Landslide.' Has a great ring to it, doesn't it?"

It does. But I can't stop looking at Christopher. Christopher, who pursues his passions no matter if the faces that come out to see him are friendly or not. Christopher, who is unbothered by people who hate him for something he can't control, but loves the people who love him fiercely. Christopher, who just did the most badass journalism I've seen just so kids at our school can all pursue a passion and feel safe within Chitwood walls. Christopher, who has enough compassion to get a new gay like me through all this bullshit.

Christopher, who (I hope) might give me a second chance.

"I didn't think it was all going to be . . . so much."

Christopher takes another few steps closer to me. Close enough that I swear he can see my hands shaking. "Well, it gets better. And then worse. And then better. And then worse. And then you end up like me."

"Well," I say, smiling, "then I've got a lot to look forward to." I glance at the empty bleachers. "Although I could skip out on waiting in the bleachers."

Christopher laughs. My whole body feels the sound. "Well, Catherine Finney and Jaxon Pierce have been staked out behind the left half, so at least it's been entertaining."

He digs his hands into his pockets, rolling back and forth on the balls of his feet. "Well, you've come out, you're on track to win the championship, and I hope you've realized by now that you're not destined to die at sixty-seven. So what're you gonna set that countdown clock to?"

I try to think of an answer, even as a joke, but my mind's drawing a blank. The urgency of the last few months is suddenly gone.

After all these months of talk about bravery and gestures, though, I finally know what the big brave thing is. What I need to do. And I can do it right now. I take a deep breath, less sure but so much more hopeful than the last time I confessed something in this gym.

"From the moment I saw you, you scared me," I say. "You were a future I could never imagine. And the more I got to know you, the more I just—I started seeing *you*. This guy who was not only brave enough to be out in Middle of Nowhere, Georgia, but who was so talented, passionate, determined, so much *more* than I thought. And every little thing about you got me hooked. The way you light up talking about movies. The way your hair falls into your eyes or how you adjust your glasses. The way I learn new things about you just looking at what print is on your shirt or shoes. The way you talk about changing the world. The way you saw me before I saw myself." I take a deep breath, eyes still on Christopher. Not focusing on him, though. I can't until I'm done. "The way your lips felt against mine, and the way you held me so tightly when we were together. I'm so sorry for everything I've done to hurt you. I was selfish and scared and pulled you into a storm you never asked to be a part of. But I promise I'm working on it. I'm going to be better. A better friend, a better person, a better . . . boyfriend. If you'll have me."

Finally, I look to Christopher.

He's gazing straight at me like a laser. Hands still tight in his pockets.

Then he smiles.

He leans in and presses his forehead to mine. The warmth charges between us, that hair that always falls in his face is caressing my skin. "So you *were* paying attention to all those rom-coms I showed you."

When our lips meet this time, it's less like a roller coaster and more like breathing. It's cleansing and it feels like the most natural thing we've ever done. I weave my fingers into Christopher's soft hair and he wraps his other arm around my back, tugging us so close that our heartbeats reverberate off each other. It feels like it's been no time since our last kiss, yet like mountains have shifted. There're no more unspoken feelings, no more shoving things down, no more turmoil swirling me around so much that I have to pull Christopher down as I try to catch my balance. No, I'm solid. I'm planted here with him.

I'm not even scared that at some point this kiss will end. Because tomorrow we'll knock on doors, keep fighting our good fights, and at the end of the day we'll get to do it again. Yeah, not all of it will be easy. Challenges will pop up and threaten to throw me off my feet. But they won't. Because I don't think happiness is as fleeting as it felt when

Scratch died. I think it's strong and it can weather a hell of a lot. I'm content to let the storms come when they may, knowing Christopher and I will be okay.

We can enjoy this perfect moment. We can enjoy every perfect moment that'll come after we break away from this kiss, and every time we come back together afterward.

Our happiness is just beginning.

ACKNOWLEDGMENTS

I'd like to thank my good friend Justin Chanda for always being willing to give me a shot and for creating a safe home for Todd, Carlyn, and me to tell this story. And thank you, Alexa Pastor, for your invaluable guidance.

My other safe home was created by my husband, Scotty, and my close friends in the LGBTQ+ community who always provided a supportive environment for me to be myself. There's nothing more impactful than that.

—Sean

First and foremost, I'd like to thank Michael, my mom and dad, and my sister, Courtney. Without my family, I'd never have been able to tell this story. Maybe any story. Next, I think I have to thank my work partner, work husband, and work soul mate, Sean Hayes. My relationship with Sean and our unique childhoods are really the basis for this book. If Christopher and Barclay are lucky enough to have their relationship evolve into the loving and trusting adult relationship that Sean and I have, then I think they are going to be just fine when they grow up.

I'm also incredibly grateful for the team at Simon & Schuster and especially our writer, Carlyn. Sean and I started to tell this story in a television script. Not only did we find someone who could take what we were trying to say and turn it into an important, compelling, and fun novel, but we found a special person who sees the world similarly to us and also brings her own authentic voice, which just makes the journey better along the way.

I'd be remiss if I didn't thank Michael Kricfalusi. He's part of the team at Hazy Mills, and his input and faith helped us keep going when we thought that perhaps a literary path might not be for us.

—Todd

As someone who, up until maybe the last three years, thought I'd exclusively be working in Hollywood and who has always dug deep into the world of entertainment and celebrity, celebrity collaboration with books was something I'd put down as a ten-years-from-now bucket list item. The fact that it happened now and is actually my first book deal . . . I definitely have people to thank for that kind of miracle feat.

First and foremost, I have to thank my absolute superstar of an agent, Janine Kamouh. When we first started working together, when my original work was dying on submission, I told her that I was open to any and all opportunities to get my writing out there and she really took it to heart. The elation of that call on the last workday before the winter holidays in 2020 is still seared in my mind as one of my career highs and I can't thank you enough for believing in me and fulfilling my dreams in every way we could come up with. Your kindness, patience, loyalty, and incredible advocating abilities continue to warm my heart and make me so grateful we connected.

A huge thank-you to my fearless collaborator on the publishing house end, Alexa Pastor. Your kindness, openness, and willingness to go above and beyond to make sure this book became the best story that it could possibly be mean so much to me. I'm so glad that this story is finally out in the world and shining the way it is. And a huge thank-you to everyone on the BFYR team, including Justin Chanda, Alex Kelleher, Dorothy Gribbin, Chava Wolin, and Brendon MacDonald, as well as Steffi Walthall and Laura Eckes for such a beautiful cover (that coincidentally pairs really well with my debut cover on my walls).

While this project called for a smaller group of beta readers, I did have a lovely, encouraging group of folks who would bounce around excerpts with me that I'm eternally grateful for, including Kaylee Hirzel-Duff, Amy Carr, Kate Koenig, Will Miller, and K Dishmon. Beyond that, I wouldn't be where I am without my wonderful writer groups, including the LA Crew, my New School MFA cohort, OG Pitch Wars Friends, Screenwriting Friends, and Twitter Friends. You know who you are and I love you. A special shout-out to those dear friends and individuals who represent the love, creativity, and vibrance of the LGBTQ+ community and welcomed me into their open arms so many years ago, particularly Kiavanne Williams and Jesse Anderson.

As always, a huge thank-you to my family, extended and immediate, for always supporting my dream. Mom, Dad, Izzy, Brandon, love you guys forever and always. A special shout-out in particular to my late and great great-aunt Sally, who not only always supported my dreams, but inadvertently gave me my first exposure to queer folks by virtue of living in WeHo for reasons I don't entirely understand to this day. I miss and love you and I'm making this a part of your fabulous legacy.

Finally, the hugest thank-you to Sean Hayes and Todd Milliner for picking my words and trusting me to go on this journey with you both. I still remember in 2018 I got an interview to be a PA on the revival of *Will & Grace* and when I went in to interview, the producers took one look at my resume, saw "represented by WME for books," and told me that I didn't need this job and to go write books. Lo and behold, those producers were right and I couldn't ask for a better way to meet and work with you both. Your talents and hearts are unmatched, and I can't wait to get this book into the hands of readers. *Will & Grace* truly helped pave the foundation for queer media representation and I'm so excited to be putting another brick into the house with you all.

—Carlyn